THE BLADE KINGS SERIES

Pe…
Deke

RUTH STILLING

ISBN 978-1-0686000-4-3

Cover art by Ink & Velvet Designs

Interior design and formatting by Summer Grove

Editing by Jovana Shirley, Unforeseen Editing, www.unforeseenediting.com

Proofreading by Autumn Sexton

TRIGGER/CONTENT WARNINGS

You should be aware that while this book is a work of fiction and is, of course, a happily ever after, *Perfect Deke* does contain themes of the following: discussion of the death of a spouse (not involving the main characters), sexually explicit content and strong language.

To the girls who crave the love of a boy obsessed
—and his head between her thighs.

PLAYLIST

"London Boy" by Taylor Swift
"One Kiss" by Calvin Harris and Dua Lipa
"Love Looks Pretty On You" by Nessa Barrett
"2 hands" by Tate McRae
"Bed Chem" by Sabrina Carpenter
"R U Mine?" by Arctic Monkeys
"I'm In Love With You" by The 1975
"Shape of You" by Ed Sheeran
"Sports Car" by Tate McRae

CHAPTER ONE

JACK

Violence is never the answer, but it sure as shit would feel good.

That's my very first thought as I pull my truck into the training center car park, or parking lot. I've spent over six years living stateside, and at this point, my brain is half British, half American.

But what nationality I am these days has zero impact on the main challenge facing my first day of training camp—trying not to punch Tyler Bennett in the face.

It's been a year since I graduated alongside him in college. After that, he entered the NHL to play for the New York Blades, and I joined their AHL team in Connecticut.

It was the best season of my career so far and, incidentally, the worst of his.

I haven't spoken to him since the graduation party that ended with him being carried to the bathroom by our teammates, and being honest, that surprises me. He belonged in the AHL with the way he was playing. There wasn't anything I was surer of. He's a dick, plain and simple, and the only drawback to finally living out my dream of playing pro.

Growing up in the UK brought few opportunities in ice hockey, but if there was one thing my biological dad did for me, it was moving our family across the pond, which consequently gave me a shot at playing in the NCAA.

Even though it's been a year, I have zero doubts that Tyler has changed. In college, you could cut the tension between us with a knife, and the animosity wasn't solely limited to the ice. He knew what I thought about his antagonistic game, and he was painfully aware of my thoughts of him as a man too. Especially when it came to the way he treated his girl. A girl I shouldn't have cared about as much as I did based on the amount of attention she paid me in college. But Kendra Hart was—and still is—way out of his league.

Focus, Jack.

I slam the door on the truck and swing my bag onto my back, ready to make for the training center. But not before I catch a glimpse of the initials stamped across the dark blue hoodie I'm wearing.

JM.

It still feels surreal, even now. Twelve months ago, I was Jack Thompson—son of my mum's former husband, Elliott Thompson. The kind of guy Tyler Bennett could sit down and have a few drinks with. Now I'm Jack Morgan, NHL player and, for all intents and purposes, stepson of Mum's new husband and ex-pro hockey star, Jon Morgan. The same guy I idolized as a kid and watched play for the Seattle Scorpions when I first moved to the US. The same guy who is now coaching the NHL team I just signed with and is likely standing on the other side of these double doors.

So, yeah, there are plenty of reasons why I can't punch Tyler in the face. Most notably the fact that he's once again my teammate, but also the center my stepdad is pinning his hopes on this season.

When I push through into the meeting room, some of the team is already waiting, scattered around various tables. There's a substantial spread of breakfast items lining the back wall, and when I turn around, a large projector is set up, the screen reading, *The season of the Kings*.

At heart, I'm a social guy. I've never had a problem making friends, but this atmosphere feels ... different. I estimate there to be at least ten guys in this room, all faces I know well, but none friendly enough to approach. And that's before my ex-college teammate makes an appearance.

I make my way to the back and grab a Gatorade from the stand, leaning against the wall and scanning tables for an option. I wasn't especially nervous driving here today, more excited. But equally, I wasn't expecting this kind of muted response to rookies. In only one season as head coach, Jon has at least lifted them off the bottom of the league, but given some of the beatings they took last season were cringeworthy, I figured a few new faces, especially new wingers, would be appreciated.

Obviously not.

I'm headed for an empty spot to the right when an arm in the air catches my attention.

Sawyer Bryce.

Undoubtedly the team's best defenseman and also our captain.

He flips his hands toward him, motioning for me to join him and two other guys. But despite entering a parallel universe, surrounded by players I hung on my bedroom wall as a kid, I'm actually taken aback by the smile on Sawyer's face as I take a seat next to him and dump my bag down on a spare chair. He might be the captain and acknowledged as one of the best defensemen in the league, but he's also known for telling reporters to fuck off in interviews.

"You'll have to forgive my guys for their less than warm welcome this morning." Sawyer maintains his smile as he thumbs at the rest of the room, his southern accent noticeable. "Seven a.m. start after a long offseason will do that to them."

He leans back in his chair, arms folded across his chest. "Jon's kid, right?"

I bristle and flip the cap on my drink, taking a pull before setting it down on the table. As much as I respect my stepdad and feel lucky we have him in our lives, especially Mum's, there's one thing I hate about it—living in his shadow. I took his name because he's my hero and I didn't want to play under my dad's, but with it comes pitfalls.

"Officially, Stepson," I say on a long-drawn-out breath.

Sliding a couple of documents toward me, Sawyer rests his forearms on the table, his dark hair curled around the sides of his Blades cap. "Seen and heard good things about you. I was kind of shocked you stayed in the AHL for an entire season. Could've used you earlier. But ... being totally honest with you" —Sawyer puffs out his cheeks—"there are a few guys on the team who think you landed a pro contract because of daddy." He chuckles low. "There aren't many British guys in the league, and, well, you started playing really late. You getting your shot in the pros just doesn't track for some."

I open my mouth to speak, but he's clearly not finished.

"That said, you're a killer in front of the goal, and *I'm* sold on you joining us. You might just need to win a few of the other guys over."

The double doors at the front open, and laughter immediately follows. Tyler and a couple of other guys who play on the second and third forward lines filter into the room, but the moment he claps eyes on me, his smile fades.

Yeah, I was spot-on. He's not changed one fucking bit.

He holds eye contact for a few seconds before he's broken away when one of the guys nudges him on the arm, asking him to look at something on his phone. Tyler grins in response, but I can tell it's muted. Part of me wonders if his reaction to whatever he's looking at would be different if I wasn't watching. The other part of me doesn't give a fuck.

"Played with him back in Seattle, right?" Sawyer nods his head toward Tyler.

I run my tongue across my bottom lip, a sour taste overtaking the Gatorade. "Yeah," is all I say, hesitant to add any more at this point.

"I don't like him," Sawyer says.

I snap my head to him, staggered the captain went there with a player on his team, especially one who's still considered a rookie after only a single season with the Blades. "Why?"

He dips his head and lowers his voice a couple of octaves. "There was this guy who used to play for us a few seasons back. He was our assistant captain before he basically got kicked off the team when the Blades refused to renew his contract."

"Alex Schneider?" I ask.

Sawyer nods subtly, his brows lifted in Tyler's direction. "Well, he gives me Schneider vibes, and I don't like it. Something tells me you aren't his number one fan either."

"How can you tell that?" I ask, offering a casual shrug.

He picks up his bottle of water and unscrews the cap, a smirk tracing his lips. "Because right about now, your faces match."

I blow out a low-grade laugh. "I've got my thoughts on him."

"Yep. And he has his on you—most of them he's said out loud as well. He's your main skeptic for sure."

"Oh, I don't doubt it," I counter. "So, is there anyone nice around here?"

Sawyer snorts a laugh. "Yeah, pretty much the entire team."

"Feels like it," I reply sarcastically, tracking Tyler's movements to where he joins the table directly in front of us.

The doors push open again, and Jon walks in, a binder tucked under one arm, a blue cap covering his brown hair, and a coffee in his left hand.

Setting the cup and file down on a small table at the front, he props his hands on his hips as he waits for Tyler to stop talking.

Clearing his throat, Jon finally has everyone's attention, and he tips his head over his shoulder toward the projector behind him. "All right, now that I've got everyone's attention, I guess we can get on with things. First off, welcome back. There are a few new faces that I'm sure you're all familiar with. Take the time to speak to each other because I'm not about to start carrying out kindergarten introductions. Second, the next couple of weeks are going to be like nothing you've experienced before. Some of you have been playing pro for years, and others are fresh into it. But let me tell you, this is going to be your hardest preseason yet."

When Jon pauses, Tyler turns over his shoulder, grinning at me, but I ignore it, used to his games.

"There are no free passes here. Everyone will fight *and earn* their place on the team. Last season was one up from the shit show the fans had previously witnessed, but this right here is where we turn it all around. From now until June, you will live and breathe hockey, every single one of you."

"Wait." Tyler speaks up. "June? Like, that's playoff territory."

Jon's hands slide into the pockets of his dress pants. "Damn right it is. You got a problem with that? Have you developed an allergy to success?"

I press my lips together to fight back laughter, and out of the corner of my eye, I notice Sawyer swipe a hand across his mouth.

"No," Tyler replies.

"Good. And, yes, very astute, Bennett. June is indeed playoff time and not jet-off-somewhere-hot-and-tropical territory, like many of you here seem to think it is. This time in nine months, you will be a different player, a better player. You'll all look back on this morning and wonder if you were the same person. There's a lot of talent in this room, and I'm tired of watching it go to waste. The league is coming for us this season, and most of the teams are viewing games against the Blades as guaranteed *w*'s. And to them, I say, *Fuck that*."

A few claps and appreciative grunts echo around the room, and I turn to Sawyer. "I don't believe he's giving anyone on this team preferential treatment."

His green eyes settle on me. "Play your best game, get along with the guys, and you'll be just fine."

As the room begins to empty, I push my seat back and stand, ready to head toward the locker rooms and change for our first conditioning session when I feel a hand land on my shoulder.

I spin around, expecting it to be Jon, but instead, I'm greeted with a mass of dirty-blond hair and gray eyes.

The corner of Tyler's lips tips up as he looks around at the rest of the room and then back at me. "Welcome to New York, Morgan."

CHAPTER TWO

KENDRA

"I think we need to talk about that header. Seriously though, girl, you rose like a freaking salmon."

My lip throbs as I bend down and unlace my cleats.

I face my goalie and closest friend, Jenna, and point to my lip. "And in the process, I took one for the team."

"Yeah, well, you might've taken an elbow to the face, but you kept the ball out of the net and my run of clean sheets going, so drinks are on me tonight. Even if it is just Diet Cokes."

Standing from the bench, I slip off one cleat and then the other. Swiping them underneath with my foot, I don't respond to Jenna or even look at her. I'm not ready for the inquisition about to come my way when I tell her I don't want to go out.

"Okay, I'll upgrade it to a Mountain Dew," she continues, pulling off her jersey and hanging it on one of the hooks lined up above our heads.

I remain quiet, undressing as quickly as possible so I can make it to the showers and then back home to my apartment across town.

When I wrap my towel around me and pull out a shampoo

bottle from my wash bag, I make to leave right as a manicured hand lands on my upper arm.

"You are coming out tonight, right?"

I shrug. "I don't know. It was a nil to nil draw. There isn't much to celebrate, and I'm tired." I pull the topknot out of my hair, and several blonde strands come away with it, more than the usual amount. "I didn't sleep well last night, so I was planning on going home early."

Jenna's eyes fall to the black tie in my hand, covered in blonde. "We could do pizza night at your place instead?"

"Yeah, maybe," I say, trying to leave again.

"He didn't show up last night, did he?"

I close my eyes and swallow thickly, my mind traveling to Tyler's text, still unanswered on my phone. It was our fourth anniversary, and he promised me an uninterrupted night together. Just us. Turned out, he couldn't even make it past my front door.

"He messaged me to say he needed to report for preseason really early and he couldn't come over." I leave out the picture I saw posted of him at Lloyd's Bar later that evening. "He's got a lot going on, and so do I with the soccer season in full swing. I'll see him later in the week."

Jenna makes a humming sound like she's about as convinced of that as I am. I've been center back for the New York Storm for an entire season since leaving Seattle with Tyler, and in that time, I can count on one hand the number of date nights we've had together.

Sure, I knew dating an NHL player would be tough; the season is grueling, and there's a lot of traveling involved. But no more than what my dad did when he moved to England for his pro soccer career. Since we stayed in the US to be around Mom's family, he was backward and forward across continents. He always had time for my mom, always made the effort to put her, my brother, and me first.

"You cooked for him and everything though, Kend." Jenna's

voice sounds sad as she releases my arm, and I let it fall to my side.

The anger, which was overpowered by adrenaline during the game, returns when I remember saving what I could of dinner and throwing the unsalvageable food into the trash. I earn sixty thousand dollars a year, unlike my boyfriend, who makes well over ten times my salary. Probably way more than that, but since he doesn't tell me, I go with the minimum. The National Women's Soccer League and NHL are very different worlds—not that I train, travel, or play any less hard.

"I don't want to talk about it," I reply, twisting my long hair around my wrist, my towel still wrapped around me as the chill of the locker room hits my cooling body. "I don't have the capacity to get upset with him again."

"You can do way better, babe. Truly, you can."

I flick the lid on my shampoo bottle and bring it to my nose, the honeycomb scent comforting to me and a reminder of my dad's beehive back home in Ohio. "You're still in your honeymoon phase with Lee. We've been together for four years."

Jenna's brows pull together. "And how long have your parents been married exactly?" She waves a hand in front of her. "Forget mine. My dad was a dick. But yours—they have been together since forever, right? I don't think time has anything to do with it."

I have zero comeback or justification to her logic, but I'm saved from the conversation when our center forward and captain, Hollie Browne, approaches me with a bright smile. "Nice work out there, Hart. I thought they'd snatch the three points right at the death, but you showed us exactly why we'd signed you." She takes in my height—I'm not exactly small at five feet eight. "Genuinely, I've never seen anyone as good in the air. All their right back had to do was make any kind of connection with the ball, and we would've been done." She offers me another smile and spins on her heel, making her way back to the other side of the room.

Jenna turns back to me. "I hope you gave him a good piece of your mind."

"I haven't replied yet," I say, biting down on my bottom lip. "I have nothing to say to him right now."

She nods in understanding and then toward the showers. "Come on. Let's grab a shower and head out for a while. Even if the game was nothing to celebrate, I say we slip in a cocktail or two. Fuck men."

A laugh bursts out of me, but I can't help the feeling of sadness as it coats my insides.

When I reach the showers, I turn the faucet and throw my towel over the top of the door. I stand back from the cold spray, but small droplets hit my skin as I wait for the water to heat up.

I know exactly what Jenna is thinking—I'm being too soft on a guy who has made little to zero effort on maintaining our relationship since we moved here last year. I can't say that I disagree with her since all the signs point to it being one-way traffic. It's me who texts first in the morning. It's me who invites him over for dinners, which he then cancels on at the last minute. It's me who suggested we move in together when we came to New York. It was him who said no and he wanted to take things more slowly, that we were young, and he didn't want to get too serious, too soon.

And you know what? I believed him.

The water is warm, bordering on too hot when I step under the stream, but I don't adjust the temperature. The jets act like a hug around my aching body.

I spent all of last night trying to remind myself of the reasons *why* I'd gotten with Tyler in college, but I came up empty. He was the star center and the popular guy around campus, and I was the impressionable girl who got overexcited when he showed even a little bit of interest in me. If I'm really honest with myself, I don't think much has changed since I got with him. If anything, his absence from our relationship has only grown worse. I might've put up with it when I was eighteen, but at twenty-two, I'm increasingly convinced I'd be better off single. I thought we were forever, and each time we talked about the future, I interpreted his lukewarm responses as way more enthusiastic.

And that's why I followed him to New York.

Squirting way too much shampoo into my hand, I begin massaging it through my hair, more strands coming away easily—my body's response to stress.

I've clung on to whatever it is between us for so long that I've forgotten what it feels like to be wanted. And that's not me—that's never been me.

These days, staying with Tyler is as much about proving to myself that I made the right decision in turning down a pro contract in London, playing in front of Super League crowds, as it is hoping that I haven't been kidding myself all these years.

"Hey, babe. Have you got that massage bar you brought with you last time? My calf is aching like a bitch!" Jenna shouts from the other shower stall.

I drop my shoulders, remembering that I left it back on the bench. "In my gym bag!" I reply back.

It's even down to things like this—concentrating so much on what's going on with Tyler, like what he does on nights out that he doesn't tell me about, that results in every aspect of my life and career coming a distant second to him. And not in the good way, like with my mom and dad.

My life shouldn't revolve around a boy who doesn't seem to be concerned about me at all.

CHAPTER THREE

JACK

With a thud, I replace the Olympic bar on the rack.

My spotter and also goalie, Archer Moore, flicks his eyes over to a few of the guys as they make their way back to the locker room, all of them laughing and joking around.

Chalk clouds fill the space between us as he rubs his hands together, and I sit up on the bench and grab my towel, wiping the sweat from the back of my neck.

I tip my chin in the direction of Tyler and our teammates, raising a brow at Archer. "What's the score there?"

Archer grabs his Dri-FIT shirt from behind him and tucks it into the waistband of his shorts. He passes me mine, but I'm still too hot to put it on, so I wrap it around my shoulders.

"My best guess is, they're headed out tonight for a few drinks. Probably to Lloyd's in town. It's kind of a tradition."

I stand from the bench and pick up my water bottle, popping the cap and taking a sip. "And we're all going, I assume, or is this tradition by invitation only?"

He grins at me. "Oh, we're all going, including you, rook."

It would take an internet search of around zero-point-five

seconds to easily conclude that Archer Moore is a playboy—and a prolific one at that. His activities and hookups dwarf even what Jon did back in his day. Goalies are known to border on the crazy side of sane—I guess they'd have to be willing to stand in the way of pucks—but Archer pushes even those boundaries.

Still, in a short space of time, I've concluded I like him. He has zero agenda when it comes to team dynamics—that much is clear. His only priorities are shutouts and girls, and I appreciate his straightforward approach.

"Morgan."

I'm about to follow Archer into the locker room when I spin around at the sound of Jon's voice.

On his way over, he watches his goalie push through the door and turns his attention to me. "First night of preseason, the guys go out. It's something the Blades have done for years, so I suggest you go with them."

I swipe my towel across my forehead, sweat still pouring from me. Jon wasn't kidding when he said the next couple of weeks would be tough. "I was just talking to Archer about it. He already told me I was going."

He crosses his arms over his chest. "Getting to know the resident playboy, huh? He's a good guy. They all are in their own way. Like I told you a few weeks back, the team has been fractured by poor performances and angry fans. There's a lot of work to be done, not just on the ice, but in the locker room too."

I nod in understanding. "The trainer paired us up today, but, yeah, the team is cliquey, and right now, I'm talking to anyone who will look my way."

"Hmm ..." Jon looks down and scuffs the floor with his trainer. "Talked to Tyler yet?"

He knows the score between us from the days when he coached us both in college. Being honest, I don't know how much Jon knew about the reasons why we didn't see eye to eye, but I'm pretty sure one of them wasn't the hots I had for Tyler's girlfriend. I worked pretty hard to keep that part hidden. Even if

Tyler could tell I thought he was dating a girl way above him, we never actually came to blows over it. Jon just knew our personalities clashed.

"He welcomed me to New York," I reply with humor.

"You both need to bury the hatchet. This isn't the NCAA anymore, Jack." His tone is serious, and my smile fades when I see the look on his face, one I haven't noticed before—or at least, it's never been directed at me. "Go out tonight," he continues. "Make an effort with *everyone*, and for the love of God, stay off the booze. I have sprints lined up for tomorrow, and I'll be able to tell who made the right choices the night before and who didn't." His face softens as he claps a hand on my shoulder. "You did well today. This is all just an adjustment period, but you one hundred percent belong here. This is the beginning of an insane pro career, and your mom and I are proud of you."

"Stay off the booze and keep doing the same things," I repeat back at him. Bringing my hand to my forehead, I offer him a salute. "No worries, Jon." I spin around and head for the locker room.

"Oh, and, Morgan?"

I turn back on my heel. "Yeah?"

"Outside the training center and arena, it's Jon. But inside these four walls and on the ice, you know the drill. You might've been able to get away with it in college, but not here."

I nod lightly and take another sip of water. "Sure thing, Coach."

"So, THIS IS LLOYD'S THEN," I say, walking in with Sawyer flanking one side of me and Archer on the other.

"Sure is," Sawyer responds, pulling off his jacket and handing it to the doorman.

The bar is the exact opposite of what I anticipated. I based my expectations for this place on Riley's—the bar I used to hang out at with some of the Scorpions guys when I lived back in Seattle—but this place is different. Rather than a sports bar—which it kind of is with an NBA game playing on the overhead screens—it has more of a cocktail bar feel to it. The place is all dark greens and blacks with plush seating.

As we make our way to the back, heads turn in our direction.

There are twenty of us here tonight, and as we reach the ropes to the private area, Sawyer heads for the front of the group, leaving me and Archer toward the back.

"What do you drink?" Archer asks me, eyes already on the private bar in front of us.

"Soda," I reply as we walk toward a couple of booths set out and ready for us.

He stops dead in his tracks, his face turning white, almost like I just admitted to killing his puppy. "Fuck off."

I shrug. "We've got sprints tomorrow. Apparently, I need to stay off the booze."

He walks toward me, tapping me on the shoulder as he passes by. "Let me guess—orders from Coach Morgan?"

"Yeah."

"Well, if there was ever a case of *do as I say, not as I do*, then that is it." He tips his head over his shoulder as he makes for the rest of the guys, and I follow, noting the booth he's heading for is exactly where Tyler is sitting. "Listen, I might only be twenty-six, but I've been in the NHL long enough to remember when Jon was in his prime, and let me tell you, he did not abstain from the booze before preseason sprints."

We take a seat next to each other in the round booth. I'm opposite of Tyler, who's too busy scowling at his phone to notice me.

"So, yeah, have a *drink* and worry about the consequences tomorrow. The closer we get to the season, the more you need to hold off. Tonight is one of your last chances." He pauses and turns to me as I watch Tyler angrily hit the keys on his phone. "So, what'll it be?"

"IPA," I answer with no hesitation.

Archer nods and gets up from the booth, leaving me, Sawyer, Tyler, and his clique all in silence, the beat of the music the only sound between us.

"How many times have you messaged her?" Connor, one of the second line forwards, asks.

Tyler shrugs, clenching his jaw. "Three. She's read them all, but she hasn't responded. I thought she'd want to see me after I couldn't make it last night."

"Maybe she's pissed at you for something," Connor replies with a chuckle. "Wouldn't be the first time."

My molars meet, and like a flashback to college, I fight back the urge to push for more details on why Kendra is ghosting him. To be honest, I fight back the urge to ask why the fuck she's still dating him at all.

Tyler winces, but not in a way that indicates regret—nah, his face is too smug for that. "I had to bail on our plans last night. You know, with the early start Jon landed on us at the last minute."

I grind my teeth harder.

"Shit, man. Yeah, chicks don't like being stood up." Connor's brows shoot up as he leans back and takes a beer from Archer, who is handing them around to the group.

"Yep," Tyler replies, setting his phone down, still staring at the screen. "Especially on our fourth anniversary."

As soon as I take my pint from Archer, I instantly bring it to my lips—anything to stop me from kicking Tyler under the table.

He's a prick.

"But you were here last night," Archer says, taking the seat next to me.

Don't punch him in the face, Jack.

"You know, my dad did that kind of shit to my mum. Didn't

work out well for him in the end," I burst out, unable to stop myself. "She's now married to a former NHL star and rarely gives him a second thought."

Tyler's head darts up, his eyes narrow. Clearly, he was so engrossed in trying to contact Kendra—for fucking once—that he genuinely didn't notice me take a seat.

I nod at his phone, which shows zero notifications. "Maybe Kendra's had the same thought. You know, that she could do better."

Archer clears his throat from beside me as I watch the column of Tyler's throat work to swallow his anger.

I know all too well that I shouldn't give a fuck about someone else's relationship, and ordinarily, I don't. But I've spent way too long watching this fucker mess things up with a girl I'd give my left nut to date. I wasn't all that bothered with girls in college, too busy with trying to work on my game and get the grades I needed to catch up with all the other guys who had been playing since they could walk. But I watched my mum put herself second when she had more talent in her little finger than my dad possessed in his entire body, and this situation right here stinks of the same.

Tyler keeps his eyes on me as he sits back in the booth, running his tongue across his bottom lip. "Yeah, well, I'll make it up to her tonight. She likes to be on top."

A couple of the guys sitting around laugh but quickly fall silent, their eyes shooting over my shoulder.

"You can tell her that now, Ty." Sawyer chuckles as he motions over his shoulder, multiple eyes following because ...

Goddamn.

I've seen her pictured with Tyler a few times, but mainly from photos of her playing for the New York Storm. Though nothing—absolutely nothing—could've prepared me for the way she looks tonight.

With her blonde hair curled around her shoulders, she and

another dark-haired friend, who I recognize as the goalie on her team, come to stand at the foot of our table.

I pick up my beer, trying to concentrate on the glass rather than the low-cut black dress she's wearing or the black leather boots that stop just below her knees. Her toned thighs look incredible as she leans forward and drums her green fingernails on the table.

"Kend," Tyler chokes out, pointing to his phone. "We were just talking about you. I've been messaging you all night."

Since I'm back to staring at her like a fucking loser, I notice the way her attention briefly snags on me before she focuses back on her dickhead boyfriend.

"Yeah, I know. I just didn't feel like replying. Thought I'd just show up, see what you're up to in your favorite place." She looks around the bar area.

Archer shifts uncomfortably, his body language reflecting how the rest of us feel.

She's pissed.

Tyler might try to hide it, but the guilt across his face is unmistakable. He tips his chin at Connor. "Move over will you so my girl can sit down?"

CHAPTER FOUR

KENDRA

Of course he's here.

Even if I wasn't aware that tonight was a tradition for the Blades or he hadn't been texting me nonstop, I'd still know exactly where to find him.

As his teammates move aside, I take a seat next to Tyler. I can barely look at him.

When he started blowing up my phone, I was all for leaving him on Read, but Jenna suggested I come here and show him what he'd missed out on last night. And that sounded like the best idea she'd had all season because, yeah, I'm pissed.

I know he hates the dress I have on purely because other men love it, but he can fuck right off if he thinks he gets to call the shots on what I wear. He's called enough of them during our relationship.

My eyes are still glued to the black table in front of us when Tyler's hand reaches behind my back and palms my ass. This is his way of saying sorry since he's never been able to say it out loud, but unfortunately for him, I'm not in the mood to accept any kind of apology right now.

"Do you, um ... want a drink?"

My gaze tracks the voice and lands on Jack Thompson. Well, Jack Morgan now. I saw him the second I walked into the bar and couldn't help but steal a quick glance his way when I was talking to Tyler.

He's hot. I'm not single, but I do have eyes, and, holy moly, he just went and got a whole lot hotter these past twelve months. His shoulders are way broader than they were, and his eyes somehow look much bluer than I remember. He's also let his brown hair grow out, and it flops forward, kind of like how his stepdad wears his.

Though it's not his appearance or white shirt with the sleeves rolled up to his elbows that has my full attention.

"Wait. You're British." Jenna speaks first, his accent clearly making the same impression it did on me.

I was kind of pissed that Jack and Tyler didn't get along in college because, man, oh man, could I listen to him all day.

Jack smiles in response, popping his cute dimple, but he doesn't look at Jenna. He keeps his attention straight on me.

"I'll get the drinks," Tyler interjects, leaning down to kiss my bare shoulder.

I snap my eyes away from Jack and look at my boyfriend. "No. I'm good, thanks. I can buy my own drinks." I turn to Jenna. "Wanna help?"

Tyler doesn't argue, and I stand, pushing my way out of the booth past him and his teammates.

The second I reach the bar and set my purse on the counter, Jenna's hand lands on top of mine.

"Okay, hold up on ordering drinks because I'm going to need a minute. That's Jon Morgan's son, right? You never told me he was into you."

I drop my head forward and giggle. "Um, what? I've never said anything because he's not."

Her brows knit together in confusion. "Kend, you have got to be kidding me."

Cautiously, I tip my head over my shoulder to see Jack joking around with Sawyer Bryce and Archer Moore.

"I think you're going a little crazy." I tap my pointer finger against my temple. "I've known Jack since the beginning of college, when he started playing with Tyler, and back then, I didn't pick up any vibes either. Other than his hatred of my boyfriend."

"Hmm ..." Jenna responds. "Well, he had me with the British accent, and now I might be certifiably in love with him. He can obviously tell a dickhead when he sees one."

I'd like to have the luxury of arguing with her and defending the guy I'm supposed to be head over heels for, but honestly, other than being in complete agreement with her, I don't know what else I am right now. I definitely don't know if I'm in love with Tyler anymore, and my stomach bottoms out at the thought.

"Talk to me, babe," Jenna says, taking a seat at the bar. She looks down at the stool next to hers, asking me to join her. "You can barely look at the guy. This isn't right anymore, is it?"

I blow into my cheeks and point at a random cocktail on the menu when the bartender approaches us. I've no idea what I selected, but if it has alcohol, then that's all that matters right now.

"I don't know what to say. I came to this city because this is where Tyler got drafted before college. In reality, I should probably be in London, playing in Premier League stadiums. I think that was my chance, you know? And I turned it down for a guy who ..." I look over my shoulder to find Tyler with his head thrown back, laughter spilling out of him. The only person looking my way is Jack, and I offer him a small smile. "I guess he just isn't that concerned about us. I'm tired of doing the chasing and hanging on to something that doesn't seem worth the effort anymore."

The bartender sets a blue cocktail down in front of me, and I sniffle, my senses tingling with sadness. "You were right about time. It shouldn't matter how long you've been dating. It should still be exciting, but we've lost that, and he doesn't want to make the effort to get it back."

Jenna nods and sips her drink. "So, what are you going to do about it?"

"Talk to him, I guess. Tell him I'm unhappy, if he hasn't already worked that one out." I run a finger around the rim of my glass as it shines beneath the bar lighting.

"You okay?" A tall shadow looms over me, blocking the shine on my glass.

God, that British accent.

As he motions to the bartender, Jack turns to face me, leaning against the bar.

I shrug. "Yeah, I'm good."

"You sure about that?" he replies.

"I-I'm just going to use the restroom," Jenna announces, pushing off her stool and grabbing her bag. "Be back in a sec!" she sings.

I fight the urge to roll my eyes, knowing full well she doesn't need to pee. She just went when we left my apartment twenty minutes ago.

"Yep. Just had a tough game today, and I'm tired," I reply, still staring down into my cocktail since there's no way I can look at him with glassy eyes.

He's still standing to the side of me when he leans back further, attempting to capture my attention, and when he succeeds, the smile on his face causes my lips to tip up. Jack was always known around college as the nice guy. He spent nearly all his time at the rink or library, but for a short while, he dated a girl who was in the same English Lit course as me. She never said why they'd split, but she did say she was gutted. Although I never really got to know or see that side of him much since whenever I was around, so was Tyler.

"Is that a smile I see?"

"Nope," I reply, my smile growing all the while. "Too damn moody for that."

He blows out a breath and hands the bartender a twenty-dollar bill. "Have these two drinks been settled?"

"Nah, on a tab for Tyler," the bartender responds.

I reach into my purse to pay.

"I got them," Jack replies to the bartender before looking at me. "If that's okay with you?"

This time, when I look at him, I feel heat flush my cheeks. "You don't have to."

"I know. But what if I want to?" His voice is slightly flirtatious, or maybe that's just my imagination after what Jenna said.

"Kend, the bartender knows to put your drinks on my tab, we take it in turns to pay and it's my night."

Jack's lips morph from a smile to a scowl when Tyler sidles up beside me, taking Jenna's stool.

"You buying my girl drinks, Morgan?" Tyler pins him with a glare, but I'm about ready to explode.

"*Your* girl?" I look at Tyler and point at my chest. "First, I'm not some kind of possession you can claim, and second, so what if he was?"

Tyler rears back at the way I snapped at him, almost like he wasn't expecting me to go off, but genuinely, I've had enough.

"Let's be honest," I continue. "It's not like you were bothered when I came to sit over here a second ago or even when you stood me up last night."

Out of the corner of my eye, I notice Jack shift from one foot to the other.

"I'll be right over there if you need me," he says, gesturing toward the booth.

"Why would she need you?" Tyler scoffs. "I've got her handled."

"*The fuck*?!" I announce. "I'm sorry, you've got me *what* now?"

Tyler's face pales when he sees mine.

I snatch up my bag and slide off the stool, spinning around to face my boyfriend for what I know is the final time. My rage is at an all-time high, and humiliation flows through me. "Got me handled? Who the fuck do you think you are? You ..." I bite down on my lip, attempting to steady my emotions. "You're acting like a complete asshole!"

"Babe, are you okay?" Jenna asks as she approaches us, her head turning as Jack makes his way back to the booth.

"I want to leave," I say, not taking my eyes off Tyler.

"Baby, don't be like this."

He reaches for my hand, but I snatch it away quickly.

"Don't," I bite out.

"Let me get my jacket," Jenna says, grabbing it from the back of Tyler's stool.

Tyler throws his arms up. "So, what? That's it? You're just going to bail on me?"

I choke out a laugh and throw an arm out behind me, gesturing toward the booth. I know people are watching our fight, but at this point, I couldn't care less. "Why are you so upset, Tyler? You're practically in a relationship with everyone but me anyway."

He scratches at the back of his neck, guilt all over his face. I'm pointing at his teammates, but we both know there's a fair chance he hasn't always been faithful. I've never had hard proof, but I have seen questionable photos from away series and heard the rumors, all of which he straight-up denied when I asked him about them.

So, why have I never believed him?

Running a rough hand across his mouth, Tyler drops it to his thigh with a slap. "Let me come back to your place later, and we can talk about this. You know, rather than make a fucking scene in public. You might fly under the radar, but I'm famous, and people take pictures."

I shake my head with a sarcastic laugh. "Yeah, you're right. I am under the radar, aren't I, Tyler? In fact, I barely register anymore. Well, let me make this real easy for you." I step toward him, feeling more relieved than upset at what I'm about to say. "Don't bother coming over tonight. In fact, don't bother at all. We're done."

CHAPTER FIVE

JACK

Shortly after I moved to the US and for my eighteenth birthday, my mum, Felicity, bought me ice-level season tickets to the Seattle Scorpions. I'd watched a ton of hockey games in the UK and started playing when I was eight, but the first time we took our seats at an NHL game? Yeah, that was something pretty fucking special.

I guess that's when my commitment to the game hit overdrive, and the more people that whispered and laughed about my chances of making it pro, the more I dug my heels in, determined to prove them wrong.

My dad always said sports were a waste of time. He wanted me to follow in his financial footsteps, working in Canary Wharf, London. Being a stockbroker appealed to me as much as gouging my eyes out with a blunt knife, and when I refused to join his firm as an intern, you could say that was when our relationship really took a nosedive. I'd always been closer to my mum, so I guess it wasn't surprising when my parents divorced and I opted to stay in Seattle with her while my dad and sister, Darcy, returned to Oxford at the end of his work contract.

And that's where they both are right now, though it's only my sister I miss today as I finally live out my dreams. I don't think Dad will ever really take an interest in what I do. The only time he seemed to pay attention was when he saw the number of zeros in my pro contract.

It's true; I got a head start when Mum began dating Jon, and he started coaching me in private, but I was still way behind the standard expected of other players my age. I've always been fast on the ice, but my technical skills were ... let's just say, not where they needed to be.

I about broke myself in college. It got to the point where I was risking injury and straddling the lines of complete exhaustion as I set up camp at the rink and library, only occasionally heading out with friends.

I didn't have time to date, but at one point, I found myself seeing a girl called Olivia. She was on the same course as Kendra, and she was nice. I just never wanted to take it further than a few dates, so I broke it off, not wanting to mess her around.

Darcy is the complete opposite of me—whereas I never wanted to get serious with anyone, she's had a long-term boyfriend since she was, like, fifteen. I've watched her and Liam go through the wringer together, and honestly, that's never been for me.

There was only ever one girl I wanted to get to know seriously.

Shaking away thoughts of the last time I saw her at Lloyd's Bar, I come to a stop at center ice. Nothing could've ever prepared me for today. I could've attended a thousand NHL games as a spectator and played in the AHL for ten seasons, and I'd still be just as overwhelmed for the first exhibition game of preseason.

Fuck, this is crazy, and it's only warm-up.

"All good?" Sawyer moves alongside me, and we begin stretching out our groin, glutes, and hamstrings.

I take a look around the arena, packed with at least twenty

thousand fans. It's impossible to make out my mum, but I know she's sitting—and probably screaming—in the family box way up top.

"Yep," I say, moving to my left leg and stretching it out.

"You'll get plenty of ice time tonight." Tipping his head over his right shoulder, Sawyer takes in the orange jerseys belonging to the Dallas Destroyers. "Really going in at the deep end with these guys."

"They're tough, but we're smarter," I say, standing up as Jon approaches us.

Sawyer smirks. "Were you watching the same footage as me before this? Key thing is keeping our heads in the game and moving the puck quickly."

"And playing as a team," I reply, catching Tyler in my peripheral vision as he heads toward Archer, ready to take shots.

"All right, Morgan, I want you warming up your slap shot, as we discussed. And, Bryce, I need you for a second. I've had a last-minute rethink on a play since they aren't starting with the line I anticipated," Jon instructs.

"Got it, *Coach*." I elongate the title and smile at him, and he lifts a brow in response.

One thing about Jon Morgan: he's got good banter. But mine is better.

The second I reach Tyler, he rockets a couple of pucks my way, keeping at least a dozen to himself.

"What, are we on rations now?" I say, replacing my mouthguard and lining up in front of Archer, who's focused in on us both.

It's been nearly a week since Kendra walked out on Tyler, and I'd be lying if I said I wasn't pleased about it. Though based on his mood, I'd guess it's been that long since he heard from her.

Firing off another shot, which is easily saved by Archer, Tyler props his gloves on his hips. "There's a whole bunch lined up over there." He tips his chin in the direction of the benches, but doesn't look at me.

"Or you could just pass me half of what you have, and we can get on and quit fucking around," I retort.

"No can do. I'm gonna need all of these." He slaps another puck at Archer, and this one goes insanely wide.

I shake my head and look down at the ice. "Are we really going down this path again, Tyler? Are you not tired from your petty antics during college? Because I am. I've got a career to focus on."

I slide a puck toward myself, sending a slap shot to the goal, which finds the top right. Even from back here, I catch the appreciative look on Archer's face.

With a wrist shot that takes our goalie by surprise, Tyler squeezes the puck between Archer's legs before he can get down to it.

Satisfied with his attempt, Tyler looks at me for the first time since that night at Lloyd's. "Focused on your career? Could've fooled me, *bro*. From over here, it looks like your attention is on one thing only."

I shake my head at him and blow out a breath. "Yeah? And what's that?"

He hits another shot but misses again, and Archer throws his arms out in frustration.

"Kendra. But I guess that's nothing new either, is it?"

A few more pucks land at my feet when Sawyer slides up alongside me.

"Thanks," I say as he immediately turns and skates toward center ice.

I decide not to rise to Tyler's bait as I begin firing off slap shots at Archer—some of them he saves and others find the exact spot I picked out.

Tyler speaks again after a few more minutes. "I'll take your silence as confirmation."

With my row of pucks depleted, I skate over to him as our goalie turns to face his net, grabbing his drink bottle.

"Let's just keep this about hockey, yeah? We've never seen eye to eye, and I accept that. You don't like me, and I'm not exactly mad about you either."

I continue skating past him.

"But you like her, don't you? Just be a man and admit it."

I spin around to face him, chewing on the corner of my mouthguard. "So what if I do? I'm not dating her, and neither are you. She's a free agent and neither of our concern."

Kind of my concern.

Approaching me, Tyler stops just before our helmets touch. In the crowd, you would either guess we're good buddies, having a laugh, or the first ice fight of the season is close to breaking out.

"Oh, she's always been my concern, and she absolutely is yours too. Even if it's never been your right. Don't think I haven't noticed you checking her out. I don't know what the rules are over in your country, but in America, we don't make a play for another dude's girl."

I throw my head back and laugh. "In my country? Jesus, Tyler, I haven't once made a play for Kendra. She *was* always your girl and loyal to you. Even if you can't say the same."

I know I'm pressing his buttons, and it's a really bad idea, especially right before a game, but I can't fucking help myself. When we traveled for away games in college, I'd watch Tyler leave bars with girls who were categorically not Kendra.

"Watch your mouth, Morgan," he spits.

I slide away from him, aware that we literally have an audience of twenty thousand people. "Look, Tyler, I meant what I said. I'm here to play hockey, and you and I are going to play a lot together over the next eighty-plus games. I have zero interest in getting into it with you."

He pulls off his helmet and tucks it under his arm, his jaw clenching at whatever's going through his mind. "Stay away from Kendra, and we won't have a problem."

CHAPTER SIX

KENDRA

When I ended it with Tyler—my long-term boyfriend, the guy I'd moved across states for—just over a week ago, I figured things couldn't get much worse.

Well, I was wrong.

The morning after I dragged myself from my bed—aka my pit of sorrow because I had nothing to show for our past four years together—I expected to find my kitchen just how I'd left it the night before. Instead, I found half my ceiling missing, debris and plasterboard everywhere, dust ingrained into every soft furnishing I owned.

How in the hell I'd slept through it happening I have no idea, but I did.

It's safe to say, my place is fucked.

It's also safe to say that my landlord is an asshole of the highest order. Apparently, it will take weeks to bring my apartment back to some kind of livable state, and he doesn't seem that concerned in hurrying the fuck up about it either.

I can't say I'm shocked that half my ceiling fell in. The

building is old and was in a bad state when I moved in a year ago. Which is probably why I secured the low rental I did.

But I was determined to have a place of my own instead of moving into shared housing, like most of my team had done. I couldn't really afford the rent, but I made ends meet, and it was worth it to have my privacy. Even if Tyler had offered to help me out financially, I know I wouldn't have accepted it.

My apartment was my little haven. And now it's a construction site.

Sure, the New York Storm could put me up in a hotel, which they said they'd do, but living out of suitcases for the next however long really didn't appeal to me. I need some kind of home comforts, and staying in a hotel long-term doesn't feel all that safe.

So, it was at this point that I lost my shit, and just like my ceiling, I collapsed, every single emotion pouring out of me. Luckily, the only person to witness my meltdown was Jenna, who immediately suggested the sofa bed in her living room.

And that's exactly where I am right now. With a suitcase full of clothes and insurance claims coming out of my ears, this isn't what I expected from my life twelve months after moving to the Big Apple.

My phone buzzes in my hand as I continue scrolling for alternative places to live in the Brooklyn area, all well out of budget.

> TYLER
>
> Kend, I really want to talk to you. Can't we just try and work this out?

Ignoring this text like I have with all his other ones, I throw my phone down on the duvet in front of me and adjust myself on the sofa bed that's seen better days. The springs dig into my sides, leaving me exhausted and grouchy. Not a great combo for a pro athlete trying to break into the national squad and get a shot at the World Cup next summer.

Despite the shit show that is my life right now, one thing has never been clearer: I'm not upset over our breakup because I lost Tyler; I'm upset over the decisions and sacrifices I made for him. Yeah, there's a part of me that misses him—how could I not when he was a huge, if not dwindling, part of my life for four years? But the larger part of me feels—I don't know—indifferent toward it all. Like, deep down, I always knew it was inevitable, and I was coming to terms with the end of us for way longer than what I could admit.

But I don't have the right words for him at the moment, and honestly, I'm still pissed about the way he treated me. I can't even find it in me to tell my family we split, not that my mom or dad cared much for him anyway. They always thought someone who loved himself that much could never hold space in his heart for anyone else.

A giggle filters down the hallway, followed by a bang against the living room wall, and I sink down further under my duvet.

Another reason why I need to find a solution to my homelessness—I think there's only been one night in the past week when Lee hasn't been over, and when I say my friend has a high sex drive, I mean it.

A lot of my stuff might have been ruined in my living area, but one saving grace was, my vibrator was safely tucked away in my nightstand. If you asked me when the last time I had sex was, I'd tell you there was snow on the ground. Tyler was a guy who believed his own hype, but unfortunately for him, his skills on the ice didn't exactly extend to the bedroom. He was selfish between the sheets, and I mastered the art of faking it until my interest in sex faded almost entirely.

Replacing my earplugs so I can't hear my friend, I reach across to my suitcase and grab my red wand—which I named Scarlett because I think she works better with an identity.

The second I switch Scarlett to the first setting and dip her below the waistband of my sleep shorts, my mouth pops open with instant euphoria.

I've been way too distracted to think about getting myself

off, but when she finds my clit, sending delicious vibrations through me, I realize this is exactly what I needed.

Working the vibe slowly inside me, I can't help but feel like maybe I haven't just been missing out on career opportunities while messing around with Tyler, but maybe on hooking up too. And when the vibrator hits a spot my ex-boyfriend could never find, I start to wonder if playing the single game and having fun might be the way forward.

Jenna told me for months that I could do better, and each time, I told her that beyond my relationship with Tyler, I couldn't picture being with anyone else.

As I move the wand between my legs, my knees begin to shake under the weight of intense pleasure.

Perhaps I don't need to have a relationship with anyone. Maybe what I really need is to date and have casual sex. Maybe all I need is to take the pressure off me to find the right guy and settle down for a while.

I hit the next setting up on the wand and throw my head back into the pillow, drawing my bottom lip between my teeth.

God, this is good.

It's kind of sad that my vibrator can get me off when my ex-boyfriend couldn't.

I push Tyler out of my mind and flick Scarlett to her highest setting, suppressing a moan when the vibrations take me right there. I can feel it building, every single thread of knotted tension unraveling as blissful waves crash over me.

My orgasm threatens to break through, and I'm right on the verge of tipping over as I squeeze my eyes shut, focusing on just me and this moment.

Until I'm not seeing darkness any longer, and I fall over the edge when Jack's face comes into view, his broad shoulders and toned abs moving above me. His dimple pops on a sexy smile, and his floppy brown hair falls over his blue eyes.

"You like that, Kendra?"

I bolt up on the bed and look around, unsure if I'm hallucinating or dreaming. One thing is for sure: Jack Morgan is not in my bed, but he sure as fuck was in my head a second ago.

Pushing the covers back quickly, I lean across and flick on a side lamp, flooding the living room with soft light.

What the fuck just happened?

I drop Scarlett onto my duvet and shoot out of bed, padding into the kitchen and flicking on the coffee maker. I grab an overturned mug from the drainer and grip it with both hands as I lean back against the counter.

I've never thought about Jack in that way. Sure, I've thought he was good-looking, but never ... like that.

"Babe?" Jenna stands in the space separating the kitchen and hallway, her fluffy pink robe wrapped around her. "You okay? You look kind of shocked."

My eyes flick over to the sofa bed, and against the crisp white duvet, Scarlett is unmissable.

My cheeks flush when Jenna follows my gaze across the room, and she pins her bottom lip between her teeth, suppressing amusement.

"Did I interrupt something?" she goads.

At twenty-five, she's not exactly innocent—definitely not with the way she and Lee go at it every night—but I can't help the heat as it spreads throughout my body.

"Coffee?" I say, turning away as I grab a second cup and quickly fill it.

She clears her throat and then walks toward me, and I spin back around, offering the drink to her.

She takes it, eyeing me cautiously.

"Go on. Say whatever's on your mind," I drawl on a futile breath.

She raises a brow, bringing the cup to her lips. "I was just thinking about the last time I saw that flush on your cheeks."

I cock my head to the side, eyes narrowing at my friend. "Oh yeah? When?"

She takes a small sip but keeps the rim to her mouth, trying to hide her smugness. "Oh, I think you know when you last had that kind of reaction."

I continue to play dumb, picking up my own cup and adding sweetener. "You'll have to be more specific."

She spins around and makes her way back to the bedroom, but not before she stops, turning to look over her shoulder. "I'll give you a hint: you told me he was the only guy you accepted a drink from that night."

CHAPTER SEVEN

JACK

The start of my pro career has been, on one hand, awesome —having made two assists and scoring a goal against Dallas. There's no doubting I'm happy with the way things are going. Even Tyler's set aside our differences on the ice, and the past four days have been less dramatic.

Though that's where the positives have stopped. Off the ice, he won't even look in my direction, let alone speak to me. It's possible he thinks I care about his cold shoulder.

Too bad I don't.

I've been living in Brooklyn for just over three weeks, and other than my teammates, Jon, and Mum, I know next to no one.

What I have found is the best bakery a couple of blocks down from my three-bedroom apartment. And it sells cakes that are almost as good as being back home in the UK.

Almost.

Rise Up is jam-packed as I push through the door and pull off my beanie, shoving it in my jacket pocket. It's early October, and the temperatures in Brooklyn have already fallen to below freezing.

As the line of customers moves forward, Ed—the owner and main guy who usually serves me—approaches with an extended arm and shakes my hand over the counter. The first game of the regular season is in two days, and I probably—definitely—should not be here. But whatever. He makes scones the way they should be made.

"Jack, nice to see you, man. What can I get for you?"

I tap the glass a couple of times and point to a cherry scone and then a brownie right at the back. "These two, please, Ed."

He nods and gets to work. "To eat in or take out?"

Since I don't have practice or any commitments today, I have time to kill. I swivel round, searching out a place to sit. Every table in the small café is taken, but as I'm about to give up and ask for them to be bagged, my attention snags on a mass of blonde hair. Her back is to me as she bends over the table, tapping away on her phone.

I turn back to Ed, my day already feeling a little fuller. "Eat in, please, and can I take an extra scone?"

With a plate in each hand, I come to stand in front Kendra as she remains focused on her phone. I realize she's calculating something when I see the app she has open. As she hits the total button, she lets out a forlorn sigh and drops her head down on the table, the screen reading, *-200*.

I pull out the chair opposite Kendra, setting the plate down in front of her, jam and clotted cream on the side of the scone. "Is this seat taken?" I ask, sitting down anyway.

"Huh?" She lifts her head, and it's then I see the dark circles around her eyes.

Fuck.

"Hey," I say when she looks from the scone to me and then does a double take.

She pushes her hair away from her face, straightens in her

chair, and quickly locks her phone. "Jack, um, what are you doing here?"

My eyes are still fixed on her, and I lean back in my seat and pick up my brownie, taking a bite. She's not wearing an inch of makeup, and her hair isn't styled, but fuck if that doesn't make her more beautiful.

Even more stunning than when I saw her at Lloyd's.

Swallowing my mouthful, I try to act like I've casually bumped into a friend on a whim and I'm not fantasizing about the way I'd bring her here for breakfast the morning after having her in my bed all night.

I normally smile a lot, but I'm starting to realize I wear a particular one around Kendra, and it's all over my face right now.

"I live a couple of blocks away, and this is the best café I've found so far."

I move my plate to the side and lean on my forearms, eyes still on her and the smile aching in my cheeks. "What about you?"

She glances down at the scone in front of her and then back up at me. "I don't usually, but I was in this part of town, and it's freezing outside, so I came in to get warm and grab a coffee."

I take in her face as she tries to smile but fails.

"What's this?" she asks, pointing at her plate.

I pull back, my eyes wide with shock. "Please tell me you're joking."

"Um ... no, I literally have no idea what it is." Her brows knit together.

I tip my chin at her plate. "It's probably easier if you try it."

She scrunches up her nose, which makes her even fucking cuter. Like a kitten refusing to follow instructions. "Do you dip it in the jam?"

A laugh bubbles out of me as I clasp my hands under my chin. "What, like a fry in ketchup?"

"Yeah?" She shrugs her shoulders, lifting her deep brown eyes to mine for the first time.

Jesus.

We maintain eye contact as I reach out with one hand and pull her plate toward me. Picking up the knife set on the side, I cut the still-warm scone in half. "These are English scones. You can get them plain, with currants, or flavored with cheese."

She motions to the scone. "I've only been to England a couple of times, and that was when we watched my dad play. We never ate those when I was there."

I flick my gaze up to hers and find her watching me intently. "Back home, there's this ongoing debate about whether you should put the cream on before the jam or the other way around."

"Which way do you take it?" Kendra asks.

To prevent my laughter, I bite on the inside of my cheek. There are so many ways I could turn this conversation in a completely different direction.

I spread cream and then jam on one half and do the opposite on the other. And when I slide the plate back her way, this time, she reaches out and brings it in front of her.

"Why don't you settle opinions for a nation and tell me?" I reply.

The second she brings one half to her lips, I instantly regret throwing on gray sweatpants to come down here. I'll freely admit that I've thought about how Kendra's mouth would feel more times than I probably should have, but letting her know that with my dick is not ideal.

She swallows down her first mouthful and twists her lips to the side.

"Good?" I ask.

"Hmm ..." She rests her cheek in her left palm and then picks up the untouched half in her other hand, this one with the cream underneath. "I need to compare before I give you my decision."

When she finishes her second bite, she sets the remainder of the half down and looks intensely at the plate.

"I like how seriously you're taking this," I say.

For the first time since I sat down, she smiles, and even if it's only brief, it makes me feel good, knowing I've distracted her from whatever is responsible for the circles under her eyes.

"It feels kind of weird to have the jam on top of the cream." She points at the second half she bit into and pins her bottom lip between her teeth. "I'm saying jam first, cream second."

I sit back in my chair and run a hand through my hair, and she tracks my movements.

Is it possible Kendra Hart finds me attractive?

"Good answer," I reply.

She breathes out a sigh of relief as she crosses her legs underneath the table, picking up her phone in the process. "Okay, phew. That was a lot of pressure for a Wednesday morning."

I nod at the phone in her hand, remembering her reaction to the calculator. "Wanna talk about it?"

She pockets her mobile and brings her hands to the table in front of her, twisting them together. "No offense, Jack, but why do you care? I'm the enemy, aren't I?"

I can't stop the way my brows pull together. I don't like her thinking my issues with Tyler extend to her. Because of her? Yeah. But again, how the fuck am I supposed to tell Kendra that I've harbored a crush on her for years?

"You aren't the enemy, Kendra," I reply.

"Because I'm not with Tyler anymore?" she asks.

I shake my head, my smile obvious. "You've never been the enemy. I care because I saw." I pause, sitting forward and drumming my fingers lightly on the table, searching for the right words. "I care because I saw a girl being treated like shit by a guy who was supposed to care for her. And nearly two weeks later, I see her with her head in her hands and circles around her eyes. I was brought up to give a shit about others."

Her full lip makes its way back between her white teeth as she nods subtly. "I ... ugh ... I'm kind of in a bit of a jam, and I'm running out of options beyond my teammate's sofa bed."

"Wait," I say, rage tearing through me. "You're telling me you lived with him and he kicked you out?"

She shakes her head. "Nah. It's actually worse. I had my own place, but the night after I ended it with Tyler, the ceiling in my apartment fell in."

I sit up. "Shit. Fuck. Are you okay?"

"I'm okay. My apartment? Not so much. My landlord initially told me it would be several weeks to get it fixed and livable again, so I figured I'd ride it out in Jenna's living room. But since the mattress is like sleeping on nails and she's, well, in a new relationship ..."

Her cheeks flush as she looks up at me, and, fuck, I'm growing hard again.

She clears her throat. "So, yeah, last night, my landlord called me to say the contractors working on the repairs had found asbestos."

"Shit," is all I can manage.

"Yep." She pops the *P*. "I'm being released from my lease early since the entire building is now condemned, and I'm left trying to find a new place on a limited budget and a pathetic contribution from my team since the league isn't made of money ..." She pauses and takes a deep breath. "And moving into team housing is not what I want to do."

I go to open my mouth, but she cuts me off.

"Oh, and before you ask, no, I don't want to ask my dad for money or my brother or anyone else for help. I made it as a pro soccer player, and at twenty-two, I'm not about to ask my parents for handouts." She sits back in her chair, arms crossed over her chest in frustration.

Her eyes narrow at me as I smile at her—again.

"It's not funny, Jack."

I hold out a hand in defense. Yeah, this girl is definitely giving me kitten vibes. "Whoa, whoa. I never said it was."

She huffs and looks down at the floor, pinks still painting her cheeks. I know Kendra's dad was a big-time Premier League player back in the day, and her brother, Ollie, is also playing in Europe right now. They could easily put her up in a penthouse, but something tells me this girl has fought her way to the top of a game that's male-dominated, and it's that same determination that's causing her to hang back from going to them for money.

"I respect the fact that you don't want to go to your family for help. Also that you want to have your own space."

"Thank you," she replies on an exhale.

"Was that how much you're short for a new place? Two hundred?" I ask, remembering the figure on her phone.

She uncrosses her legs before crossing them over again in the opposite direction. "Yes. I was viewing a place not far from here. It was perfect, but with the bills and even with the contribution from the Storm, I'd fall way short each month, and I can't get by on that, obviously."

Even in my first season in the NHL, I earn way more than I can spend. Both my parents are comfortable, and my sister is just like Kendra—fiercely independent and working two jobs to get her through the last year of college.

"I'm sorry, Kendra," I reply. "What about farther out of Brooklyn?"

She shakes her head. "I guess that's my only option other than sharing a house. I can't *wait* to get up at four a.m. and ride the subway across town. A pro athlete, and I can't even afford my own place." Her voice wobbles on the final word, and, fuck, now I want to wrap my arms around her.

Silence stretches between us for a few seconds, and then it hits me.

My place.

Sure, she'd be living with me and not on her own, but I'm about to start a season where I'll be away as much as I'm at home.

As I fight with the fear of her laughing straight in my face, I open my mouth to suggest my idea when she pushes back from the table and swipes a quick hand under her eye.

She swings her rucksack onto her back and throws me a brief glance, eyes shining with tears. "Thank you for the scone and for making me smile today. Trust me, I needed it." She pushes her chair back under the table and looks at me again. "I hope you kill it this season. Ty always said you were riding on your stepdad's success, but from what I've seen in preseason footage, you absolutely aren't."

Before I get a chance to reply, she's past me and heading for the door.

I lean back in my chair and squeeze my eyes shut, knowing this is an awesome but also incredibly stupid idea.

"Kendra," I say, opening my eyes to see her already out the door.

"Kendra," I repeat, hot on her heels and waving to Ed on my way out.

"Hart!" I shout down the bustling sidewalk as I push through bodies, trying to get to her.

Jesus, this girl walks fast.

Since I don't have her phone number and no clue where Jenna lives, this is my one opportunity. And as I reach a crossroads, I look left and then right, but can't see her, and my heart drops an inch in my chest.

Fuck, Jack. You should've just asked her in the café and not pussied out.

"Jack?"

I spin around to find Kendra standing behind me, pulling a purple beanie over her head.

"You basically ran straight past me, calling my name." She chuckles.

When I step up to her, we're only a couple of feet apart as the Wednesday morning crowds continue to push and knock past us.

"So ... this might sound kind of crazy." I shove my hands into the pockets of my sweats, already prepared for the look on her face when I say it.

"Go on," Kendra says cautiously.

I thumb over my shoulder. "You remember I said I only live a couple of blocks away, right?"

She nods and then checks her watch. Fuck, she needs to be somewhere.

"All I'm saying is, I have a three-bedroom apartment with a solid ceiling, and I'll be away a lot of the time so you could ... if you wanted ..."

Her eyes grow wide as she connects the dots. "Jack, are you suggesting I—"

I can't fucking stop myself when I place a palm on her upper right arm, and she cuts herself off. The second I touch her, I expect her to move away and for me to be filled with regret, but she doesn't, and I'm not.

"I get it," I reply. "Tyler, me, and the possible complications that could bring. But I can't let you walk away from me and not offer the huge amount of space I have. You can treat the place like it's yours. You won't need to pay rent because I don't fucking need it. You can save up for something, you know, that won't collapse on you. You won't even need to use the same bathroom as me."

Stop talking now, Jack.

Kendra continues to stare at me, her face about as shocked as I expected.

I pull out my phone and bring up my number on the screen, handing it to her. "You don't need to make a decision right now. Think on it if you want. But here's my number."

She types my details into her Contacts and then hands me my mobile, her upper lip raising slightly. "I don't even know what to say."

I shrug like I'm not fucking desperate to hear her thoughts. "It's nothing. I could use a few more friends around this city anyway."

When she flips her hair out of her jacket collar, I'm hit with something sweet I remember from college, and it takes me right back to the house parties we both went to, but never really spoke at.

Checking her watch again, she winces. "I need to get to an appointment, but is it okay if I think about it? It's just ... with Tyler and—"

"He doesn't need to know," I interrupt.

On another wince, she takes a step around me before turning and smiling again. "I've got your number, Jack. I'll be in touch. And thanks again for ... well, everything."

CHAPTER EIGHT

JACK

Jon nods at me, and I stand from the bench, ready to switch out for the line change in the third period of my NHL debut.

The second my blades hit the ice, I'm traveling down the right wing to support Tyler, who's getting into it with one of Boston's defensemen. He's played like shit all game, and I can feel his frustration simmering, especially since Jon started him tonight.

The puck spills just as I approach them, and I pick it up, using my momentum to carry me away and behind the net.

As another defenseman comes crashing toward me, I scan the ice for an option to pass it off since I'm absolutely hitting the boards in the next two seconds.

Matt Rice, our assistant captain, is the closest, but still too far for me to make a pass and not risk a turnover.

Fuck.

Knowing I have speed on my side, I pull the puck back between my skates and spin away from the defender right at the last second, heading back in the opposite direction. I've evaded him, but he's still hot on my heels.

While I feel like I'm buying time with the puck rather than doing anything positive with it, Tyler pulls himself away from the goal and drags his defender with him. Their goalie is too busy tracking his movements rather than what I'm about to do.

It's the cheekiest goal in NHL history when I slot the puck past the inside pipe and send us two to zero up in the last few seconds of the game.

A fucking goal, on my debut.

I barely have the time to process the thought when Sawyer comes crashing into me.

"Morgan, that was fucking wild!" he screams above the noise inside our home arena.

"Rook's got skills and sass." Matt holds his fist out to bump with mine.

I shrug as we turn and skate by the bench, high-fiving the team. "Saw the opportunity and took it."

I'm heading back to center ice when Tyler rushes past me, narrowly missing a shoulder barge.

"Yeah, well, I was wide fucking open, but you're welcome."

Sawyer spins around to face me, one eyebrow raised in question.

I shrug again and look over at Tyler, who's back in position with a face like we just leaked a goal and aren't two ahead.

The remaining ten seconds plays out when the final buzzer goes, and the first game of the season ends in a *W* for the Blades.

Exchanging words with a couple of the Boston players on the way over to the benches, Jon stops me by the arm just as I'm about to step off the ice and head down the tunnel.

"Got a second?" he asks.

As the ice clears and the benches begin to empty, Jon turns to me. "Nice intuition out there, Morgan."

I set my stick against the boards. I know there's something else to this as I begin pulling off my gloves. "But?"

He looks off toward the locker room, where all the players are disappearing. "How are things with you and Bennett?"

My first thought should definitely be about his shitty comment when I put us two up deep in the third, but instead, my mind travels to Kendra. It's been three days since I offered her my place, but so far, I've heard nothing.

This is the issue with your coach knowing you so damn well—he can read you like a book.

I look at him and portray a casual stance. "I think things are better. On the ice for sure."

He runs a hand through his dark hair. "And off it?"

"No different. We just don't match up, and it's as simple as that."

As the last of the crowd filters out of the arena, Jon takes a seat on the bench. "Make an effort with him. Be the bigger man."

Pulling off my helmet next, I nod and move to walk past him toward the locker rooms. "Sure," I reply.

He grabs my arm again. "Why do I get the feeling you're holding back on telling me something?"

I smirk at him, knowing this is absolutely not the right time to tell him about the offer I made Kendra. He's my stepdad, and I trust him, but he's also my coach, who just asked me to try and rub along with Tyler.

I tip my chin at his dark hair and blow out a mock sigh. "I don't know how to tell you this, Coach."

"Tell me what?" Jon's face turns serious.

I reach out and ruffle a hand through his hair, pealing away and making for the tunnel. "You're turning into a silver fox."

I'm halfway to the locker room and fighting back laughter when I hear him grumble, "Cocky bastard."

"I think you've just gotta give her space, man," one of our defensemen says to Tyler as I push through the doors.

Tyler drops to the bench and starts pulling at his pads, throwing them onto the floor in the process. "I don't like the fact that she's ghosting me. I got, like, a one-worded answer last night when I asked if I could collect my stuff from hers."

As I unlace my skates, I casually zone in on Tyler's response, trying to make out their conversation above the noise. I can't help but wonder if Kendra has told Tyler about her apartment.

"She said she'd get it back to me ASAP," I catch Tyler say.

"That was it?" one of our defensemen replies.

"Yep. I just don't like being ignored." Tyler pulls his phone out of his bag, checks it for a second, and then throws it back inside. "I think she's seeing someone else."

The moment the words leave his mouth, his eyes flick to mine, and we hold contact for a beat before I'm looking back at my laces.

If Tyler found out about my proposal to Kendra, there's no doubt his fist would be in my face at any second. I knew when I put it to her that I was treading on dangerous ground. But even if I wasn't attracted to her, I couldn't leave her with the options she had when I have two unused bedrooms and bathrooms in my place.

"For someone who just scored in his NHL debut, you're really fucking quiet." Sawyer breaks me from my thoughts. He's standing directly in front of me, a towel wrapped around his waist.

I rise to my feet and pull my jersey overhead. "Just processing it all, I guess."

"Hmm ..." He scratches his bare chest in thought. "Your pensive attitude has nothing to do with the conversation going on behind us then?"

"Nope." I speak as quietly as he did, preventing eavesdroppers.

"But you're sweet on her, aren't you?"

I can't put my finger on what it is when it comes to Sawyer Bryce. Despite what the media says, I like him. Granted, he's the captain, and you'd expect him, at thirty-four, to be using his experience to make rookies feel welcome. But he was also the only guy who made any kind of effort with me back at the training center, and somehow, I know he's got my back.

I nod my head and figure that's enough to answer his question.

He crosses his arms over his chest, tipping his head toward the ceiling. "Fucking knew it. It was written all over your face that night at Lloyd's."

I pull off my Dri-FIT shirt and grab my wash bag before facing my captain. "Nothing is going on between us. You couldn't even classify us as friends, to be honest."

From behind Sawyer, I watch as Tyler and a couple of other guys head for the showers.

"I can trust you, right?" I ask. "Outside of hockey?"

Just like I did before, he nods once, and I take a deep breath.

"I've known Kendra for as long as I have Tyler, and let's just say, I don't blame her for ending it and ghosting him afterward. Plus ..." I sigh. *Here goes fucking nothing.* "She's kind of got a lot on her plate right now."

Sawyer quirks an inquisitive brow, but doesn't speak.

"She's basically homeless. A few days ago, I ran into her in a café, and we got talking. I'll spare you the details, but she's in a tough spot, trying to find somewhere to live since her ceiling fell in and now her building is condemned."

"Fuck."

"Yeah, fuck indeed," I reply.

A laugh bursts out of him, catching me by surprise. "Let me guess where this is going." He continues to laugh. "You offered her your spare room."

It's the first time I've heard Sawyer laugh properly, and my face breaks into a smile in response as I scratch at the back of my neck.

"Yep."

He claps a hand on my shoulder, turning to walk away. "Secret's safe with me, Jack. I'd just hold off on telling Tyler anytime soon."

When my phone buzzes in my bag, I reach behind and grab it before I look back at Sawyer. "It's an arrangement to help her out while she gets back on her feet. She has about as many friends in this city as I do, and she can't exactly move in with her ex."

He nods in understanding. "I get it, and it's the gentlemanly thing to do. I'd still probably hold off for a few weeks though." His laugh begins to fade out. "For the record and from a captain's point of view, this is a bad idea. But we're all pros here, and I'm not about to stand in the way of my guys' personal lives. Just approach this with caution, all right?"

"I got it. You don't need to worry," I reply confidently. "She might not even accept the offer anyway."

I'm alone for the first time when I turn my phone over in my hand, and my pulse picks up.

KENDRA

Hey, sorry it took me a few days. Life has been crazy, and we only just got back from an away game in Texas. Does your offer still stand? Nice goal, BTW.

I'd ask how her game went, but since I already know they won, I leave that part out. The fact that she watched my game though ... well, that sends my pulse racing a little faster.

ME

Hey, yeah, course it does. When do you want to move your stuff in? I can help if you need.

KENDRA

I have a grand total of one suitcase and two duffel bags, one being Tyler's. So, thanks, but I'm good. I was thinking tomorrow morning if that works?

Fuck, tomorrow. I mentally walk through my apartment and think of all the prep I need to do and which room would be best for her. Thank fuck Mum insisted on me making up one spare room when I moved in. To say my place is a bachelor pad would be an understatement.

ME

Was literally everything destroyed?

KENDRA

Pretty much, but my apartment came furnished anyway. I just can't reenter while there's asbestos exposure.

I head on an away series the day after next, but I'll be home tomorrow morning.

Okay.

And thank you for this. Seriously, you are a lifesaver. I promise it will only be a few weeks until I can get a place. In the meantime, you can put me to use to make up for the favor. I can't cook that well, but I'm not totally useless in the domestic department. *smiley face*

I close out of the message and squeeze my eyes shut, dropping my head between my shoulders.

Kendra around my place, probably dressed in sweats and T-shirts, with her hair in one of those messy buns girls casually throw up but know exactly what they're doing when they wear them.

Jesus.

What the fuck have you gotten yourself into, Jack?

CHAPTER NINE

KENDRA

Standing outside Jack's apartment door with two duffel bags on my back and a suitcase by my feet is the strangest kind of surreal.

Single, homeless, and about to move in with my ex-boyfriend's rival.

"Jesus, Kendra," I whisper under my breath as I lift my hand and knock twice on the white double doors.

I don't need to see inside his apartment to know that this place is an NHL player's stomping ground. The lobby and hallway were enough to clue me in. But when Jack pulls the door open and light cascades in through the huge windows, bouncing against the vast white walls and marble floor, I'm reminded of the other side of pro athlete life.

"Hey." Jack speaks first, swiping the back of his hand across his brow.

"Hey," I reply awkwardly as I try—and fail—to disguise the once-over my brain can't seem to prevent.

Today, he's wearing light-blue gym shorts and a dark blue

Blades T-shirt, and by the flush on his face, I assume he was working out.

He moves to one side, opening the door slightly wider, and when I step through, he reaches out and takes my suitcase from me, our fingers brushing in the process.

"You found it okay then?" Jack closes the door behind him as I continue taking in the open plan living space.

As I swivel around, I wear a sarcastic look that could be interpreted as confidence, but really, I'm nervous as shit and way out of my depth. "You mean using the directions to one of the most exclusive apartment buildings in Brooklyn? Yeah, the taxi driver found it just fine."

He huffs out a laugh and sets my suitcase by the side table, shoving his hands into his pockets. "I don't own it or anything."

"Is this the kind of living budget the Blades offer then?"

On a wince, Jack scratches at the back of his neck. "It's Jon's. Last year, he bought five apartments to rent out, this one included."

I nod my head lightly, but don't move.

"I pay him market rent though. Wouldn't want to take handouts now, would I?"

When I look up at him, his cheeks are still flushed red, and his hair is a cute, disheveled mess.

I can't help but press my lips together with amusement. "That would never do, Morgan."

He rocks back on his white Nike sneakers, which look brand-new, just like this apartment.

"You keep the place nice," I say, taking a step toward the insanely big kitchen situated behind Jack. When I reach the island, I pull off my duffel bags and dump them on the counter.

"Not always," he replies, following me and heading for the fridge.

Opening the door, he pulls out two bottles of water and holds one out for me, which I take.

"Ah, the cleaner just left then." I smile, swallowing my first sip.

He sets his bottle beside him and leans back against the counter, gripping the gray granite in his palms. "Speak for yourself, Hart. I clean up my own mess."

Silence spreads between us as he picks up his bottle and takes another sip, and as I do the same, I find myself trying to work out the atmosphere between us. Would I call it awkward? Not exactly since it's clear Jack has no problem making eye contact with me. In fact, he hasn't stopped watching me since I walked through his door. Still, whatever it is settling in the room between us, it's charged to fuck.

I clear my throat, trying to move past the feeling. "So, which one is my room?" I ask.

"Shit. Yeah, sorry." Jack pushes off the counter, almost like he was locked in the same kind of thought process as me.

Walking over to my suitcase, he picks it up and then heads straight for the island, grabbing my bags and holding them in his other hand.

When he reaches the threshold to a long hallway, he pauses and turns to me. "I gave you the room that overlooks the city. There's a good view of the bridge, and the bed is bigger in this one." He closes his eyes, but only for a millisecond before they're back on me. "In case you like to, you know, spread out and have lie-ins."

After the best part of two weeks living out of a suitcase, unpacking my clothes and organizing them into a dresser was nothing short of therapeutic. And the same with this apartment. Jack's spare room and en suite about brought me to tears when he opened the door and the cityscape and large black bed came into view. The room has a monochrome finish with low-level lighting around the floor. Which, incidentally, is also heated.

After I finished unpacking, I tested out the rainfall shower and threw my hair up into a messy bun. And as I stand, staring at myself in the full-length mirror, dressed in sweats and a Storm T-shirt, I run through how long I can feasibly stay here rent-free before I feel like I'm taking advantage of him.

Which I already sort of am.

"Kendra?" Jack's voice filters into my bedroom.

Tucking a piece of loose hair behind my ear, I continue facing the mirror. "Yeah?"

"Can you come here for a second?"

When I reach the living space, I find Jack sitting at the island with his back to me, head down and deep in concentration.

"How can I help?" I say, taking a seat next to him and studying the grocery app he has open on his iPad.

Once another item has been added to the cart, totaling in excess of three hundred dollars, he turns his attention to me, his eyes landing on the pile of wet hair on top of my head.

He doesn't say anything as he slides the iPad across to me. "I was going to do this earlier, but then I realized I don't know what you like. So, just add what you want, and I've reserved a delivery slot for late afternoon."

Checking out the contents of the cart, I select a couple of things I'm running low on, including deodorant. "I can give you half of the total cost," I say, continuing to check out the list. Which is everything I could think of.

I pause on the clotted cream and look up at him, grinning. "But I'm not paying for this."

With his chin resting in his palm, Jack braces his right elbow on the countertop. "Let's not get off to a bad start now, Kendra. We both know you love a scone."

I refocus on the grocery cart, but pause and scroll back up a couple of items. "Candles?"

Jack's eyes fall to the list, his lips twisting slightly. "So, my sister, Darcy, really likes candles. She's a similar age to you and says they make anywhere feel homey. I figured that, you know, you might like to have some here. In your room or whatever."

He swipes a hand across his mouth as I continue to look at him, probably with mine hanging open.

"Sorry, it was a stupid idea."

He reaches out to hit the Remove button on the list, but I beat him to it and cover the screen with my hand.

"No, no. Your sister is right. I love candles, and it's true; they do make any place feel homey."

I retract my hand, but Jack's remains hovering.

"I'm surprised my apartment didn't burn down, to be honest. Flames everywhere," I muse.

Clicking the plus sign next to the vanilla-scented candle, he adds a few more. "I don't want any money for groceries, unless you insist because it makes you feel uncomfortable or something."

"It makes me feel uncomfortable," I immediately confirm. "Just give me your details, and I can transfer whatever you need."

Leaning back in his chair, he crosses his arms over his chest. I clocked his broader shoulders the first time I saw him at Lloyd's, but today is the first time I've noticed his thicker forearms.

He also has a face, Kendra.

"Okay, deal," he replies. "But that's it. I don't want anything else. Save the money you earn; otherwise, me putting you up for a few weeks is pointless if you go right back to square one."

"Thank you," I say quietly. "I can use it to subsidize rental payments until I sign a new contract later this season. Which will hopefully see an increase in my wages."

Hitting Order on the app, Jack pulls the iPad back toward him and locks the screen. "I find it kind of gross that male pro footballers earn what they do, but not the women. It's the exact same back in the UK."

I run my tongue along the roof of my mouth. "Yep. Ty always

said it was a male-dominated sport, and so it's natural to have a pay gap." I laugh sarcastically. "I'd love to see him survive on sixty thousand dollars a year."

Jack's eyebrows shoot up. "Yeah, it would last him a week."

"This summer, I'm hoping to secure another twenty thousand since it will be my third season in the NWSL. That's what Jenna thinks I'll be offered anyway."

"Did you tell her about moving in here?" Jack asks, changing the subject.

I shake my head. "Told her I was going to stay in a hotel a couple of blocks from our training center for a while. Said I wanted to give her and Lee some privacy. I'll tell her tomorrow at practice."

And I can't wait for the look on her face when I do.

Silence stretches between us again.

"I'm leaving pretty early in the morning for my flight, and I'll be away for three nights." Jack reaches into his pocket and pulls out a key. "I got this cut for you, and I left the code to get onto the floor in your bedroom. The one you were given downstairs is a guest code."

I take the key from him. "I saw it. Thanks."

When he runs a hand through his hair, I can tell he wants to ask me something.

"Go ahead," I say, granting him the opportunity.

"Does Tyler know about your place?"

I shake my head, thinking about all the times he's tried to reach out to me over the past few days. Every single one is about him and the way I'm "ignoring" him. Not one asks me how I'm doing.

"No. I'll tell him when I get set up in a new place. He didn't really come around when we were together, so no danger of him turning up, unannounced. Even if he does keep blowing up my phone."

For the past few minutes, Jack's expression has been relatively relaxed, but I can't mistake the way his jaw clenches.

"He's bothering you?"

My hands immediately find my hair, and I rearrange my bun.

"Kendra, is he bothering you?" Jack repeats, more concern than any anger in his voice, which takes me by surprise, given his history with my ex-boyfriend.

I puff out a breath and drop my hands into my lap. "It's always the same type of message. He says he's sorry and wants to talk it out. But the thing is, I don't. I want to get on with my life and soccer because, as I see it, there's no way back for us."

Jack pins his bottom lip between his teeth. "Then reply and tell him that."

I nod, knowing he's right. "I just don't want to talk to him again. If you'd told me this time six months ago that I'd be in this situation—single and homeless—I'd have probably cried more at the single part. But honestly, I'm struggling to feel anything toward him. I just want him to leave me alone."

Jack goes to speak, but I continue, feeling some kind of relief to say everything out loud.

"If anything, I'm kind of excited about the single part."

His eyes grow wide as he runs a palm over the scruff of his jaw. "What do you mean?"

I pull out my cell and scroll to the Tinder app. "I've only set up a profile for now, but I'm thinking I'll go out and have a bit of fun. I've been in a relationship for four years, and I'm two weeks away from turning twenty-three, so, yeah, I feel like maybe I've been missing out."

The giddiness in my voice is not reflected on Jack's face as he looks off to the side and then back at me, concern lacing his features.

"Yeah." A gravelly noise escapes his chest. "I mean, yeah, for sure, you should enjoy yourself. Just be careful with"—he points to the phone in my hand—"guys you don't know. Be safe, I mean," he finishes, shifting awkwardly on his stool.

"I won't be bringing anyone back here; you don't need to worry about that." I chuckle.

He scratches at his temple, blowing out a laugh that feels kind of forced. "Yeah, I know."

I set down my phone, dropping my face into my hands.

Who am I kidding?

"Yeah, you're right. Dating apps are probably a terrible idea for me."

With my hands in front of my eyes, I can't see anything. So, when Jack takes hold of my wrist and pulls a hand away, I feel his warm, slightly rough palm all the way to my toes.

His face is soft and comforting. "Hey, I'm not judging anything, Kendra. You do what you want, but I'm just saying, be careful. Plus, if closure is what you want with Tyler, then if I were you, I'd be getting his stuff back to him ASAP. That way, he doesn't have any reason to contact you."

I offer Jack a small smile, appreciating everything he is doing for me while somehow regretting I never got to know him better in college. "All I want to do is concentrate on playing soccer, getting to the World Cup this summer, and finding a place I can call home."

A bigger smile pops Jack's dimple. "Football."

"What?" I reply.

"Football," he repeats. "It's the second time you've called it soccer since you started living with me." He leans toward me, his smile turning cocky. "I don't have many house rules, Kendra, but this is one. Whenever we talk about the sport where you physically control the ball with your foot, we refer to it as football."

I narrow my eyes at him playfully, all the previous tension in my shoulders vanishing in an instant. "Hard pass, Morgan."

CHAPTER TEN

JACK

One thing I've never struggled with is sleep—something Jon used to comment on when I would pass out on the uncomfortable and noisy team bus. Give me any kind of surface, flat or otherwise, and I'll be drifting off in no time.

The exception to the rule? Apparently, that's when Kendra Hart is climbing into bed just on the other side of my bedroom wall.

Lying awake until the early hours, thinking over my new reality, was a unique kind of torture—a cocktail of fantasy and panic, topped off with a *what the fuck am I doing* garnish.

The team plane leaves for Colorado in three hours, and last night, I got even less than that in sleep.

Since I spent all of yesterday morning cleaning my apartment and packing for this away series, it takes me next to no time to get up, grab a shower, get dressed, and gather my bags.

It's just after five in the morning when I quietly step out of my bedroom. I do not expect the dim light that creeps down the hallway from the silent living area.

Did I leave a light on last night after Kendra went to bed?

The answer to that question? No, and also, *fuck*.

Like she can sense the presence of my eyes burning into her Lycra-covered ass, Kendra stands from a weird pose and spins around to face me, AirPods tucked into her ears, the TV lit behind her.

"Jack," she says, pulling out her earbuds. She reaches across and pauses the program, which I can now see was some kind of Pilates class.

With my case in one hand, I lift my other and motion to the screen, but instead, it looks like I'm staring at the skimpy blue crop top she's wearing.

Words try—and fail—to leave my mouth as continue pointing at her tits.

"Er you, um, you do Pilates?" I ask.

She turns to the TV and then back at me, a shine coating the skin on her chest and forehead.

Jesus.

"Badly, but yes. I try and get a session in at least three times a week."

I remain still until my brain finally kicks into gear and I drop my hand.

"Heading out then?" she asks.

"Yeah, I thought you'd still be sleeping."

She picks up her water bottle from the coffee table and shakes her head on a sip. "No. I have *soccer* practice"—she pauses and raises a challenging brow at me—"later this morning, but I couldn't sleep, so I thought I'd get my stretching in now rather than stare at the walls."

I nod. "You didn't sleep well?"

She sets her bottle back on the table and then looks down at the blue yoga mat beneath her feet—which, to be honest, has seen better days. "No. Normally, I do, but I don't know. Maybe it was just a first night in a strange place ... I mean, not that the bed isn't comfortable or you haven't been welcoming."

I can't help but return a raised brow as she continues to ramble at me.

Cute as *fuck*.

Her eyes fall to my dress shoes and she opens her palm, fiddling with the AirPods in her hand.

"Do you usually wear those to work out?" I tip my chin at her hand.

At this point, I'm now running behind schedule and risking pissing off not just Jon, but the pilot, but my feet refuse to move from this spot between my living and kitchen area.

"Sometimes. I just didn't want to wake you this morning. I wasn't sure how early when you said early."

This time, I'm successful when I look at the screen rather than her chest. "Do you find it helps you? You know, with your game?"

When she reaches up to adjust her ponytail, her crop top rides up with it, but I fight to keep my eyes on the paused instructor on the screen.

"I guess it's no secret that I have ongoing issues with my left knee. My ACL is relatively unstable, so I do all I can to strengthen it. Pilates is great for that, and with a strong core comes reduced risk of injury. I'm barely into my pro career and already facing physical battles."

I know she's struggled with sporadic injuries; I remember overhearing Tyler talk about them in college.

I reach into my pocket and pull out the keys to my truck, knowing I have to get going, but still unable to prevent myself from asking one last question. "Got any plans for your upcoming birthday?"

Last night, she dropped that she was turning twenty-three soon, but I'd already known. I never went to any of the parties her friends threw for her, but it always stuck with me that we were born exactly a week apart, and consequently, we're both Libras. When I'd found that out in our first year of college, I can't say it surprised me. Kendra and I are similar in a number of ways, but mainly in that we love to socialize.

As I stand, waiting for her to finish another sip of water, I can't help but hope that she noticed my birthday when we were in college.

She shakes her head slowly and runs the back of her hand across her mouth. "No. I was planning on having a few of my teammates over at my place for pizza and maybe a couple of cocktails, but"—she shrugs and picks up the TV remote—"that one went out the window."

A few beats pass between us until she points to the keys in my hand. "Better get going, or you'll be catching a red-eye to Colorado at this rate."

I look down at my keys and then back at Kendra, my brain in overdrive at all she said. "Right, yeah. I'll be back in three nights."

KENDRA

The second the door closes behind Jack, I look down at my skimpy black Lycra shorts and sky-blue crop top.

Nice one, Kendra. Way to make a guy feel uncomfortable in his own place.

With my focus completely off track, I point the remote at Chelsea Rayne—my favorite online Pilates coach—and the screen goes black, plunging the room into darkness.

Overflowing with frustration at my lack of awareness for my roommate, I grab my phone and open up the message thread with Tyler. The last five texts are all from him, asking if we can meet up to talk things through.

I stare down at the flashing cursor and think over the best

way to go about this, Jack's advice to bring closure repeating in my brain.

ME

How about we meet when you get back from your away series? I can hand you your stuff at the same time.

The second I hit Send, panic shoots through me. How would I know he's on an away series without someone telling me? Or worse still, me tracking his movements like I'm missing him or something.

I open up a new message and begin rushing out another response as three dots appear below. My fingers fly across the keyboard, and I feel like I'm in a race to send an explanation before he can get there first.

Tyler beats me to it, and I pause on typing to read his response.

TYLER

Yeah, sure. What about Friday night? I can pick you up, and we can go to that French place you always wanted to try out. P.S. Good to know you remember my schedule. *winking face*

I audibly groan into the dark room as I move across to the L-shaped couch and drop down with a thump. Picking me up is not an option, and no way am I letting him take me out to dinner. And to the place I suggested more times than I've run sprint drills? A little too late for that.

ME

How about a coffee somewhere?

I think back to the place I ran into Jack and smile at the way I fucking loved that scone—with or without the jam on top.

ME

There's a café not far from your place, called Rise Up. I'll meet you there at one, if that works.

Dots appear and disappear over and over again, and I'm ready to give up on waiting and head for the coffee maker when my cell finally buzzes.

TYLER

Well, it's nowhere near your place, but if you're set on meeting me somewhere and not having me pick you up, then I guess that's okay.

I'm poised and ready to shoot Tyler a reply when *Ollie* lights up my screen.

Making my way over to the kitchen, I flick on the coffee maker and hit Accept.

"What time do you call this?" I ask.

"Noon," my brother replies with a single word.

Ollie is four years older than me, but didn't go to college since he got signed by a top Spanish team at eighteen, and he has been playing in Europe ever since.

And it shows; his accent is sometimes confused—a bit like Jack's. I can still detect Ollie's strong heritage, but occaisonally, a twang of the place where he's spent years living creeps in.

"And only six here," I complain.

"Yeah, well, I figured you'd be up and busy training, like the pro you are. Or if you weren't and you were wallowing instead, then I'd stop you from being a lazy brat."

As I pour myself a black coffee, my mind circles back to his wallowing reference.

"Why would I be feeling sorry for myself?"

Since it's only ever been me and my brother, we've always been close. Although I can't deny the envy I've had over the ease he experiences in his career as opposed to mine. I remember him complaining one Thanksgiving a couple of years back that his team in Madrid hadn't paid a higher performance bonus. It'd been frozen at a casual seven hundred thousand euros. I wanted to slap him for that. Instead, I threw a green bean at him.

"Well, I was hoping you'd tell me that, Kend. You know, since you're my sister and everything." The background noise behind him disappears, and I realize he's just climbed into his car when I hear the door shut.

Still no wiser, I take a sip of coffee and pull back when I burn my lips, remembering Jack's coffee maker is way more efficient than mine when it comes to actually serving a drink hot.

"I'm sorry, but I'm lost."

He blows out a breath. "Tyler, Kend. Your now ex-boyfriend, allegedly. I thought you'd be crying over him, but apparently, you've forgotten." He chuckles. "Now, him calling me kind of makes sense, come to think of it."

My brows knit together. "*What?*"

Ollie exhales again. "Yeah, you know how I barely even spoke to the guy since he was a huge douche? Well, he called me out of the blue last night, asking me to talk with you. Sounded kind of angry more than upset though. He was fed up with you ignoring him or something."

With my elbows braced on the kitchen island, I switch the call to hands-free and set my phone down in front of me, resting a cheek in my left palm. The second I do, I remember Jack sitting on the opposite side with his cocky grin as we discussed grocery shopping.

"I ended it a couple of weeks ago," I say. "I've kind of been ghosting him, but it's not been deliberate. I just haven't had a lot to say. He wants his stuff back, and I literally just agreed to meet him on Friday, so he shouldn't bother you again."

There's a long pause before Ollie replies.

"I thought you were in love with the guy?"

I shake my head to no one. "I think I got over the breakup way before I actually ended it, Ol."

I hear the faint sound of a turn signal as he continues to drive.

"Well, for what it's worth, I'm fucking relieved. You knew my thoughts on that asshole were similar to Mom and Dad's. Speaking of which, you plan on telling them anytime soon?"

I shrug a shoulder. "At some point, yeah. I've been waylaid by trying to find a new place since mine was condemned."

"What?!" Ollie blurts out. "Kendra, why the fuck am I only hearing all of this now and after I called *you*?"

"I'm sorry," I groan. "I've been so preoccupied with getting everything organized. I've been off the grid."

"Yeah, no kidding," Ollie replies. "But you're all settled now, right? Where are you living?"

I look around Jack's lavish apartment, sunlight creeping in through the expansive windows. The place is stunning for sure, but somehow, it feels different without him here.

"Kind of," I answer with zero intention of divulging my current whereabouts to my brother.

"Listen," he says as I hear the road noise fade out to silence. "I might be a guy with absolutely no dating experience since I can't seem to hold down a relationship to save my life, but I wasn't born yesterday, Kendra." His tone is a touch sharp, and it catches me off guard.

"Huh?"

"Well, let's look at the evidence, shall we? First, you tell me you split with the long-term boyfriend you'd moved across the country for. Now, you're telling me your place has been *condemned* ..." He says that word in a doubtful way. "And suddenly, you're being all vague and shit over where you're living. Why don't you just go ahead and tell me without telling me that you've met someone else?"

My heart rate picks up. I guess it does sound like that.

"That's not true," I reply, struggling for a plausible alibi.

I rarely spoke to Ollie about any of Tyler's teammates, but he is a huge ice hockey and Seattle Scorpions fan, and I know Jon

Morgan was his number one player back in the day. So, telling him I'm shacked up with his stepson? Well, let's just say, I hope he's pulled his car over.

"So, what is true, Kendra? And what's with the secrets all of a sudden? We've always told each other everything."

The hurt in my brother's voice has me questioning—and regretting—my previous decision to withhold the truth from him.

"If I told you, you probably wouldn't believe me," I say, taking another sip of coffee now that it's had a chance to cool.

"Try me."

"Okay," I say, figuring this can be the trial run for when I break it to Jenna later today. "So, you know Jon Morgan?"

"No, Kendra. Never heard of the guy. Wait. Fuck me, he's married! Kendra, I never thought I'd say this out loud, but please tell me you aren't involved with my hero. Because if he's cheating on his wife, then I'll never look at him the same way again. My childhood will be ruined."

I burst out laughing and then halt abruptly. "But you wouldn't be bothered about my behavior?"

"Details, Kendra."

"I'm living with his stepson."

Like he's choked on his own breath or something, Ollie starts coughing. "You're getting into it with Jack freakin' Morgan? Fuck ... I don't know whether to slap you or salute you. You're straight out of one relationship and st—"

"We aren't dating," I interject. "He offered me a place to crash for a few weeks since I can't afford alternatives right now, and I took it. He's a nice guy."

"I'm not even going to get into the reasons why you didn't come to me or our parents with your financial woes since I know you're as stubborn as a fucking mule, but, Kendra, Jack Morgan? Didn't you once tell me he was Tyler's rival?"

"Still is."

The laugh that rings down my phone is enough to hurt my ears, even when on loudspeaker.

"And I assume Tyler has no idea about this?"

"Zero, and it needs to stay that way. The plan is for me to live here for a few weeks, save up some cash, and then find something else."

Silence.

"Ollie?" I say, checking the line is still connected.

"I'm here, Kendra," he replies after a few more seconds. "But I gotta ask, are you sure you aren't sweet on him? It's a pretty big deal to just accept something like that. From a guy's point of view, it's an even bigger one for him to offer."

I pause, not knowing how to answer. I know what I should say, what my head is screaming internally, but there's something else stopping me from denying that I don't feel something between us.

Crazy thinking, Kendra. He's a nice guy, helping a girl out.

"No," I reply. "He's being a gentleman, and I'm simply grateful, nothing more."

My brother exhales a long breath when I hear the engine on his Maserati fire up again. "All right. Can't say I'm not a little gutted about it, but that's just me being selfish. Tell him I said thanks for helping my stubborn, secretive baby sister out."

CHAPTER ELEVEN

KENDRA

"That's him, isn't it?" Jenna peers over my shoulder.

With a towel wrapped around me and my freshly showered hair dripping down my back, I flatten my phone to my chest. "Yes."

"Knew it," she sings, coming to stand beside me after our two to one win at home.

Somehow, I clinched the game with a winning strike on the full volley. Never in my life have I mastered that shot, but as the ball floated through the air on a corner, I thought, *Why not start here?*

Although my left knee is not thanking me for it right now.

As Jenna rummages through her change bag, I take the opportunity to read Jack's WhatsApp message.

JACK

Nice volley, Hart. That Pilates is paying off.

When I showed up for practice the morning Jack left for Colorado and Jenna immediately asked me how the hotel was, I broke the news to her.

Unsurprisingly, her reaction was similar to my brother's, but with added squealing and, "I told you so," thrown in.

She will no longer accept any other argument than he likes me, but I won't even entertain the idea.

"So, what did he say?"

On an eye roll, I accept that resistance is futile, and I show her my screen.

"Okay, so I take two things from this." She ponders, still staring at my phone as if the one line he wrote were more like a Shakespearean sonnet I studied in college.

"One, he's thinking about you, and two, he's already watched the highlights of our game."

"One," I counter, "he's my roommate and the main occupier of the apartment he just entrusted me with, and two, he likes soccer." I keep my face straight and fight back the smile tugging at my lips when I think about his hatred of that word.

"You know I'm really enjoying this, right?" Jenna's face tells me she absolutely is.

"Well, maybe you are, but you're going to be left disappointed. He's a nice guy, and I guess I enjoy his company, but I'm also not about to jump into anything."

"Oh, so you've thought about it then?"

"No!" I announce louder than I wanted. "All I'm thinking about is getting my ex-boyfriend off my back and my ass into an apartment of my own. If I make a friend along the way, then great."

Jenna zips her bag shut with force and looks at me, the freckles along the bridge of her nose prominent with mischief. "Not convinced."

"I have zero intention of convincing you with my words. I'll let my actions do the talking," I reply as I pull on some shorts and wince at the soreness in my knee.

"You need to get back in front of the physio, babe." Jenna's voice switches from playful to serious in an instant.

From my seat at the bench, I can see the slight swelling

around my patella. "I think all I need is my brace to help it for a while."

She props her hands on her hips. "And you think showing up to practice on Saturday morning, wearing a brace, won't result in questions from the trainer."

Jenna flops down next to me as I huff out a breath.

The past three weeks have *not* been the best for me.

"I know Team USA scouts could show up at any game or practice, and I know they have me on their radar. Since Laney retired last season, we've been short on center backs, and I feel like this is my shot. I don't want to wait another four years, Jenna."

She wraps an arm around my shoulders and brings me into her as the rest of the girls start to file out of the locker room.

"You okay, Kend?" Hollie stops on her way out the door.

I throw up a hand and smile. "All good, babe. Be out in a second."

With a little squeeze, Jenna pulls me around to face her. "Listen to me, Hart. When I say there isn't another defender I'd want in front of me in club or international games, then I'm not lying. You are more than on their radar; you are absolutely at the top of their list. But if you start fucking around and hiding injuries, then not only will they find out and be pissed at you, they'll also be concerned that you weren't up front."

As I stand from the bench and pull my phone back out of my bag, I know she's right.

Jenna's playful exterior returns as she swings her bag onto her shoulder. "Now message lover boy back and come join us outside."

I don't bother to argue with her as she pulls open the door, and it slams behind her, leaving me alone in the locker room.

ME

Thanks. You should give it a try sometime. One last game tonight, right?

JACK

Yeah, we need the W. How's the apartment doing? Ceiling's still in place, I assume?

Who knew the guy I barely spoke to in college was actually this funny?

When the app shows that Jack has gone offline, a wave of panic flashes through me. Was that flirty?

Damn you, Jenna, for messing with my head.

I'm hurriedly typing out a clarification that I'm grateful for his help when Jack starts typing again.

JACK

Put the flag out. Kendra Hart noticed me.

I stand in silence, staring at the message and trying to work out exactly what he meant by that. Similar to what Jenna did a few minutes ago.

ME

I did notice things about you in college.

All right, let's test that ...

I'm poised with my phone gripped tightly in my hand as he types again.

Without cheating, when is my birthday?

My brow furrows as I rack my brain for an answer that has to be buried somewhere. The temptation to bring up Google and search him has me closing out the message thread and opening up a new window. But as I type in his name, I feel like I owe him my honesty.

I want to say April.

Nope.

Well, are you going to tell me?

Nope.

A single laugh bubbles from my chest.

Okay, try me with another.

All right, last chance, Hart.

Butterflies swirl in my stomach. Why the fuck do I find something I played back in junior school so damn exciting? This is the sum of what my life has become.

JACK

What was my last name before I changed it?

I roll my eyes and type out a response.

ME

Give me a little credit. Thompson, obviously.

Good girl.

One more since that was so damn easy.

Last one, and then I have to go to skate.

Hit me with it. Give me your best.

I take a seat on the bench and hold my breath while I watch him type.

JACK

Why did we wait so long to start speaking?

My thumbs hover over my keyboard as the few very faint

memories I have of Jack in college play like a carousel in my mind. Most of them are of him on the ice or the look he would throw Tyler or his friends from across the room.

As the slideshow continues, it finally stops on one moment I was aware of at the time, but never thought—or allowed myself to think—much more about it.

I was playing in a game when my knee gave out. I was in my third year, and it was the second time in my college career it had happened. The trainer wrapped it, and when the final whistle went, everyone headed back to the clubhouse.

I stayed sitting on the bench for a while longer, staring out at the pitch and trying to figure out how long I'd be out this time.

In that moment, I felt pretty desperate. It was a game Tyler had promised me he'd come to since he wasn't busy with hockey, but he hadn't shown.

The one person who had? Jack.

My attention was drawn to a guy on the other side of the pitch, wearing a college baseball cap and jacket. I knew it was Jack, but I assumed he was here for someone else.

So, why was he still there when everyone else had gone inside?

I wanted to head over and ask him what he was doing here, but the second I rose from the bench, Tyler's voice filtered from behind me.

And when I turned back around to check on Jack, he'd left.

ME

Honestly, I don't know. But maybe a faulty ceiling isn't all that bad after all.

CHAPTER TWELVE

JACK

Watching the replay of some of my games will go down as the most painful experience of my life. Like the time in college when I missed a wide-open goal to secure a win. Damn, that's one memory that will haunt me for life.

Tonight's game though? Well, I could watch that beauty every day, and it still wouldn't be enough. I didn't score, but somehow, my role on the ice felt more dominant than ever before. Tonight, I felt less like a rookie in headlights and more like I was meant to be in the NHL. Especially when I set Matt up for a one-timer to clinch the game zero to three.

A game that, based on our performances last season, we'd never expected to win.

So, it makes perfect sense for our goalie to be sitting next to me at the bar, wearing a wide grin. He killed it tonight.

My grin? Well, that's as big as Archer's, but for more reasons than just hockey. She might not be on the same page as me when it comes to birthdays, but she is wondering why the fuck we never spoke more in college.

And for me, that feels like another big win.

There's just one thing tonight that's bothering me ...

"What's the score with Sawyer?" I cock my head in his direction.

Our captain is sitting alone on the other side of the crescent-shaped bar. Most of the guys are gathered around tables, but Archer and I are watching NHL footage on the overhead screens. I've invited Sawyer to join us on a couple of occasions, but each time, he's declined.

As he continues to stare up at the overhead TVs, the wince on Archer's face is unmistakable. "How much do you know about our captain?"

I shrug and twist my pint glass around on the beer mat. "Aside from the very little he's told me over the past three weeks ... only what you and the general public has access to."

"Hmm ..." Archer responds, picking up his beer and taking a large pull. "So, you know about what happened six years ago then?"

When I don't immediately respond, Archer assumes correctly—I have zero idea.

"Yeah, I guess you would've been like, what, sixteen when it broke?" He pauses and casts a quick glance Sawyer's way. "Look, it's not really my place to say since it's his business, but as some of it is common knowledge I'll tell you this. There's a reason you don't see Sawyer with women. When it comes to the fairer sex, he and I are polar opposites."

As I lean back in my high stool, I think about the truth in that statement.

"Sawyer was married—and when I say *married*, I mean, they were head over heels in love and gave you all the feels from just watching them. They were, at one point, considered to be the power couple of the NHL. Sophie wasn't a famous model or anything, but she was the reason Sawyer had made it to where he was—or at least that's what he's always said. Let's just say, he hadn't had a great early life until he met his wife."

"Wait, was Sophie a redhead?" I ask, vaguely recalling something reported about her.

"Yeah, and I don't think Sawyer will mind me saying *hot as fuck* too." Archer clears his throat. "So, run the clock forward a couple of years, and they had their first baby, Ezra. There was a time when Sawyer was a very different person from the guy he is today. It all changed when Sophie suddenly passed away from a pulmonary embolism. One night, he had kissed her and his four-year-old boy good night to go on an away series, and the next, he got a call from family to tell him that when he got home, it would only be Ezra waiting for him."

My eyes flick to Sawyer just as he pulls his phone out and begins swiping across the screen. "Oh fuck."

Archer nods his head slowly. "Yeah. Sawyer has never recovered. He's the greatest dad to Ezra, but all the guys on the team know what to expect when we travel to Colorado."

"It happened when he was here, didn't it?" I ask, already knowing the answer. The pieces click into place rapidly. "Do you think I should say something to him?"

Archer pulls his attention from the highlights and looks at me. "You're a good guy, Jack. I think the team needed you for more than just your ability on the ice. In the three weeks I've been playing with you, I can already see you as a captain in the future. You're like the glue that sticks a team together. But on this occasion, I'd advise you to let Sawyer be in his head. He'll come through it, as he always does."

Archer claps a hand on my shoulder, and I pick up my glass, taking a sip and giving Sawyer one more look.

"So, what's your story?" I ask, changing course.

Laughter erupts from the tables behind us, and I watch as Sawyer empties the rest of his glass and slides off the stool. He nods once at us and the rest of the team and disappears out of the bar. When I get back to our shared hotel room, I expect to find him already asleep.

"What do you mean by that?" Archer chuckles.

I shrug. "Dunno. I just feel like I know most of the guys on the team reasonably well by now, but you're kind of a mystery."

Archer looks kind of surprised by my question, but not reluctant to give me an answer. "I'm a straightforward guy."

"Yeah, I figured that part out. You've never wanted to find that one girl though, no?"

He quirks a brow in my direction. "I'm twenty-six, not dead. There's still time for me to find someone. I'm just not in a hurry."

"Fair enough," I reply.

"What about you?" he asks.

My thoughts drift to Kendra and the last text she sent, congratulating me on our win.

"Bit like you, I guess, in the sense that I'm single and I've never been all that bothered when it comes to dating. I had a brief girlfriend in college, but that didn't work out."

"You don't strike me as a playboy," Archer replies.

I shake my head. "I'm not. I've slept with a few girls, but other than Olivia, no one was more than a one- or two-time thing."

Finishing up his drink, Archer tips his empty glass in my direction. "Why do I get a strong past-tense feeling about all you're saying right now?"

I'll give him one thing—he's fucking perceptive.

I pull at the back of my neck. My attraction to Kendra is nothing new, but the feelings I'm developing and trying to suppress are starting to play havoc with my head.

"I know the phrase *it's complicated* is overused, but in this case, it's definitely true—as is the term *unrequited*," I tag on, a tug pulling in my chest as I do.

Archer blows out a long breath. "In one sentence, I think you've summed up the exact reasons why I fuck and flee."

I'm practically howling when I set my eyes back on Archer, and his shoulders shake too.

"Jesus, you got a way with words, buddy."

His smile turns cocky. "Yeah, that's what they all say right at the critical moment."

Laughter continues to spill from me when I feel a presence from behind.

Sensing it's our coach, Archer pushes his glass toward the barman and throws down a twenty. "I'm gonna head to bed."

As Jon takes a seat next to me, I call after Archer, "For real?"

He scratches at the scruff on his jaw, his cockiness returning. "I never said alone, did I?"

"Jesus, just looking at him resurfaces memories of me fifteen years ago," Jon groans.

I turn to him. "More like twenty, no?" Lifting a hand at the barman, I ask for two more pints of IPA.

"Really, Jack?" Jon asks as I feel my cheeks flush.

"What? We're celebrating a win, aren't we?"

He nods at my empty glass. "What number was that one?" Jon sits back in his stool. "All right. You played your most accomplished game tonight, so I'll let this one slide."

"You're too kind," I reply on my first sip.

As the rest of the team filters out of the bar, I watch Jon's demeanor shift from a coach to family.

"Your mom said she messaged you yesterday, asking if you'd be over for your birthday on Sunday."

I wince when I remember reading the text and forgetting to reply. "Kind of have plans. Maybe later in the week?"

Jon's eyebrows shoot up. "Sure thing. But with who?"

I stare at the condensation as it runs down my pint glass. "A girl."

To prevent his pint from landing in his lap, Jon quickly sets his glass down. "I'm sorry, what?"

On a wince, I know it's time to give him the truth. "When I say plans, they're kind of not fixed in place yet. I plan on speaking to her about it when I get home."

"Jack, I'm really going to need you to start talking English as soon as possible."

I puff out a laugh and decide just to go for it. "Kendra Hart. She's staying at my place for a while. Long story short, she's basically homeless, but not because she recently split with her boyfriend. I said she could stay with me, and, well, since she doesn't have any plans for her birthday, which is a week after mine, I figured I'd see if she wanted to celebrate. As friends," I clarify.

Jon holds up a shaky hand. "Wait, Kendra? As in Tyler's ex?"

I nod once.

His head falls into his hands. "Oh fuck."

"Yep." I pop the *P*. "It's just a case of me helping a friend out," I repeat.

He tips his head toward me so I can see one very doubtful eye. "Yeah, the look on your face tells me a *friend* is exactly how you see her."

I lift a shoulder. My concern over what Tyler finds out is really only centered around the team and Kendra. "So, what if I do like her?"

Jon sits back in his chair as he drops his hands and drags his palms across the bar top. "You're not breaking any rules with what you're doing, but you are running the risk of a broken nose. If Tyler finds out about any of this, he will go nuclear on your ass. I can already see how their breakup is eating away at him."

"For all the wrong reasons," I say under my breath.

"Maybe so, but if he gets wind that she's shacked up with you and you're hot for her? Prepare for pain." Jon's face switches back to coach mode. "If you want to go after a girl, then be my guest. If anyone is all for finding their person, it's me, but if any part of this affects team dynamics and performances, then you know I'll come down on you both. We're just starting to make some progress in the league."

I can't deny the sense of dread as it flips through my stomach. "I'm not planning on pursuing a girl who just got out of a long-term relationship and needs my help."

A rumble of agreement radiates from Jon's throat. "And I get that. I'm just saying, I think you're living dangerously when it comes to your teammate and your feelings."

CHAPTER THIRTEEN

KENDRA

I'm curled up on Jack's couch, watching reruns of *Friends*, when the apartment door opens, and Jack appears in his postgame suit, carrying his suitcase in one hand.

I'm not sure if he sees me buried beneath the blankets when he sets the suitcase down and pulls off his shoes before making his way into the kitchen and opening the fridge.

He unscrews the cap on a bottle of water and takes a couple of sips before bracing his palms on the counter in front of him.

My initial reaction was to say hi, but my gut tells me he's having some kind of private moment as he squeezes his eyes shut and whispers something inaudible under his breath.

A few more beats pass before I sit up and clearly scare the living shit out of him. "Everything all right?"

"Fuck. I thought you'd gone to bed and left the TV on or something." He brings a palm to his chest.

"I was falling asleep but ..." I reach across the couch and check my phone for the time, a message from Tyler lighting up the screen.

TYLER

See you tomorrow at one. I miss you. x

"I could ask you the same thing," Jack says, pushing off the island and coming to sit on an empty chair opposite me. "Everything all right?" He points at my cell.

"Message from Tyler. I took your advice, and I'm meeting him tomorrow. He says he wants to clear the air between us. I'm happy to hear him out, but my main objective is getting his stuff back to him and closing this chapter of my life."

Maybe it could be described as relief on Jack's face. Whatever it is, I can tell he thinks I'm making the right decision.

"You hungry?" I ask.

"Starving."

I thumb over my shoulder to the kitchen. "I'm not exactly Chef Ramsay, but I made a chili earlier and set some aside for you. Just needs to be reheated. That is, if chili is your thing? Because I personally love it."

A smile I'm starting to become familiar with spreads across Jack's face. "I love chili."

I rise from the couch and pad toward the kitchen, pulling down my long T-shirt, which falls just below my sleep shorts.

When I turn around to ask about sides, Jack's head is bent over and between his shoulders.

"Are you sure you're good?"

He keeps his head down and nods once. "Yep. I just have a headache coming on. Probably because I'm hungry."

"Well, I can definitely help with that," I say turning to the burner and firing it up. "And I'm sorry if it's shit," I shout.

"Whoa, okay. Now I'm deaf as well as starved," Jack muses from behind me as he peers over my shoulder and into the pan.

From the second I started living with him, I haven't been able to figure out the earthy scent filling his apartment, but from this proximity, I realize it's his cologne.

My senses tingle as I grab a ladle and stir the chili.

"Can you cook?" I ask.

He pulls off his jacket and throws it over a barstool, then spins around and opens a top cupboard, fetching out a bowl.

"I'm not bad. My mum, Felicity, and Jon are insanely good in the kitchen, and a lot of their relationship revolves around cooking and going out for meals. Jon's in the process of buying an Italian restaurant in Seattle. It came up for sale a few months back, and it's always been a popular hangout for him and his friends. I guess their passion has rubbed off on me and Darce."

When the chili starts to bubble, I spoon it into the bowl, and Jack adds corn chips and sour cream.

"I think I might like your sister; she sounds like my kind of girl with a love for food and candles."

With the ladle still in my hand, I look up and find Jack hovering over me. At six-four, he's a similar height to Tyler, but something about Jack's presence feels way more dominant. And not in a bad way.

"Chili's ready," I whisper.

Jack holds his bowl in a vise grip, and his voice is gravelly as he says, "I'll have to cook for you sometime."

We're only inches apart as I stand motionless, the ladle still in my hand, hovering midair.

"What kinds of things do you like? I'm thinking a British classic," I say, trying to summon my best accent.

He grins playfully. "Well, we've established that you don't mind scones, so maybe we'll switch it up and try something savory. Shepherd's pie maybe."

My eyes flick over to the TV, *Friends* still playing in the background. "That's probably my favorite episode—the one where Rachel gets the pages stuck together and mixes a pie with some random jelly dessert."

Jack continues to smile down at me as his breath fans my face. "Trifle, Hart. She makes half a trifle and half a shepherd's pie."

Every part of me feels like jelly as Jack's usually bright blue eyes turn darker.

As if checking himself, he shakes his head briefly and refocuses on the bowl still in his hand. "What time are you meeting Tyler tomorrow?"

I feel some kind of way when he pulls back from me and takes a seat at the island, immediately digging into his food.

"One p.m. at *Rise Up*. I'm dreading it, to be honest."

With a mouthful, he nods. "What have you got planned this weekend? No games, right?"

I pull at my messy bun, and as hair cascades around my shoulders, Jack's eyes track the movement. At least, these days, it's not all falling out, like it was.

"I have practice first thing on Saturday morning and then nothing until Monday. My plan is to binge-watch TV, if you wanna join me?"

He sets his spoon down, and I take a second to process the speed in which he just finished his chili.

"Did you drop that or something?" I say, leaning down and checking the floor beneath him.

A rogue grin tips up Jack's lips. "I wasn't lying when I said I was hungry, and that was fucking good." He points to the empty bowl, and I feel a flush of pride paint my cheeks.

"I'm down for bingeing *Friends* with you." He leans forward and picks up his water bottle. "But I did want to ask you something."

My stomach swirls at his question, and I press my ass into the granite countertop. "What's that?"

"I don't know if you ever looked it up, but this Sunday is my birthday, and yours is a week after. Since neither of us seems to have any plans, I wondered if you wanted to"—he pauses and swallows thickly—"head out for something to eat or maybe catch a movie?"

I open my mouth, but Jack speaks again.

"As friends, obviously." He blows out an awkward laugh. "Just feels like a shame not to do something."

"I'm sorry," I start.

Jack holds up a quick hand, his face twisting with unease. "It's fine. I get it. It's weird."

I shake my head at him, and my stomach continues to swirl. "No, no. I wasn't going to say that I couldn't or didn't want to. I was going to say that I'm sorry I didn't realize your birthday was coming up."

Jack's dimple pops. "So then, you're up for doing something?"

"Yeah, absolutely."

When I pull out a stool and sit opposite him, I find myself fidgeting again with my hair.

Jack motions to my head. "Your hair looks good either way, but down is really pretty."

"You think?" I ask. "It needs a cut, and normally, when it grows to this length, it becomes unmanageable. So, that's when I start piling it on top of my head and get it out of the way."

I swear I see Jack's cheeks flush slightly, but then it could also be the way he just nailed an entire bowl of spicy chili.

"I never really saw you with your hair down at college. It was either in ponytails for *football* and the gym or like you wear it around the apartment." He reaches up and circles the top of his head. "All casual but with pieces that frame your face. It's nice but also different when it's down."

With my elbows braced on the counter, I lean forward, eyes narrowing in his direction. "Soccer," I say, flicking my long hair over my right shoulder for effect.

He doesn't say anything as he pushes the stool back and rounds the island with his bowl. Coming to stand by my side, he swivels my chair around to face him.

"I like having you around the place, Hart, especially when you make chili like that. But there are certain boundaries I said you couldn't cross."

The tension between us is thick as I start to wonder if this conversation is really about the name of my occupation.

"Okay, noted. But I can't promise my compliance."

His jaw clenches as he reaches across and sets the bowl down by the sink, the clatter of his spoon against the ceramic echoing around the apartment.

"What are the other boundaries?" I ask, unable to stop myself.

Jack runs a hand through his hair, his biceps straining against his white dress shirt.

On a long-drawn-out breath, he slaps his hand against his thigh, his gaze dropping to the floor. "Nothing that you need to be concerned about, Kendra."

CHAPTER FOURTEEN

KENDRA

It's fair to say that fate hasn't exactly been on my side lately, and apparently, not much has changed as I push through the entrance of Rise Up to find Tyler already seated at the same table I shared with Jack not all that long ago.

With coffees and cakes already in front of him, he waves his arm in the air to attract my attention.

"Hey," Tyler greets me cautiously as I take Jack's previous seat and hang my jacket on the back of the chair, setting a duffel bag down beside me.

"I, um ..." He points at the blueberry muffin and millionaire shortbread on the plate in front of me. "I wasn't sure which one you preferred, so I went with both." He smiles. "I know you like blueberry and chocolate, so I figured they were the best options."

I continue staring down at the treats in front of me, not really processing what he's saying, consequently allowing my mouth to get ahead of my brain. "I'm actually going through a bit of a scone phase right now, but these are also delicious. So, thank you."

Tyler tips his head to the side, his hands clasped together on the table. "You've never mentioned that before, but if you want me to change it ..."

"No, no, it's fine," I rush out and then clear my throat, frustrated with myself for saying anything in the first place. "So, you wanted to talk?"

With his left hand, Tyler scratches his temple. "Yeah, I do."

"What about?" I ask, determined for him to show his cards and lead the conversation if only for once in his life.

The time it takes him to speak again is probably only a couple of seconds, but it feels like forever. "About us."

Adding a sweetener to my coffee, I pick up my spoon and begin stirring—any excuse to avoid eye contact. I don't want to be rude, but the atmosphere between us feels awkward, and I'm struggling to sit through it.

Return his bag to him and find closure, Kendra.

I draw in a breath before I speak. "There isn't an 'us' anymore, Tyler. I thought I was here so we could clear the air and move on."

Reaching down, I pick up his duffel bag and hold it above the table between us. "I think this is everything you left at my place. There wasn't much, so I could fit it all in here."

I continue holding the bag on an outstretched arm, but when Tyler doesn't take it, I finally find the courage to look at him.

"Take it, please."

His face is full of frustration when he reaches out and hooks his hand around one of the straps. "This is your bag."

"Keep it," I reply, waving a hand in front of me. "It's an old college one I don't use anymore."

General conversations go on around us, punctuated by the clatter of plates and noise from the coffee machine as I wait for Tyler to speak again.

He pulls at the back of his neck and looks toward the ceiling. "I'm sorry."

I nod my head in acknowledgement. I wasn't necessarily

looking for an apology, but I appreciate the fact that I have one, even if it's years overdue.

"Can we at least try and be friends?" Tyler asks.

I think we both know the chances of us being friends are slim, especially since the only thing we have in common is the city we live in. But I don't want to risk another argument.

"Sure," I reply, offering my best but ultimately weak smile.

Tyler pulls out his phone and starts scrolling. I force back an eye roll. He never could give me his full attention; the pull of social media and engagement updates on his latest post always proved way more captivating to him.

He presses his lips together in thought. "In that case, I think it's a good idea for us to go to the gala next week as a couple. I know we'd be friends, but my mom and dad have been asking questions about us since they read rumors that we'd parted on bad terms, and Dad's concerned that it reflects badly on my character. So, if we go together and make it clear we're attending as friends, then I guess that would help."

"Gala?" I ask on a long breath. "What are you talking about?"

Tyler's brow furrows. "The annual pro athlete gala, Kend. The one we attended last year. You know, the one for chari—"

"I remember." I cut him off.

Fuck.

My stomach drops. With everything going on, I somehow managed to forget that the NYPAG—New York Pro Athlete Gala—was scheduled for next Saturday night. All the email reminders about it are still unopened in my inbox.

Taking a sip of coffee to buy myself another few seconds of thinking time, I set my cup back down and look at Tyler. "So, you want me to go with you to help with your reputation?" My voice is incredulous. I never liked Tyler's dad, but now I'm starting to see exactly where my ex-boyfriend gets his egotistical hang-ups. "I don't think that's a good idea."

"Why not?"

I take another sip of cool coffee. "Because I'm not a pawn in your PR game."

"Huh," he huffs out and strokes his rough jawline. "Is it because you have a date to the gala?"

I shake my head in disbelief. "Why would you think that?"

"Because, Kendra"—he holds out his hand, motioning toward me—"you seem to have gotten over us really fucking quickly. Four years." His voice rises, and his eyes dart around the café to make sure no one noticed. His voice drops to a whisper. "Four years of being together, and you've moved on like I never even existed."

For the first time since I can remember, I see something that resembles regret on my ex-boyfriend's face.

"I'm not seeing anyone," I confirm. "I'm just taking time for myself and setting boundaries right now. A lot of my hurting came months, maybe even years before we split. A year ago, you gave me an ultimatum—soccer in the UK or you. I chose us and followed you to this city, only to be left out in the cold."

"Well, all I can say is, I'm sorry." There's an edge to Tyler's voice that tells me his words might not be all that sincere.

I don't need his pity. "It's fine. All water under the bridge now."

When silence falls between us again, I push back my chair, unable to stand the atmosphere any longer.

"Where are you going?"

I push the muffin and shortbread toward him. "Here, you have them. I think we've said everything we need to."

I'm reaching for my jacket on the back of my chair when Tyler's phone catches my attention. It's on the other side of the table, but the message is unmissable.

UNKNOWN

Just wanted to say the other night was amazing. You were amazing. We should definitely do it again sometime. *winking face*

When we were dating, the thought of Tyler moving on with another woman made me feel nauseous. To some extent, that might have been what stopped me from ending things between us sooner—fear of hurt.

But as I shrug on my jacket and pull my hair from the collar, I feel nothing. Complete indifference. The only emotion running through me is the simmering anger I feel at his audacity to have an issue with me potentially dating someone else.

This was the closure I needed.

I point toward his phone as Tyler continues to watch me, for once unaware of the lit screen to his left. "Looks like *Unknown* might be able to be your date next Saturday."

THE INDIFFERENCE I was feeling ten minutes ago didn't last.

The second I walked into Jack's apartment, I went straight for my bedroom, not even stopping to check if he was in the living area.

I've never been someone to cry, but as every possible emotion hits me like a tidal wave, the tears begin to flow.

What my life could've looked like right now if I'd only chosen myself over a boy.

The London-based team that offered me a contract has been at the top of the Super League since it got underway, making them current favorites to secure a place in the prestigious Champions League. Something that would've undoubtedly helped my chances of making the national squad.

I look around the luxurious room and run a hand along the Egyptian cotton duvet as I dump myself down on the bed.

I can't stay here and live off Jack's hospitality. These were decisions I made, and I can't expect other people to pick up my pieces.

Trying to sob in silence, I sit up and reach over to the nightstand, uplugging my phone charger and stuffing it into the suitcase at the foot of my—*Jack's*—bed.

A soft knock stops me in my tracks. "Kendra?"

"Just give me a minute, okay?" I ask Jack in an unsteady voice.

"Are you dressed?"

"What?" I ask, a laugh threatening to break through the sobs.

A long sigh filters through the door. "Are you decent?"

"Yeah," I answer.

Jack's face is full of concern when he opens the bedroom door and sets his eyes on me. He then looks to my opened suitcase. "Where are you going?"

I shove my long hair behind my ears. "I can't stay here. I'm taking advantage of you."

"You aren't."

"I am," I counter, standing from the bed and heading for the dresser next to Jack.

In a hurry, I pull the drawer open, and Jack reaches out, placing his big hand over mine as I grip the handle in my palm. Anything to prevent the tears from flowing freely again.

"Talk to me, Kendra." His voice is soft and understanding, like a warm blanket cushioning my troubles. "Did Tyler say something?"

"No," I reply on a deep breath. "I just think my bullshit bucket might be at full capacity."

"Bullshit bucket? That's one I haven't heard before."

I press my lips together, my mood switching from desperate to kind of amused. "Can you not for just a second?"

"Not what?"

His hand is still resting over mine as I look up at him, and my attention snags on the popped dimple in his cheek.

"Not make me smile when all I want to do is throw my clothes around the room and yell into one of your unnecessary Egyptian thread pillows."

His smile grows wider, and his blue eyes sparkle with mischief. "But you have to admit, Hart. Life's more fun when you smile."

"I'm not preventing you from smiling all you want," I huff, trying to maintain my mood.

It happens before either of us can register it—his other hand reaching up and tucking a lock of hair behind my ear.

"My original statement is still valid. Life is more fun when *you* smile."

A different kind of silence from the one shared with Tyler falls between us. One I don't want to bring to an abrupt end.

"He's sleeping with other people," I say. "I guess he can do what he wants. But what really irked me was, minutes earlier, he asked me to attend NYPAG with him. I told him no because the last thing I want is to be on his arm, as a friend or otherwise."

I puff out a frustrated laugh, and Jack drops his hand from over mine.

"But I can picture it now—me standing alone and next to the bar while he carries on with some random girl he's been boning. All while at a gala for a city I never wanted to be in." My voice grows increasingly harsh as frustration overtakes me. "I should be playing in London right now."

As the tears start to build, I quickly swipe underneath my eye.

I *won't* let him get the better of me.

"What if you didn't have to be alone?" Jack's voice breaks me from my spiral, and I look back at him.

"What do you mean?"

His anxious eyes search my face. "I mean, what if you didn't have to worry about showing up alone? What if ..." He pauses, and I watch his throat work. "What if you were on my arm instead?"

JACK

Did I just say that out loud?

Kendra's eyes grow wide.

Yep, I said it.

"What?" she replies.

On a wince, I motion between us. "You could come to the gala with me."

Kendra looks down at the dresser in front of her, clearly processing what I just said. She shakes her head. "If we go as friends, he'll say I was doing it just to spite him since that's precisely what he suggested."

Well, there goes my fallback plan.

The temptation to reach out and tip her chin up to look at me is strong, but I keep my hands firmly by my sides this time. I already pushed boundaries when I tucked her hair a second ago.

"So, what if you pretend to be my real date?"

Christ, the words just keep spilling from my tongue today.

Kendra's head whips up to mine. "You're serious, aren't you?"

I can't tell if her smirk is in response to my proposal or the suppressed excitement I'm feeling too.

In for a penny, in for a pound.

"Deadly," I reply, holding contact with her deep brown eyes so she can see just how serious I am.

"Jack, he will *annihilate* you and call me out for being a liar. I told him I wasn't seeing anyone."

I balk. "He asked you that?"

She presses her lips together and nods. "That's why he thinks I've gotten over him so quickly. He thinks I've moved on with someone else as a rebound."

"Who gives a fuck what he thinks? I mean, truly, you've spent so long fitting around his needs. It's time to start thinking about what you want."

A subtle smile brightens her face. "And you think fake dating you is what I want?"

I shrug. "You did say you wanted to have some fun. Sure, it won't be real, but I can show you what it's like to date someone who actually gives a fuck. Plus, if it gets him off your back and out of your messages, then that's an added bonus."

I know my smile has turned cocky when she rolls her eyes at me in jest.

"You think you'd be a good date, do you, Morgan?"

Determination fills my chest. I know none of this is real, but I can't help the rush of adrenaline when I think about Kendra Hart on my arm. Even if it is followed by a broken nose from Tyler. Provided I keep things professional and don't react, he's the one the Blades will take issue with.

"I'll sure make you smile a whole lot more than Tyler ever did."

When she finally releases the dresser handle from her palm, I reach out and push the drawer closed.

"I don't have anything to wear since I didn't think I'd be needing a dress anytime soon. I'll have to head out this weekend and grab one."

"Sunday," I reply. "I could take you shopping for a dress and then out for something to eat. We had plans anyway."

And I can't think of a better way to spend my birthday.

Kendra holds up a hand. "Oh, no way am I letting you pay for a dress."

I take her hand in mine, and a breath catches in her throat when I interlace our fingers and drop our joined hands between us. "If we want to make this believable, then we need to start practicing now. Getting used to holding hands and being intimate in public. If you were my girlfriend for real, then I would one hundred percent be hands on with you. I'd also treat you. Because that's what it is, Kendra—*a gift*. Not a display of ownership and definitely not a threat to your independence. So, let's make this as authentic as we can. Starting on Sunday."

She's looking at our hands when I finish speaking. I can't see her face, but I don't miss the way her chest rises and falls more rapidly than before.

And when she finally lifts her gaze to mine, relief floods my insides.

"You'd do all of this for me? You're risking a lot for not much in return, Jack."

Memories of the way Dad hounded my mum for months after they split resurface. It's possible that Jon is right, and I am risking my feelings. But if I can help Kendra break free of the web Tyler seems hell-bent to ensnare her in, then that's reason enough for me.

"Yeah, I would." I swallow thickly. "Not all guys are as selfish as your ex, Kendra."

CHAPTER FIFTEEN

KENDRA

Just like the first day I moved into Jack's apartment, I find myself staring into the full-length mirror, trying to decide if the skinny blue jeans and black V-neck sweater I'm wearing for our "date" today are suitable.

Around five minutes ago, I heard Jack's bedroom door open, and I know he's out in the living area, waiting for me.

But I'm nervous—I can't deny it. When Jack suggested we fake date, I could see all the reasons why it was a great but also terrible idea, and I went to bed on Friday night with my head full of overwhelming thoughts. And by this morning, not much has changed.

Will he hold my hand today? Hug me? *Kiss* me?

Giving myself another once-over, I conclude that even if this outfit isn't right for what he has planned, it's not like I have many other options anyway.

Turning back to the bed, I pick up the card and gift I ran out to get Jack yesterday. Sure, money is tight right now, but there's no way I'm letting this day pass without getting him something.

On one final deep breath, I push down the handle on my bedroom door and head out into the hallway.

Reaching the living area, I find Jack with his back to me. Perched on the arm of his couch, he holds the remote in one hand as he watches hockey highlights from last night's games.

"Happy birthday," I say, the butterflies in my stomach an alien sensation. I've never had this feeling, even when I was dating Tyler for real.

Swiveling around, Jack flicks off the TV, all while keeping his attention firmly on me.

I hold his gift out to him and wince at the level of cringe it is. I don't know much about his dad, but I'm sure Jon and his mom and probably even his sister will blow what I got him out of the water.

Jack still hasn't said a word to me as he tosses the remote on the couch cushions and makes his way over to where I'm standing.

In the past, I've admired how good-looking he is, and maybe today heightens everything due to the circumstances, but I find my eyes ascending his body. From his gray sneakers to his tailored black jeans and fitted sweater. The zip on the collar is all the way down, revealing a flash of his chest, and his floppy brown hair is styled forward in a messy but incredibly sexy way.

Yeah, he's fucking hot.

Not just in the way he looks, but in the way he carries himself too. With the right balance of humility and confidence. But the hottest part right now? Well, that would be his unwavering attention when he comes to stop in front of me.

He still hasn't looked at the gift in my hand when he takes it. "You look ... really great, Kendra." A smirk tugs at his lips as I feel my cheeks heat. "You wore your hair down."

I run a hand through it and shrug, trying to remain passive. "Someone mentioned that it looks good like this, so I thought *why not* since it's their birthday. Twenty-three, right?"

Jack bites down on his bottom lip as his eyes drop to the gift. "Did you get me a boyfriend card too?"

I inwardly cringe again at the theme of the card and gift I chose. "Was I supposed to?"

As he tears the envelope open, he turns the card over, and his shoulders begin to shake. "No, and this is way better than a soppy card. I love it."

I stare down at the crown-wearing British bulldog. At the time, I thought it was cute, and now, not so much.

Walking over to the kitchen island, he sets the card on the side and then begins tearing at the paper as he makes his way back over to me.

"Kendra, these are awesome." He opens the box of Union Jack coasters and begins taking them out; each one is in a different color.

He's about to toss the paper in the trash when I hurry over and stop him.

"Wait, there's something else tucked inside."

Tearing the paper open further, he pulls out a twenty-dollar gift card for Rise Up.

My cheeks flush again. Jesus. I'm also twenty-three next Sunday not sixteen.

Jack shakes his head as his eyes find mine. With my back against the countertop, his close proximity would easily allow him to take a single small step, and his body would be pressing into mine.

The flutters make a return, but this time, they're joined by a tingling in my core.

Several beats pass between us as I wait to see what he'll do next.

"Thank you, Kendra. This is probably one of the most thoughtful gifts I've ever gotten."

The second his soft, full lips find my right cheekbone, my eyelids flutter closed.

"You ready for me to take you out?" he whispers against my skin, his breath and cologne firing off sparks all over my body.

I can't help the whimper as it emanates from my throat. "Yeah, sure."

As Jack pulls away, the darkness in his eyes—the same as on the night he returned from Colorado—is unmissable as he reaches up and runs a hand through his hair.

"Okay, Hart. First stop, breakfast, then the boutiques."

I FELT sure I'd find something in this store. The first two places we'd tried had nothing that suited my curvy and muscular figure. That's the one drawback with being an athlete—trying to squeeze my quads into tight-fitting dresses.

I unzip the latest dress before I even pulled it up fully, and the black gown pools around my feet. I picked out six different options here, but again, nothing looks or feels right.

"Everything okay?" Jack asks from where he's been patiently waiting for the past half hour. Just like he has in the previous two stores.

"Ugh." I huff out a breath and step out of the gown before picking it up and hanging it back on the rail. "Nothing works in here either. Maybe we should just give up and go for lunch or something."

"Then what will you wear on Saturday?"

"I don't know," I reply with a frustrated breath. "My robe."

I've got one leg in my jeans when the curtain behind me moves.

"Could you do me a favor and try this one on?" Jack's voice sounds a touch nervous, and he pokes a light-olive satin dress through to me.

I look back at the rack of dresses I picked out—three of

them black, one light blue, and two more in a baby pink. "Green?"

"Matches your nails. Plus—I dunno—I saw it on the model out front, and I immediately thought ..." He pauses, and the dress slowly withdraws.

"Let me try it. Nothing to lose, right?" I say, stopping him from taking it back and immediately pulling it off the hanger, ready to try it on.

"Jack?" I say, my jaw agape as I twist and turn in the surrounding mirrors.

He was right. The cowl neck makes the most of my moderate cleavage, but it's the way the sleek satin material clings to my small waist and full thighs that really steals the show.

Not in a million years would I have picked this out.

"Yep?"

"Did you by any chance go dress shopping with your sister back in London?"

He huffs out a laugh. "Nope. She'd rather die than parade around in front of me."

I think about Ollie and how accurate that statement is. "Well, maybe it's beginner's luck, but I think you nailed it the first time around."

Jack clears his throat. "Well, I guess I'd need to see to be sure."

My stomach flips. Obviously, I'll be wearing this in front of hundreds of people on Saturday night, but something about walking out in front of Jack feels way more intimate than it should.

I pull back the curtain and step out in the strappy sandals I picked for the other dresses, but somehow, they suit the length of this one much better.

"What do you think?" I say, turning around slowly and feeling like an idiot.

When I complete the circle, Jack is standing only inches

away from me, his eyes roaming my body. If I didn't think this was the right dress before, there can be no doubting it now.

He shakes his head, a sweet smile tracing his lips. "It doesn't matter what I think, Kendra. How do *you* feel in it?"

Despite myself, I can't deny the way it makes me feel. My eyes drop to the flowing gown. "Amazing."

"Then that's all that really matters."

With a finger under my chin, Jack pulls my attention back to him. Right here, in the middle of an empty dressing room, is the closest we've ever been. His breath fans my lips right before his eyes drop to them.

I've only ever seen the playful side to Jack Morgan, but from the way he's currently looking at me, I know there's so much more lurking behind the light exterior he portrays.

"Is this how you would treat your real girlfriend?" My voice is breathy, and I'm unable to stop the question as it tumbles from my lips.

"No," he replies, his voice more of a rumble.

Bringing his hand to my left hip, he pulls me closer to his body, and any air left in my lungs leaves in a whoosh.

"The dress is stunning, but if you were mine, the only place it would be right now is the floor."

CHAPTER SIXTEEN

JACK

"You weren't lying when you said you love chili," I say with a smile that's been plastered on my face the entire day.

Kendra picks up a corn chip and scoops a generous helping of chili and sour cream, swallowing it in one bite.

I haven't touched my enchiladas since the server brought them out a couple of minutes ago, and I'm painfully aware of the reason—I can't stop staring at the girl in front of me. Truth be told, I've never been able to tear my eyes from her. But seeing her step out in that dress earlier and knowing she'll be wearing it while on my arm this Saturday? It's safe to say the feelings I've always harbored for Kendra are no longer at risk, but certifiably fucked.

I know none of this is real to her, even if I find myself questioning the way her cheeks flush and her breath catches. She might find me attractive, but I know that's as far as it goes. She's fresh out of a relationship with an asshole, and I can't say I blame her for wanting to find some fun after four years of bullshit.

Trouble is, I was sure I could be the one to give her what she wanted instead of searching for it via dating apps. Now all I can think about is not just showing her what it's like to date the right type of guy. I want to be him.

"It's superior. I could probably go for it multiple times a week if our nutritionist let me." She picks up another chip and crunches down.

It's only lunchtime, but the dim lighting in the restaurant I chose makes it feel like an evening date, the soft glow of the candles scattered around our table warming Kendra's face.

She picks up her mocktail and takes a sip, pointing to my food. "You haven't eaten any of yours, birthday boy."

I reset my focus and look down at my plate. "Not that hungry."

She cocks her head to the side, narrowing her eyes in my direction. "But you're *always* hungry. What's the matter?"

Oh, just falling for you. Nothing major.

I open my mouth to offer a completely different response when I'm interrupted by a vibration, followed by a text alert.

"Sorry," I say, reaching into my jeans pocket. "I thought I put this on si ..." I trail off when a name I haven't seen in a while is on my home screen.

Kendra sits up straight and points to my phone as I continue to stare down at the short message that doesn't need me to open it to read it in full.

"Who is it?"

I swallow thickly, my appetite now completely depleted. "My dad."

DAD

Happy birthday, son. Proud of you.

She sets her spoon down, her face full of concern. As far as I'm aware, she doesn't know anything about my family. Only that I have one sister, my mum is called Felicity, and Jon is both my coach and a future NHL Hall of Famer.

"By the look on your face, I'd say that message is out of the blue and only because it's your birthday."

My thumb hovers over the Delete button. I haven't heard from Dad in months; the last time was when I signed my pro contract with the Blades. I didn't miss him when he returned to the UK and I stayed in Seattle for college, and I miss him even less now. If my sister wasn't still in contact with him, I'd have probably severed ties altogether.

I close out the message, but don't delete it.

When I repocket my phone, Kendra is still watching me expectantly, and I take my first bite of food, attempting to eat something.

"You can talk to me, you know?" she asks.

There's not much to tell when it comes to my dad. His existence is one I prefer to ignore, but that would also mean shutting out Kendra, and a larger part of me doesn't want to do that.

I swallow my mouthful and chase it down with a sip of water.

"Sometimes, I'm tempted to ask Mum if she had an affair with the milkman since my dad and I couldn't be any more different."

"So, he's an asshole?" she asks with a raised brow.

"Something like that, yeah. He's not a regular fixture in my life, and I can't say I'm sad about it. He gets on better with Darce than he ever did with me. He and Jon have had several run-ins, and I can't say I blame Jon for hating him."

I think back to the first Christmas following my parents' divorce. I was in my first year of college, and Dad and Darcy had returned to Oxford. Mum had just started seeing Jon but was determined to spend the holidays with us. We were supposed to all stay together in our old house for few days, but the second we arrived, the tension was palpable. I could tell my dad was waiting for an opportunity to grill Mum on her new relationship. He said he wanted to try again with her, but really, it was more about his own ego and the fact that she'd moved on, which motivated his actions.

Just like Tyler with Kendra.

We didn't even make it past Christmas Day. When Darcy and I were out of the house, seeing friends, Dad started verbally attacking Mum. He'd been harassing her for a while, but the only thing that stopped him? Jon's fist to his face.

That was the turning point for me. The day I told myself I might have his DNA, but I'd never be like him.

"Jack." Kendra breaks me from my thoughts as she reaches across the table and finds my hand, taking it in hers.

I look down at the connection between us and then back up at her. "Yeah, Hart?"

"Can I ask you something? No pressure to answer or anything." Her voice is as soft as the palm in my hand.

"Anything," I reply.

"You had loads of friends in college, but you only ever dated one person that I remember. I knew her from my class. She seemed really into you, but you broke it off with her after a few weeks. What's the story there?"

It's possible Kendra thinks the brief relationship and abrupt ending with Olivia is down to the insecurities I have from my dad and his absence from my life.

But she's wrong.

I adjust my hand, interlacing our fingers. I'm not sure how much of this right here is real for Kendra and if she feels the undeniable connection between us.

"Dating wasn't in the cards for me at college. I spent way too much time playing and studying. I'm not the kind of guy who dates someone just to mess around, and neither was Olivia. I took her out a few times ..." I pause, not wanting to add anything about us sleeping together. "It was fun, but I couldn't offer her enough of my time." My eyes find Kendra's big brown irises. "And I realized after a few weeks that I kind of didn't want to either. I wasn't about to start leading her on, so I broke it off."

Instinctively, I run my thumb across the top of her hand. "I've always trusted my gut—on the ice and off it. I couldn't see anything more with Olivia, and I largely kept to myself for those four years. It was touch and go for my pro career. I didn't get drafted like Tyler and a couple of others on the team. I had to put in the work."

She offers me an appreciative smile. "I get that—like, I really do. I should be in the UK right now and not hovering around a strange city. You made the right decision with Olivia. I know she was gutted, but she'd probably thank you today."

My face looks smug, and Kendra quirks a brow as she breaks away and leans back in her chair.

"She was gutted, was she?" I ask.

"Apparently, yeah. I don't see it myself, but maybe she liked scones and called soccer football."

I throw my head back and laugh. "She wasn't a bratty little kitten—that's for damn sure."

Kendra's shoulders straighten as she grabs a corn chip and raises her eyebrows, threatening to launch it at me. "I'm sorry, Morgan. What did you just call me?"

"Brat." I lean on my forearms, taking a chip from her bowl and dipping it in the remaining chili and sour cream. My mouthful is huge, and I smile as I chew.

She holds up a hand. "No, no. Not that. Being called a brat is nothing new to me—my brother made sure of that. I'm referring to kitten."

The chili is one of the spiciest I've ever had, but the flush spreading throughout my body has fuck all to do with it.

"Kitten," I repeat. "You're soft, fluffy, and cute on the outside, but you're also likely to stomp your feet and show your claws at any second."

The chip sails over to me, and I catch it, demolishing it in one bite.

"I was actually starting to like you. But now I kind of agree with Tyler."

"Oh, fighting talk," I muse.

"In all seriousness though, I'm nervous about his reaction on Saturday. What if he punches you?"

I shrug my shoulders and take a sip of water. "Then he does, and he'll face the consequences. We aren't doing anything wrong, and he knows it. As long as I can stop myself from landing one on him, it'll be good."

"You genuinely don't care, do you?"

I roll my tongue along the roof of my mouth. "Yeah, I guess I am risking a long-term, loving friendship."

Kendra snorts and slaps a palm over her mouth. "That was ladylike," she groans.

When the server asks us about desserts, we both turn them down since one of us has eaten their body weight in chili and I barely touched my main course.

The check lands in front of me, and Kendra reaches for her purse.

"Unless you're about to head to the bathroom with that"—I nod at her bag—"then don't even think about it."

Her eyes are challenging as she slowly unzips it.

Pulling out my Amex, I throw it over the check and lean back in my chair. From this angle, I notice how low her V-neck sweater drops, revealing part of her cleavage.

Yeah, now's not a great time to get hard, Jack. Jesus.

I love it when she smiles, but when she turns bratty, I start to think about all the ways I could put that pouting mouth to good use. If she'd let me, the things I would do to this girl would border on criminal.

So far, her experience of me is the nice guy everyone knows. But given half a chance, I'd fucking love to show her not just what it felt like to date a guy who treated her right in public, but the way he would put his hands on her in private too.

CHAPTER SEVENTEEN

JACK

"Great practice this morning."

The entire locker room falls silent, not just because Jon entered, but also because of the compliment he just paid us.

I thought, over the years, I'd seen all sides to my stepdad's personality. Turns out, NHL Coach Morgan wasn't one of them.

"We've ground out some unexpected results against teams that were predicted to hand us our asses. That means, going forward, the league will be more wary of coming up against us. Bar a couple of you who I'll speak to in private, I'm happy you stepped up the intensity out there this morning."

Beside me on the bench, Sawyer is still hunched over, his forearms resting on his knees. He left it all out there in sprints and drills and led like a true captain.

I clap a hand on his back, noticing his shirt is slick with sweat. "Doing all right there, old man?"

Without moving the rest of his body, Sawyer turns his head to look at me. "I often ask myself why I like you. This is one of those times."

My palm circles his back as he brings a clenched fist to his mouth.

"If you're gonna puke, please make sure it's not on my new Nikes," I plead.

Sawyer waves a hand, indicating he's fine, before my attention snags on Jon and Tyler in the corner of the room. Tyler shrugs with his palms out at his sides as Jon continues to talk. I don't need to hear what he's saying to work out he's not happy. And I'm not surprised either. Of the few exceptions Jon just mentioned, Tyler is definitely at the top of that list. Truth is, he has been for a while, and that has everything to do with him substituting extra gym and ice time for nights out. If Kendra has seen the evidence of his antics online, she hasn't said anything.

As Jon finishes up his conversation with Tyler and stalks out of the room, my mind drifts involuntarily back to Sunday. The way she looked in that dress I'd picked out for her for the gala, the way she genuinely cared about the still-unanswered message from my dad.

The way I left at the crack of dawn this morning. I wish I were racing to grab a shower and heading back home to climb back into bed with her before she had a chance to get up.

"If I wasn't already nauseated from practice, I sure as fuck would be from the look on your face."

"Say what?" I reply, Sawyer's voice infiltrating my thoughts.

He swallows thickly and stands, pulling off his shirt. "You look like a lovesick puppy or something."

I mirror Sawyer's actions. "Stuff on my mind—that's all."

With our backs to the guys, we both face the bench and work on getting ready to hit the showers. I swear I can physically see the cogs turning in my captain's head.

"Why don't you just come out and say whatever's on your mind?" I ask, peering into my change bag to see if Kendra is up yet and has seen the overnight oats I left her in the fridge last night.

It's a part of her training routine, I've noticed, but when she got home late after a heavy practice, she headed straight for bed and didn't make them herself. So, I did.

"I don't need to since I know you aren't that fucking stupid."

I'm still smiling at Sawyer, but I can't help the twinge of dread that creeps into my brain. He's talking about the gala.

"You're going to have to be more specific." I play dumb.

He scratches at his chest in the usual way. "Kendra. You're taking Kendra, aren't you?"

I open my mouth, but he holds up a hand.

"And don't ask me how I guessed. Your smile has gone from annoying as hell to all-out sickening, and since I'm the only one who knows about your living arrangements and your feelings for her ... well, let's just say, I won't be rivaling Sherlock with my conclusions."

Pausing on getting undressed, I prop my hands on my hips. In three days, it'll all be confirmed anyway. "Yeah, I'm taking Kendra to the gala."

"*What the actual fuck?*" Tyler's breath blasts at the back of my neck.

Fuck. This is not the way I planned on him finding out. Truthfully, I didn't have a plan since I seem to have lost my fucking mind when it comes to this girl, but him overhearing it in the locker room would *not* have been my first choice.

Bringing a towel to the back of my neck, I wipe away any remnants of his rage and then turn to him.

His face is exactly how I pictured it would be—beet red. His eyeballs are practically bursting from their sockets, and he clenches his jaw so tight that it's likely getting a better workout then the rest of his body has in weeks.

"You'd better be so damn straight with me right now, Morgan. Tell me you aren't taking my girlfriend to the gala."

"Ex."

"What?" he replies, too enraged to process my response.

"I said, ex, Tyler. She's your *ex*-girlfriend."

With his jaw still tighter than the deke I pulled off earlier in practice, he drops his head to the floor and huffs out a laugh.

The uppercut he lands on the underside of my jaw is painful, but not exactly surprising.

I bring my palm to it; it hurts like a motherfucker, but I keep my eyes glued to his and rub at it lightly. It's clear he only knows about the gala and not where she's living. If he knew both, I'm pretty sure I'd be nursing more than a sore jaw.

"Still working on lifting three sixty on the bench press then, Ty."

He rears back to hit me again when Sawyer steps in front of him, catching Tyler's fist in his palm. "Hit my winger again, and this will go a whole lot further than these four walls."

Tyler maintains eye contact with me as he drops his fist down and Sawyer steps away.

The first drops of blood land on my chest and make their way down to the waistband of my shorts.

Tyler steps even closer, his eyes burning into me. "Have you fucked her?"

"I don't think that's any of your business, do you?"

"Have you fucked her, Morgan?" he repeats.

The entire locker room is deathly silent as at least a dozen guys look on intently. I could easily claim I have, if only just to wind Tyler up further. But Kendra means way more to me than that. She isn't a pawn in some game.

"No," I breathe out. "Things only just started up, and I want to take it slow since she just got out of a toxic relationship with an asshole."

His lips curl into a filthy sneer. "Story of your life, isn't it, Jack? I mean, first you get shipped to the farm team for a season. Then you're fighting for your place on the third line. And now you're biding your time, waiting for Kendra to let you put your dick in her when, for years, she was only too desperate for mine."

I swipe at the blood on my chin. "Sloppy seconds never felt so good."

Tyler throws his head back and laughs darkly. "You think she's dating you for real? Here's my best guess." He gets fully in my face, our eyeballs near enough to touching. "This is one of two things: She's using you to get over me. Or this is all just a ruse for her to piss me off and you to finally get one over on me since you can never do it on the ice. I don't believe for one fucking second that you dating Kendra is real. She barely looked your way in college. In fact, I'm not a hundred percent sure she even knew you existed."

The locker door bangs against the wall, and Jon strides back in. "I walked out of here, leaving calm and order, and walk back into shouting." Scanning the room, he finally lands on me and Tyler, and his eyes drop to my jawline. For the briefest moment, they flash with concern before he blinks it away and thumbs over his shoulder. "Morgan, Bennett. My office."

"But I was ab—"

Jon cuts Tyler off immediately, "Don't give a shit. Put your shirt back on. I want you both in my office, stat."

The door crashes against the wall once again, and Tyler waits for Jon to leave before he looks back at me. "This isn't over, not by a long shot."

He spins on his heel and makes for his side of the room.

Grabbing my shirt, I pull it overhead.

"Here, take this. The bleeding has almost stopped, but it's gonna bruise up good," Sawyer says, holding out an antiseptic wipe for me to use.

"Thanks," I say, swiping it across my chin and throwing it into the rubbish bin next to me.

Sawyer clears his throat from beside me. "He's not going to drop it, you know."

When I pick up my mobile, there are still no messages from Kendra, and I tuck it into the pocket of my shorts.

I'm about to head for the roasting of my life when Sawyer prods a finger into my shoulder blade, and I turn back to him.

"I still think you're fucking crazy, by the way. But you made the right call in not hitting him back."

JON HASN'T SAID one word since Tyler started giving him a detailed rundown on what happened. Conveniently, he's relayed the entire story, bar the uppercut he landed on my already-bruising jaw.

"So, yeah"—Tyler crosses his arms and sits back in his chair opposite Jon like some kind of petulant teenager—"Morgan thinks it's okay to move in on another guy's girl. Fuck bro code and especially fuck teammate respect."

I want to bend over in fits of laughter at the way this guy clearly lives in the 1950s. But instead, I work to keep my face serious and cross a leg over at the knee, waiting for Jon to say something—fucking *anything*.

Clasping his hands together in front of him and leaning forward on the desk, he drops his head between his shoulders and blows out a long breath. "Can someone explain how Morgan's face looks different from how it did when practice ended?"

I look at Tyler, who raises a brow at me. He has zero intention of throwing himself under the bus.

"Bennett lost his cool for a second, but was in the middle of apologizing when you walked back in," I lie, and Tyler's brow furrows at me in question.

"That true?" Jon focuses on Tyler.

A few beats pass as I watch my teammate gradually wade through his options before he nods his head slowly.

Leaning back in his chair, Jon drums his fingers on his desk, eyeing us both cautiously. "I think it's fair to say, there is zero love lost between the two of you. The tension has been simmering since college. Back then, I'd have handed you both a warning and dropped you for the next game, but now you are pros, and with that comes a level of responsibility."

He points at Tyler. "The second you laid a finger on your teammate, you opened yourself up to the risk of being put on waivers. Alex Schneider was the last guy that happened to, and let me tell you, our GM won't hesitate to do it again. I have to report this to him, and the best you can hope for is a heavy fine. The worst-case scenario is, we make you available to trade."

Tyler swallows and runs a stressed hand through his hair.

"I will, however, make it clear that you immediately recognized the error in your ways."

Jon's attention lands on me. "Morgan, I don't know what the fuck to say to you, to be honest. It's clear you didn't retaliate, and for that, you just saved yourself the same fate as Bennett here." He raises his brows at me. "That said, I don't think I need to remind you of the stupidity of your actions. You're a fucking *professional,* and while you're not breaking any kind of terms in dating a teammate's former girlfriend, you are putting the locker room at risk. And that's all I care about. You fuck around with my team's dynamics, and you find out just how far I'm willing to go."

"I'm not planning on letting this interfere with my game," I reply.

"Oh, it'd better not." Jon looks between us both. "Because if I pick up on even the slightest undercurrent of tension"—he pinches his thumb and forefinger together, leaving only a tiny space between them—"then you are both being recommended for the farm team. That is, if you're still here and playing at all, Bennett."

His anger nearly reaches boiling point when he stands abruptly from his chair, and it rolls back into the wall. "Now get out of my office."

Tyler's already out of the door. I'm hot on his heels when Jon calls my name, and I let the door close in front of me.

"Yeah?" I ask as I turn to face the guy who straddles the line of stepdad and coach with expert precision. To an unknowing spectator of that conversation, you'd never know he was family.

Jon looks down at the floor, his hands stuffed in the pockets of his sweats. "I really hope you know what you're doing with this girl, Jack. I also really hope she's worth it. You realize this doesn't look great right now. To everyone, this doesn't look great."

My phone buzzes in my pocket, and I pull it out to see a message from Mum.

MUM

Jon just told me. Jack, what is going on?! You never get into fights ON THE ICE, let alone off it.

Jon juts his chin at the phone in my hand. "That Felicity?"

"Yep."

"She called me right after I walked in on you and Tyler getting into it."

I repocket my phone and shrug a shoulder. "It's fine. I'll call her later and explain."

I'm about to head out, feeling like there isn't much left to say, when Jon stops me again.

"You and Kendra—is it serious?"

I close my eyes and depress the handle on his office door. "For me? Yeah. For her? I don't know."

Deep down, I know even that's pushing it since Kendra only sees us as fake. Though, somehow, I can't bring myself to admit that out loud, even if I know Jon wouldn't say anything. Other than telling me I was an even bigger idiot.

He blows out a harsh breath. "I'd be a hypocrite to tell you not to chase the girl you want since I spent months going after your mom." His voice softens. "You're a good person with all the best intentions, Jack. Just make sure she's on the same level, yeah?"

Looking over my shoulder, I hold eye contact. "I will."

The second I step out of the office, Tyler is in front of me, his face still contorted with anger. "I meant what I said, Morgan. This isn't over."

I smile mockingly. "Maybe not for you, even though it should be. That's exactly why I lied and said you regretted punching me."

He looks on, still as confused as when I told Jon.

"Kendra has nothing to do with you anymore. She isn't your concern, and she *definitely* isn't—and never has been—your possession. I told Coach you apologized because that's exactly what you should do, right after you leave my girlfriend the fuck alone."

CHAPTER EIGHTEEN

KENDRA

"You know I'll be seeing you in around two hours, right?" Jenna says as she picks up my call.

"I know, but I didn't really want to tell you in the middle of a packed locker room," I say, flicking on the coffee maker as I stifle a yawn and wait impatiently for my first—and much needed—caffeine hit of the day.

"Well, color me intrigued. Spill," Jenna replies as I hear the sound of a door closing on her end.

"So, the gala this Saturday ... I'm not going alone."

"Please, on all that is holy, do not tell me that you're going with Tyler. I don't think my sanity can take it."

I blow a laugh down the phone. "If you think I'm that stupid, then maybe you should reconsider your choice of center back."

"Okay, good. You had me worr ..." Jenna trails off, and a couple of beats pass before she speaks again. "Wait, if you aren't going alone and it's not with Tyler—oh crap, you're going with Jack Morgan, aren't you?!"

As the coffee maker finishes its prep, I pick up the jug and begin pouring myself a steaming cup. "Good guess."

"I wasn't aware there was going to be a fireworks display this year, but maybe I just didn't get the memo until now," Jenna replies. "Like, for real? You're going with him for real, as a date?"

This is the part where I could say yes and allow my closest friend in this city to believe our ruse. But our relationship has always been based on truth, both on and off the pitch.

Pulling myself up onto one of the stools around the island, I press my lips together and decide to go for it. "Tyler asked me to go with him, and I turned him down. He's been a grade-A asshole lately—"

"Tell me something I don't know," Jenna interjects, which has me nodding in agreement.

"So, yeah, after I met Tyler for a coffee, I get back to the apartment, and I'm upset but more just pissed off, to be honest. Everything with him has an agenda, and all I wanted to do was return his stuff to him and move on. Jack caught me in the midst of my mini meltdown and made the suggestion that we go together. That way, I'm not alone, and Tyler has to start backing off."

"And since then, you've fucked in every room in the apartment, just to test out your compatibility and for practice."

How Jack's kitchen isn't wearing my coffee I'll never know. I forcibly swallow my mouthful and burst into a coughing fit.

"Oh, come on now, Kend. You can't bullshit a bullshitter. This arrangement is convenient for the both of you—and in more ways than one."

"Actually, no. You're wrong. We already went on a *practice* date, and we didn't even kiss, so your theory is dead in the water."

Silence falls between us, and I feel the mood shift from playful to something more serious. In a bid to keep my mind off the memory in the dressing room, the one where Jack explained exactly where my dress would be if we were for real, I push off the stool and head for the fridge.

"But you understand he likes you, right?" Jenna eventually speaks.

Rolling my eyes, I pull open the door to find something for breakfast. "I don't know how many times I need to say it—Jack and I are just ..." The rest of my sentence dies on my tongue when I find a jar of overnight oats, complete with my favorite blueberry compote.

Taking it out of the fridge, I see a note stuck on the outside.

Even if my girl forgot to make her overnight oats,
she'd still get them.
Hope they're not shit.
J
x

"Earth to Kendra?"

I blink a couple of times and come to. "Yeah, sorry. W-what was I saying?"

"You okay?" Jenna asks.

Lifting my cup, I take a seat back at the island and down another sip of coffee as I try to regain my composure.

No wonder Olivia was fucking gutted.

"Jack wants to help me out, and neither of us wants to go to the gala alone. So, it's a mutually beneficial arrangement." I finally finish my sentence with a confident pep to my voice.

Jenna blows out a long breath. "So, if you guys are playing this off as real, when does it all end? Right after the gala?"

She makes a good point. I've been so caught up on Saturday and Tyler's reaction when he sees us that I haven't thought much beyond that night.

"We haven't talked about that," I reply.

An unconvinced murmur sounds down the phone. "I will say this, for what it's worth: if this 'arrangement' between you both is 'mutually beneficial,' then maybe you could go after some of the fun you were hoping for with guys."

"Meaning?" I ask, knowing full well what she's insinuating.

"Hook up, fuck buddy–style. If he is down for a few benefits along the way, then replace that red wand of yours with Jack Morgan."

The morning Jenna caught me having fun with Scarlett races back to me, as does the image of Jack hovering above me. My thighs squeeze together of their own volition, and I bite down on my lip.

"I don't know if I could do that."

When a key slides into Jack's door, I immediately uncross my legs and reset myself.

"I have to go," I whisper-hiss to Jenna.

Jenna chuckles down the phone. "Tell Mr. Morgan I said hi."

Jack strolls into the apartment and throws down his training bag as he kicks off his sneakers by the door. I'm certain he hasn't noticed me when he reaches into the pocket of his gray sweats and pulls out his phone. I look on from the kitchen island situated behind him and watch his shoulders drop an inch before he repockets his mobile, and I set mine down on the counter in front of me.

The sound has him whipping around to face me, and his eyes immediately land on the unopened jar of oats.

"You found them then?"

My thighs squeeze again as he walks toward me. His hair is still damp from practice, and his black Dri-FIT shirt clings to every line of his well-chiseled body.

Oats, Kendra. Talk about the oats.

"I totally forgot to make them last night. Thank you," I tag on.

Reaching the coffee maker, Jack grabs himself a cup and begins pouring. He looks over his shoulder at my half-finished cup. "I don't know how you can take that without at least a drop of milk."

"Need the caffeine kick badly. And if all I'm allowed is one cup a day, then I'm making the most of it," I reply, another yawn overtaking my body.

Maybe it was because his left side was away from me when he walked into the kitchen, but the second he turns to face me fully, I see it. The bruise across his jawline.

Guilt tears through me.

"Jack, what's that on your jaw?" I whisper.

Heading over to the fridge, he fetches out the milk and pours a small amount into his cup. "Oh yeah." He chuckles. "So, Tyler knows."

I climb off the stool and approach him as he stands with his back against the fridge. "This is all my fault." I inspect the purple bruise more closely and notice a small cut too. "Is it painful?"

Jack shakes his head as he looks down at me.

"Did you hit him back?"

"No. Tempting as it was."

I drag a hand down my face and pause over my eyes. "I knew this was a bad idea."

"Like I said the first time, Hart"—Jack wraps his palm around mine and pulls my hand away—"who gives a fuck what he thinks? Has he messaged you this morning?"

I pause and think over my recent texts. Only one from my brother, talking about the national squad announcement dates. "No. He hasn't actually."

Jack smiles. "I told him to leave you the fuck alone."

"I'm starting to feel like a broken record. All I seem to do is thank you." I blow out a breath.

He takes a sip of coffee and sets his cup down beside him. There's an entire apartment behind me, yet I still haven't stepped away from him.

Finally, I turn to move away and head for the hallway. "I have something that might help with the bruising."

When I reach my bathroom and begin searching through the contents of my medical bag, I find what I'm looking for.

"What's that?" Jack's voice shocks me, and I turn around to find him standing in the doorway, hand braced on the frame above his head. His eyes briefly fall to my bare legs since I'm only wearing my sleep set and a loosely tied robe.

"Arnica cream." I hold the tube up to him. "Mom always swore by this when we were kids. It helps the healing process and brings the bruising out faster." Unscrewing the lid, I squeeze a small amount onto my forefinger and then cringe. "I guess you don't need me to apply it for you like she did for me." I laugh.

Jack's arm drops to his side as he steps into the bathroom, and I back up a couple of paces.

"If you were my girlfriend, would you then?"

I look down at the cream and then back up at him. "Perhaps." Butterflies swirl in my stomach at the thought.

Jack's eyes fall to my mouth and then finger as he stands right in front of me. "No harm in getting in some more practice then, is there?"

I reach up and begin applying the cream to his bruise, being careful to avoid the small cut in the center. "I never realized how tall you actually are," I muse.

In a split second, Jack sets my ass on the counter.

"Is that easier?" he asks, his eyes planted firmly on mine.

Every muscle in my body contracts when he steps forward a few more inches and stands between my legs.

"Much," I whisper.

His hands are braced on either side of me, and I feel the way his breath fans my face. If I closed my eyes, every nerve in my body could sense how close he was. Somehow, I want him closer.

Would I sleep with Jack Morgan? Every time the thought has crossed my mind, I've pushed it away. Determined that it could only make my life even more complicated than it already is.

As I finish up with the cream, Jack closes his eyes and then reopens them. "Tyler's a fucking idiot."

"I thought you'd already worked that one out," I say, screwing the cap back on the cream and tossing it back into my bag.

Jack doesn't move from his position, and when I find his eyes again, his gaze drops to my mouth once more.

"On Saturday, will you kiss me?" The question is out before I can stop it.

His dimple pops. "Would that be a problem? It would be kind of weird if I didn't."

"It's not a problem." I shake my head slowly. "I just want to make sure I'm prepared, is all."

I can't deny the shot of need as it races through me. I want him to suggest we practice right now.

"Kendra," Jack starts, "do you w—"

His phone buzzes several times in the pocket of his pants, and we break eye contact.

"It's Darcy. Mum must've already told her about us since Jon witnessed my confrontation with Tyler and hauled us into his office for an explanation." He smiles as he scrolls to read the rest of the message. "She wants to know who Kendra Hart is and when she gets to meet her."

CHAPTER NINETEEN

KENDRA

From the outside, I look like I'm wearing an expensive designer dress and I have my shit together. On the inside, it's anything but.

Sitting next to me in the executive SUV he booked to take us to the gala, Jack looks as calm as can be in his black tux and bow tie. He also looks hot as fuck with his hair styled back and clean-shaven jawline—the punch from Tyler nowhere near as visible as it was three days ago.

"What's on your mind, Hart?" Jack's gaze drops from me to my twisting hands as they rest in my lap.

I stare out of my passenger window, Brooklyn passing us by in a flash of street and car headlights. Up until the past couple of days, so much about tonight has centered around my ex-boyfriend—when he'll see us at the gala, how he'll react when he does, if he'll be with another girl. And now that the night has finally rolled around, Tyler is no longer the reason why I'm nervous.

"Yeah, I'm good," I reply quietly.

"You don't even have to speak to him, you know?" Jack's voice is as soft as mine.

I want to tell him it's not the thought of seeing Tyler that's got me all twisted up. I couldn't care less if he turns up alone or with three supermodels on his arm. I couldn't care less if he tries to speak to me or even launches his drink in my face.

When Jack suggested we go together, the only reason I hesitated was out of fear of my ex's reaction. Now it feels like my reservations over us doing this have shifted to something completely new. Because all I can focus on is when Jack plans to kiss me.

His trademark smile is ever present when I turn to face him. "I'm sure he'll be avoiding us as much as we will him."

Jack shrugs as we pull up outside the same venue the gala was held at last year.

Jesus, it's insane how different your life can look in just twelve months. It's even more amazing how blind we can be to the one we convinced ourselves was right.

"Jon seated us directly opposite him. I think it was his personal way of punishing me for causing a locker room fight. That, and the fine I was given. Which was half of what Tyler eventually got."

I pull back as we come to a stop. "But you really didn't retaliate?"

Jack swings the door open and rounds the car quickly. When he opens my door and holds his hand out to mine, I take it and step out into a sea of flashing lights.

"I didn't hit him back." He interlaces our fingers. "But I couldn't resist antagonizing him a little."

I want to ask him what he said to Tyler, but the beating music from the venue, combined with hollering reporters, makes it near impossible to hold a coherent conversation. Last Sunday, we kept a low profile, but tonight, there's no hiding our relationship status as Jack leads me onto the red carpet. And as we make our way toward the entrance, I don't miss the nudges and whispers between some of the reporters as they focus their lenses on our joined hands.

Maybe Jack can sense the tension running through me because he squeezes my hand and pulls me to one side just inside the entrance. "Still okay?"

I bite the inside of my cheek as couples continue filtering into the venue and then blow out a long breath, focusing on Jack. "I'm good. Just nervous." It's as honest as I've been with him all night.

When his huge palm wraps around the nape of my neck and pulls me into his chest, I loop my arms around his waist. I've spent the past four years with Tyler, refusing to show vulnerability. The determination that got me to the top of my sport also became a fixture in my relationship with him. Each second of our time together felt like running on loose sand. Everything felt like the biggest effort with the least reward. But being around Jack feels easy, even when our history tells me it absolutely shouldn't. I should feel awkward around the guy who I barely spoke to for years. But I don't.

"Jenna's here tonight with her boyfriend, isn't she?" he asks, tucking a piece of wavy hair behind my ear.

I nod.

"Then try to focus on them and not the asshole sitting opposite us at dinner."

I STAB INTO MY DESSERT, and my fork is halfway to my mouth when Jack leans down and whispers in my ear, "Want some clotted cream with that cheesecake?"

I narrow my eyes playfully. "American desserts are superior."

Jack picks up his beer and smiles around the glass as I cast a quick glance at Tyler.

I was correct on two counts. He didn't attend alone, and I definitely don't give a shit about the blonde who's been all over him this entire dinner.

In fact, I've barely paid any attention to my ex all night—if only the same could be said for him. I've felt his eyes burning into me since the second we sat down, and even with Jack next to me, I've been uncomfortable as fuck.

On my final bite of cheesecake, I set my fork down and push back my chair. "I'm going to go to the restroom."

Jack reaches out and grabs ahold of my hand as I turn to leave. "Do you want me to get you a drink or anything?"

I look down at our hands and then across at Tyler, his eyes laser-focused on them. I know I have a match tomorrow, but it's also my birthday, so why not?

"Yeah, thanks. How about a prosecco?" I reply, turning to leave the main room.

Standing in front of the bathroom mirror, I'm searching through my bag for blush when the door swings open and Jenna strides in.

"Well, that dinner was ... something."

I nod as I reapply my makeup. "You noticed."

She comes to stand beside me and watches me in the reflection. "Babe, I could've noticed from Sydney. Who's the girl he's with?"

I shrug. "Who knows? Could be one of many he likely has on call." I snap the lid shut on my compact. "Not that I care."

Jenna gives me an appreciative look. "That's my girl. Although you know Tyler isn't the only one who can't stop staring at you. I mean, other than me because ... damn." She drops her eyes down the length of my dress. "You are a smokeshow."

I bite my lip and check out Jenna's strappy black gown. "I can't say I haven't thought about spending the night with you either. Lee had better watch out."

She chuckles and spins back to the mirror. "But seriously, Jack is a boy obsessed."

I pick up my clutch and drop my shoulders in the reflection. "As my date. It would be kind of weird if he didn't pay attention to me, no?"

She scrunches up her nose. "Still not buying it. Anyway, I need to pee. See you back out there."

I get as far as stepping out the restroom door when I come face-to-face with Tyler, waiting on the opposite wall.

"Kendra," he calls.

I opt to ignore him and make a break for it down the hallway and back toward Jack.

"Kendra!" he repeats, but I keep walking.

"Kend."

A hand falls on my upper arm, maneuvering me around to face him.

"What do you want, Tyler?" My voice is full of exasperation as I thumb over my shoulder. "I have a drink waiting for me."

He shakes his head. "Is it true?"

I look down at the floor, tired of seeing the anger in his eyes. "Is what?"

"Morgan? Is it true you're dating Morgan?"

"Well, I'm here with him, aren't I?"

Tyler's hand is still on my arm, and I pull it back to break free, but he tightens his grasp around me.

"And can you let go of me, please?"

He ignores my protest. "Why are you playing games with me, Kendra? Is this all about making me jealous, huh?"

I pull away again, but his grip tightens even further. "I'd have to care to want to make you jealous. The only thing I want right now is for you to get off me!"

The Blades captain, Sawyer Bryce, approaches Tyler from behind and pulls him away.

And that's when I see Jack. With a face of thunder.

"Don't, Jack. Remember what I said," Sawyer shouts after him.

I'm motionless as Jack stalks past Tyler and heads straight for me. His eyes fall to my upper arm before returning to mine.

He doesn't say anything as he reaches out and takes my hand in his, and as he guides me back to the function area, he briefly pulls up alongside Tyler. "That's the last time you'll ever get to look at my girl, let alone touch her."

Jack doesn't stop walking until we reach the bar at the back of the main room.

Two glasses of untouched prosecco sit on a black tray, and he reaches out and passes me one.

I take a sip and try to steady my emotions, although I know I'm doing a better job of managing them than Jack.

"Did he hurt you?" he asks in a clipped voice.

I shake my head and take another sip as I notice Tyler enter the room with Sawyer hot on his heels. "No."

"Your arm is covered in red marks."

Jack gently traces them with his thumb. "What did he say to you?"

I look up at him. "That I'm playing games with him and trying to make him jealous. That he knows this is all fake."

Jack breathes out slowly, and as a few strands of hair fall over his blue eyes, he shifts his attention from the marks to my face. There's nothing but serenity in the way he looks at me. "Are you trying to make him jealous?"

"No. I want him to leave me alone," I whisper, my senses alive with anticipation.

"Are you still in love with him?"

"No," I repeat.

Taking my drink in his other hand, he sets it on the bar next to him and then turns back to me.

The hand stroking my arm comes under my chin, demanding all my attention.

But he already has it.

"You deserve so much better than what he can give you, and the only time a man should put his hands on you is to make you feel like a queen."

I didn't even notice we were moving until my back finds the wall behind me.

His thumb and forefinger still hold my chin when his lips hover over mine. "I know he's watching us."

"Probably," I reply, not caring either way.

He smiles down at me. "Remember when you asked if I'd kiss you tonight?"

"Yes," I whisper.

"Was that because you wanted me to?"

My heart races in my chest. Every part of me wants Jack to take my mouth with his and kiss me in the way I've been thinking about for longer than I care to admit. Yet I still can't shake the uncertainty pooling in my gut. What if none of what I'm feeling is real for him? What if this is his way of proving to Tyler that we're real and to back the fuck off me?

My head wars with my heart.

Jack's eyes search mine. "Talk to me, Kendra."

"I-I want you to kiss me."

When his hand finds the back of my neck and pulls me closer, he brushes his lips over mine. "How does that feel?"

I roll my lips together. The taste of him is faint but incredible. "More."

"Do you want my tongue, Kendra Hart?" Jack teases as his breath fans my damp lips, and I can't fight the smile that pulls at them.

"Yes."

This time, when he presses his mouth against me, I part for him, and the first stroke of his warm tongue against mine sparks an outbreak of goosebumps across my skin.

This is what it's like to be kissed.

Jack's hand ascends my neck until his fingers play in my hair.

His kisses are demanding as his tongue licks into my mouth, and I whimper at the sensation.

The temptation to grind against his knee as he pushes it between my thighs is so overwhelming. If this is the way he kisses, what the hell is it like to spend the night with him?

I want to find out. I hope I get the chance.

"Wow, Kendra," he whispers against my lips, resting his forehead on mine. "That was ... definitely believable."

CHAPTER TWENTY

JACK

SAWYER

Evening, lovebird. Just checking in to make sure Tyler hasn't hidden a hit man in your apartment and my winger is in fact still breathing.

ME

Still breathing, but I haven't checked all the rooms yet.

Listen, I might not be Cupid's biggest believer these days. But from what I saw, death might be worth it.

I sit on the end of my bed with my shirt undone, bow tie hanging loosely around my neck.

You saw the kiss?

Sweetheart, EVERYONE saw the kiss.

If it looked anything like how it felt, then it was likely the greatest show of their lives.

ME

She's incredible.

I dump my phone down on the bed beside me. So much of me wants to tell Sawyer about the arrangement Kendra and I made, and being honest, I don't know why I haven't.

I pick my phone back up and begin typing out another message.

ME

Can I trust you?

SAWYER

Have I given you a reason to doubt me yet?

True.

Kendra and me—well, we're fake dating. I offered to take her to the gala to help keep Tyler off her back and so she wouldn't feel so uncomfortable if he turned up with a random date. That kiss you saw earlier—it wasn't exactly real.

I hit Send on the message and instantly feel like my efforts to be straight with him are anything but. *Everything* about that kiss felt real.

SAWYER

It's real. Trust me when I say, you can't fake that. I don't care if you've won a hundred Golden Globes and Oscars line your trophy cabinets. That shit was real.

ME

I won't deny that it was for me. I felt everything between us. I'm in deep with her. But how can you tell with Kendra?

Because that's the way my wife used to look at me.

I feel the punch to my gut on his behalf. What can I say to a message like that? How can I—or why would I want to—argue with that kind of statement?

Reaching under my bed, I pull out the present I have wrapped for Kendra's birthday tomorrow and then the card, all signed and ready to go.

The entire ride back was charged to fuck after the kiss, but neither of us spoke about it. And when we got back to my apartment, Kendra headed straight for bed without saying much.

I figured that would be the last time I saw her before she headed out for her game tomorrow. But when I see a dim light cast beneath my door and then hear hers close with a soft click, I realize she isn't asleep.

Pulling off my shirt and bow tie, I throw on a training top, along with a pair of athletic shorts, and make my way toward the living area, but stop when I find Kendra curled up on my sofa, a couple of blankets thrown over her and the usual *Friends* playing quietly in the background.

"Can't sleep?" I ask, knowing she hasn't slept well since the day she got here.

She props her head up with her hand. "Looks like we're in the same boat."

I nod and make my way over to a chair on the opposite side of the room when Kendra sits up and pulls back the blankets.

"You promised me a *Friends* binge session, if I remember correctly."

The blankets are already warm from her body heat when I take a seat next to her and pull them into my lap. "I also promised you shepherd's pie."

Her pink cheeks flush in the light casting from the TV. "I'm still waiting on your cooking. Eagerly waiting, if your overnight oats are anything to go by."

"Oh, so they were a hit, were they, Hart?"

She brings a hand from underneath the blanket, holding it out in front of her. "I'd say fair to good."

Leaning toward her, I stop inches from her face. "You're definitely a brat."

She shoots back in mock hurt, "Must be a nightmare having me around."

My face breaks into a cocky smile. "Fucking torturous."

I continue to stare at her as my expression shifts from playful to a whole lot more. She took her makeup off and piled her hair into a messy bun since we got home. Honestly, this is the version of Kendra that I'll remember when she moves out and finds her own place—relaxed and watching repeats of her favorite programs in my living room. This is the everyday version of the girl I'm falling for and the one I never want to end.

More silence stretches between us as the TV continues to play in the background, though I can't take my eyes away from hers.

"You excited for your birthday tomorrow?"

Her tongue peeks out and swipes across her bottom lip, and when her gaze falls to my mouth, my cock stirs at the intensity in her eyes. The way it felt to kiss her earlier—no kiss with any other girl has ever come close to that.

"It depends," she replies cheekily. "Did you get me anything?"

"I did."

Our lips are centimeters apart. I want this girl so fucking badly. I'm right there, dangling on the precipice of my willpower.

"Can you show me now, or do I have to wait?" she asks, her voice barely a whisper.

If I make the move to kiss her, alone and with no one to see, then she'll know it's real for me. All I have to do is pray she'll kiss me back.

Sawyer's message repeats in my head.

"Fuck it."

My mouth crashes against hers as I brace my hand on the

sofa behind her body. Her tongue is hot and smooth as I leisurely tease it with mine, savoring the way she whimpers and melts beneath me. I want to taste every single part of the girl who's invaded my mind since I was eighteen, but I also want to take it slow so I can remember all the ways she responds to my touch.

I thought the kiss earlier was special, but, fuck me, this is so much more. I feel myself sinking into her further, the lines of reality blurring completely.

But I'm too far in to pull back—or maybe even care. If fun is all she wants with me, then that's what I'll give her because the alternative is not an option.

Breaking from her lips, I start kissing across her jaw. Her skin is soft, just as I imagined it would be. Maybe even more perfect. When I start licking and sucking down her neck, her breathing picks up, as do her moans, and, *fuuuuuck*, my cock is so desperate to bury itself inside her.

"More," she pleads in a voice I can scarcely hear. "More."

My hands come under her ass, and I lift her up and onto me, throwing off the blankets in a single motion.

In tiny pink sleep shorts and a cami top, she looks like a wet fucking dream—*my* wet dream—as she straddles my lap and grinds down into me. She throws her head back and I watch from beneath her with fucking heart eyes.

Is this really happening right now? Or am I going to wake up, frustrated and with the bluest balls in history?

Gripping her hips tightly, I grind her harder against me, if only to realize my reality when she reaches up and pulls the tie from her bun, hair cascading around her shoulders.

"You like it like this, don't you?" Her pupils are blown as she rocks into me, bracing her hands on my shoulders.

"Fucking stunning, Hart," I breathe out, my cock threatening to blow at any damn second.

It's been a while since I was with anyone, and right now, I'm in danger of going off before we've even gotten started.

My fingertips sink into her soft hips. "What do you want?" I ask.

Her hair falls around my face as she leans down and kisses me. "I want you to take me to your room and not hold back. I want you to make me come until I see stars."

I bite down on my bottom lip. "Is that right? You want me to fuck you hard?" My hand falls to her ass, where I slide my fingers underneath the hem of her sleep shorts, and I immediately feel the heat radiating from her. "How wet is this pussy of yours?"

"Dripping," she moans.

My fingers continue moving until they find the seam of her panties. "Can I be the judge of that?"

Kendra squeezes her eyes shut. "Touch me."

I push two fingers underneath her already-soaked underwear, and when I feel how wet she is, my balls contract to the point of pain. "Is this all for me, Kitten?"

It's the first time I've called Kendra the name I've associated her with since we met in the café, and by the feral look in her eyes, I know she likes it.

One swipe of three fingers through her pussy not only has her moaning out loud, but me as well. She spreads her thighs wider, granting me better access.

"I have every intention of fucking your brains out tonight." I push the tip of my finger inside her tight entrance, and I hear the way her pussy takes me. "But I'm a guy who likes to play with my meal before I devour it. Would you be okay with that?"

"Ohmygod," she gasps as I push my finger deeper, quickly adding another. "What do you have in mind?"

My mind wanders to the way I've always imagined Kendra beneath me, and I know she'll look perfect.

I bring the hand that isn't fingering her to a strap on her cami and pull it down over her shoulder, a breast spilling free. My tongue teases it, sucking and biting on her round, perfectly pink nipple.

I pop off and stare up at her as I sink my fingers deep and find her front wall.

Her head flops forward. "Oh fuck!"

She's not coming yet, but I let her savor my fingers for a few more seconds before I pull them out and bring them to my mouth.

I'm like a starved animal as she watches me swallow down my first taste.

"I want to tie you to my bed and treat you like the queen you are, Kitten." I wrap my hand around the nape of her neck and pull her face down to mine. "I want to watch when I make every single nerve in your body fire off. I want to do to you exactly what I've been thinking about since I laid eyes on you years ago."

Her nipple hardens further, and I smile around it as I bring it into my mouth, pulling down the other strap on her top.

"Y-you want to tie me up?" Her voice shakes with lust.

"Only your hands," I say as I switch to her other nipple. "I want all the work tonight to be mine. I want you at my mercy."

"When will I get to touch you?"

Picking her up with my hands underneath her soaked sleep shorts, I stand, and she wraps her legs around my waist.

With her suspended like this, all I can think about is how easy it would be to push down my shorts, pull her underwear to one side, and slide all the way inside her tight pussy.

Fuck, don't blow yet, Jack.

My tongue licks against hers. "You'll get to touch me when I've made up for years of wanting you."

I begin walking us to my bedroom, and her full tits bounce against my chest.

"I can't believe you've wanted me for that long."

I stop just at the entrance to my bedroom. "Kendra"—my lips find her collarbone as she tips her head back and moans—"I've had to endure years of watching an asshole mistreat the woman of my dreams." I whisper against her pebbled skin, "And even if tonight is my only chance with you, when the sun rises tomorrow morning, you'll know what it feels like to be worshipped."

CHAPTER TWENTY-ONE

KENDRA

Four years. He's wanted me for that long.

Jesus, I really have been blind.

My brain is still trying to catch up with the bombshell Jack just dropped as he lays me down on his duvet.

Standing at the foot of his bed, he reaches behind his head and pulls off his training top. In the soft glow from the lamp on his nightstand, his chest and abs are exactly as I thought they would be. Perfection.

My mouth waters, and I grow wetter at the thought of him tying me up and living out his fantasies. I want him to steal my words with his mouth and keep me awake all night with his dick.

His dark blue athletic shorts ride low on his waist as he reaches over, picks up a wrapped box, and sets it on the floor. "This part of your gift can wait a little longer."

Next, he moves across to his dresser and pulls open the top drawer. Turning over his shoulder, he throws me a panty-melting smile as he reaches inside and grabs a black tie, pocketing it in his shorts.

I've never been nervous to sleep with a guy. With Tyler, I was way too focused on trying to reach a climax to even think about what I was doing or who I was with.

But as Jack Morgan crawls over me and lifts my cami top overhead, butterflies swarm my body in response to the way he drinks me in.

I sit up on my elbows and drop my gaze to the hard bulge tenting his shorts.

He chuckles, leaning down to take my mouth with his, massaging our tongues together.

"I've never had a problem speaking my mind." He drops his forehead against mine. "But you do things to me I don't think I'll ever have words for. Never in my wildest dreams did I think we'd be here, and I feel so damn lucky right now."

He pulls out the black tie, and I pulsate with need.

"Have you ever done this before?"

With our foreheads still pressed together, I shake my head. "Never."

A dark rumble rises from his throat, almost like that turns him on further. "Lie back and lift your arms above your head for me."

I do as he asked, and Jack sits up on his knees, taking my hands in his. As he wraps the tie around my wrists and secures it to his headboard, I know I'm completely at his mercy. The thought alone has me biting down on my bottom lip, the excitement and anticipation bordering unbearable.

My experience with guys is limited, but one thing they all shared was reaching their climax as soon as possible. So, when Jack straddles my waist and his lips fall to my upper left arm, emotions I wasn't expecting from tonight stick at the back of my throat.

Truth is, I don't know what I want with him. I have so many confused feelings that are ultimately overpowered by need. We've been dancing around each other for too long, and I need to know what it feels like to be in his bed.

"Promise me you'll never let a guy touch you like that again.

And if they do, then I want to fucking hear about it, Kendra." One at a time, he kisses the five marks Tyler's fingers left and then brings his eyes back to mine. "Promise me."

"I promise," I whisper.

"I don't know if you're aware of how special you are. I don't think I've ever met a woman more determined to go after what she wants. Do you know how beautiful that is?"

His hands fall to the waistband of my sleep shorts, and carefully, he peels them down my legs. When they pass over my knees, his lips hover over my left kneecap—the place where I feel constant pain.

I'm left in only my black thong when Jack tosses my sleep shorts onto the floor.

"Jesus Christ." He swipes a hand over his mouth, shaking his head in disbelief.

Crawling back over me, he frames my face with his palms as he kisses me deeply. His tongue, his breath, his scent, his moans—they all overwhelm me in the best way possible. The only way I ever want to be touched.

He pulls my lower lip between his teeth before releasing it, working his mouth down my neck and toward my breasts.

"How do you like to come, Kendra?" he asks between kisses.

My jaw hangs open when he glides his tongue from one nipple to the other, circling each one in turn.

"I-I don't know." I swallow thickly, knowing I'm already so close.

Jack lifts his head as he descends to my navel. "What do you mean, you don't know?" He narrows his eyes at me.

I shake my head at him. "Most of the time, I've only ever come with the help of Scarlett."

Jack's face breaks into a cocky smile. "Oh, yeah? And who is she?"

Other than the color of my cheeks right now ...

"She's my vibrator," I reply. "Something Tyler fucking hated."

He sits up on his haunches, hands falling to my thong. "Diamonds might be a girl's best friend, but toys are also ours. What guy wouldn't want to see his girl take a vibrator and his cock at the same time?"

As he backs off the bed, he takes my panties with him. "You're so damn wet. Part those pretty thighs for me, Kitten."

As I spread myself in front of him, a rumble leaves his chest.

"Let me see you." I tip my chin at his shorts.

His smile breaks out. "You want to see my cock?"

I want to do a lot more than just see it.

"Yes."

In a torturously slow move, he pushes his shorts to the floor. I wanted him to steal my words tonight, but I never expected his cock to achieve that just by looking at it.

"Holy hell," I gasp.

He wraps his fist around the base, and the tip shines in the light cast from his bedside lamp.

"You like what you see?" he asks.

I nod my head with need, and he climbs back onto the bed.

"Well, if you're a good girl, I'll feed it to you later ... but first" —his hands find my inner thighs as he spreads me wider—"I need to eat."

His tongue follows the trail of my release left from when he removed my thong, and when he switches to the other thigh and does the same, I can already feel my first orgasm as it overpowers me.

I shake and shudder, the sensation made stronger by Jack's fingers swiping through my pussy and circling my clit.

"I'm going to come," I moan. "Right now, I'm going to come."

His thumb replaces his fingers and applies pressure to my clit as he continues to nip and suck at my inner thigh. He's not even looking at my pussy, but somehow, he knows exactly where to touch. "Best you do it all over my fingers then."

The moment two fingers push inside my entrance, I begin to contract around him.

A guttural groan vibrates against my thigh while his mouth moves toward my apex, and I throw my head back into the pillow, straining against the tie around my wrists.

"You're coming all over my hand, Kitten."

His fingers continue pumping me, his tongue lapping up my release. Every time I think I've gone as far as I can, Jack finds a deeper spot inside me, triggering another wave of bliss, which he happily swallows down between groans.

Even if I wanted to stand up, I don't think I could. Every bone in my body has melted into the mattress beneath me.

Jack reaches beside me, grabs a pillow, and slides it underneath my hips. I raise an inquisitive brow as he brings his fingers to his mouth and sucks them on a cocky grin.

"Since you taste so good, it's inevitable that I'll be here for a while. Makes it more comfortable."

I don't get a chance to respond. In fact, I am officially nonverbal. Jesus, this man's mouth.

"So fucking delicious," he rasps against my clit, sucking it mercilessly.

My hips shoot off the bed, but he brings an arm across them and holds me in place while he drives his tongue deep inside my pussy.

"Jack, Jack, I'm going to c-come again."

"I know," he replies. "Let go, Kendra. Give me all of it."

I've never been loud in bed—maybe because I've never had a reason to scream. But as Jack lifts one of my legs onto his shoulder and drags my lower half up with him, the way he eats me has me crying out his name on repeat.

That's where I stay, suspended and pressed against his mouth, working me into a frenzy. I'm locked in a permanent state of bliss, unsure where my last orgasm finished, and a new one begins.

As his tongue slows over my clit, Jack's brown hair falls across his eyes, and he watches me unravel once more. The only sound in his otherwise silent bedroom is from the way he devours me.

I've never come so hard or fast before. I didn't even think it was possible.

He pulls away the pillow and lowers my hips back onto the bed, reaching up to untie me. "I was going to keep you like this for longer, but I want to feel the way your nails dig into my skin when I push inside you."

"Let me ride you," I say, sitting up and finding his lips again. "I want to feel how big you are."

My hand falls to his dick as we both rise onto our knees in front of each other.

Jack wraps his hand around mine. "You want to play with me?"

I pump him once and watch as a bead of pre-cum leaks down his shaft, trailing over my hand. "You untied me and released the beast. I want to hear you scream my name too."

He runs his tongue across his bottom lip, and I swipe my palm over the head, using more pre-cum to lubricate my grip.

"Jesus," he growls as he drops his head down, "I'm this close to shooting."

When I bend down to take him in my mouth, he wraps my hair around his fist, pulling me back up to face him. His eyes are hooded and dark—a far cry from the playful Jack I'm used to.

"You going to ride my dick or what?"

I inch closer, our lips a whisker from touching. "Anyone ever tell you that for a boy with a posh accent, you have a really filthy mouth?"

He reaches down and swipes a finger through my soaking pussy, offering it out for me to taste. "Maybe you should find out what all the fuss is about. Taste all the reasons why you drive me wild."

His jaw hangs open as I suck myself clean from his finger, releasing it with a pop.

"I need inside you—right now," he grits out, falling back onto his bed and gripping his cock tightly.

I'm ready to sink onto him when Jack's hands find my hips, halting me.

"We haven't spoken about protection, but I'm tested regularly, and I haven't been with anyone in ... a while."

I reach forward and kiss him. "I got tested after Tyler, and I have an IUD."

From the moment I saw him, I knew Jack was big. But I could never have been prepared for the way he stretches me out. Lowering further down, I pause when he's halfway inside me, and he sits up on one elbow, circling a hand around the nape of my neck.

"You're swallowing me so fucking well." His eyes fall to where he's disappearing, and he lifts up his hips, pushing in another inch.

"You're so big." My head lolls forward, but the hand around my neck finds my chin and tips my face back up.

"Eyes on me, Kendra. Let me see you as I claim you as mine."

I want to tell him that he isn't just claiming me tonight.

He's ruining me.

When he's all the way in, I expect him to lie back and let me do all the work. But he stays resting on his elbow, pushing his hips to drive further inside, and I rock over him for the first time.

He's so deep that I feel sure he'll break me.

"That's it, Kitten. Take what you need from me. Let me be your toy tonight."

I rock over him again and hear how wet I am. Jack must notice it too.

"Can you hear how soaked you are?"

"Never—been—this—wet," I pant, my hips losing rhythm as the pleasure builds to uncontrollable levels.

"Yeah, time for me to fuck you now."

In one smooth motion, I'm on my back, and Jack's pushing

inside me from above. His face is exactly like I pictured that morning at Jenna's.

On his knees, he thrusts into me hard and spreads my legs as they rest in the crook of his elbows. "Tell me, did you scream Tyler's name when he fucked you?"

"No," I cry.

He thrusts into me again, his dick growing harder. "Who makes you scream, Kendra?"

Falling over the edge, I do exactly that. "Y-you do. Only you."

His hot cum spills inside me, but Jack keeps moving until he's emptied all he has.

He collapses onto his elbows, bracketing me in with his arms as we kiss and settle into a peaceful and satiated bliss.

"I've wanted this for weeks," I tell him.

Jack releases a long, relaxed breath. "I'll raise you by several years. Jesus Christ, you're fucking incredible. Better than I could've ever imagined."

CHAPTER TWENTY-TWO

KENDRA

It's not even morning. I know because it's still pitch-black outside Jack's window, where I can see the lights from the Brooklyn Bridge shining bright since we both fell asleep and didn't bother closing the curtains.

When we finished having sex the first time, we went at it again. And again.

Tucked under his arm and pressed against him as he breathes softly from behind me, I squeeze my thighs and don't just remember but *feel* the things we did last night. I came more times than I could count, and I smile lazily into the duvet, the scruff of his jaw still tingling between my legs.

"Hold still, Kitten. I haven't gotten it all."

My stomach flips at the memory. His dirty words, his wicked tongue.

And I'm so here for it.

With no idea if it's two a.m. or five, I find myself grinding back into his hips, totally insatiable and needy.

I grind a few more times and feel his hard cock between my

bare ass cheeks, but there's no change to the pattern of his breathing.

Fuck, I'm so horny.

Beneath the duvet, I bring my hand to my apex and slide a finger through my pussy, my eyes fluttering shut.

"Are you still wet from my cock?" Jack whispers into the hairs at the back of my neck.

I stroke myself again and reach behind me, searching for what I want.

My fingertips graze him, gathering pre-cum, which I bring to my mouth, and he flips me onto my back, hovering over me.

His usually styled hair is messy from the way I ran my fingers through it all night. Reaching up, I play with the strands as they fall over his eyes.

"Happy birthday." He whispers the words, finding my breast with his tongue.

I writhe beneath him and bring my palms to either side of his face, pulling him back up toward me. "I want you inside me again."

"And you think there was a realistic alternative?"

I pulse at his heady voice, thick with lust. "Well, I was hoping not, but ..." I trail off, not wanting to spoil the moment.

Jack's lips find mine. "Not what, Kendra?"

I swallow down his words as memories come back. "Just thinking about how last year looked very different from the way this birthday has started out."

From above me, Jack closes his eyes. "You should've been in my bed last year too."

My heart races just a little faster. "What are we doing, Jack?"

"I don't know, Kitten." He opens his eyes and strokes a thumb across my forehead. "Following what we want?" he breathes out and notches his cock at my entrance. "Having the best sex of our lives."

When he pushes inside me, I wrap my legs around his waist. I'm still deliciously sore from last night, and it only adds to the intensity from the way he fills me. We both groan into one another, our mouths hanging open, tongues tangling.

"I think I'm addicted to you, to this body." He trails his fingertips down my side, rolling his hips against me.

I press my heels into his lower back, already wanting him deeper. "I can't get enough."

Every movement Jack makes finds a different spot from before. Every kiss he places against my skin I feel all over my body, leaving me trembling.

"Relax for me, Kendra. I'm gonna make this so good for you."

Jack sits back on his heels and brings me with him. He's still inside me when he moves us toward the edge of his bed and sets his feet on the floor.

Completely naked and straddling his thighs, the lights of Brooklyn reflect in his eyes.

"Ride me like this. Come on my cock with the world behind you."

I chase my high, fingernails digging into his shoulders.

"Tell me, do you feel as sexy as you look right now?" Jack's hands come under my ass as he lifts me off him, hovering me above just above his cock. "Do you, Kendra?" he repeats.

I nod my head. "Yes."

"Good girl."

He lowers me back onto his dick, and I gasp. I feel even fuller than before.

"I've never been this hard—ever." Sweat beads on his forehead, a few damp strands of hair falling over his eyes. "Only you do this to me, make me feel so turned on."

Lifting up, I slam back onto him, and we both cry out together.

"Fuck, Kitten, do that again. I love it when you use me."

This time, when I drop harder, his lips find my neck. Normally, he kisses or lightly nips, but this time, Jack sucks—hard.

"W-what are you doing?"

The sting flirts with pleasure as he releases my skin and licks over it with his tongue.

"Proving every part of this is real." He brings his eyes back to mine and wraps his palm around the back of my neck. "I'm never going to forget this, Kendra. Last night, this morning—it's a part of me now."

"Me too. Best day ever."

A giggle spills out, and he thrusts into me from below, setting me off like a fucking firework. I was teetering on the edge, but all it took was a deep stroke, and I'm seeing stars.

"I'm gonna blow right inside you. You want that? Huh? You want my cum, dirty girl?"

I spread my legs wider and reach behind me, massaging his balls in my palm. "I'm feeling greedy. Blow, baby."

On a deep roar that I'm certain his neighbors hear, Jack spills inside me. Last night, I could feel his release, but as the sun rises behind me and casts an orange glow into his bedroom, my body heats at the way he fills me up so well.

"Jesus Christ." Jack's forehead falls against my chest. "You think you're greedy? I'll never get enough of you."

"Thanks. Well played," I say, shaking Casey Robinson's hand.

"You too, Hart. You're hoping for a place in the World Cup squad, right?" Cleveland's goalkeeper asks. Robinson has been to more major tournaments than I can recall.

I nod and adjust my stance, taking some of the pressure off my knee. Securing the win against the top of the league has left me more than just a little exhausted. Although I'm not sure how much of that is due to the three hours of sleep I got last night.

"Yeah. Fingers crossed I make it."

"Well, let's put it this way: they'd be crazy not to select you."

"Hey there. Back off my girl, all right?" Jenna throws an arm around my shoulders and drags me away from Robinson. "Find your own center back," she calls behind her, giggling all the way.

I shake my head and chuckle. "So possessive."

Releasing me and jogging over to her goal, she picks up her towel and water bottle and makes her way back. "How was last night?"

I narrow my eyes at her in question. "You saw me last night."

She squirts water into her mouth and seals the cap on her bottle, grinning. "Yeah, but I'm fairly certain you weren't sporting a Jack stamp when I last saw you."

"Oh fuck." My face flames as my hand darts up to my neck, tracing the mark he left.

"I mean, I thought you had a little more pep this afternoon." She steps forward, her blue eyes glittering with mischief. "Now I know why. Was he amazing? I imagine he was."

I turn and head for the locker room as the crowd around us fully disperses. "I'm not talking about it."

Jenna throws her head back like a child. "Oh, come onnnn. I'd spill on Lee."

I nudge her and laugh. "Oh, I bet you would."

Catching my hand in hers, Jenna stops me just before we push through the door. "Seriously though, Hart, you're smiling. You look happy."

For once in my life, I don't try to hide it. "Yeah, I am."

She beats her boot against the designated mat. "Does this mean things are ... more permanent?"

I roll my lips together, uncertainty combining with unease. "I don't know what we are. Things are kind of blurry right now."

Jenna's shoulders drop. "Have you spoken—"

"Miller, can I borrow you for a second, please?" Coach's voice cuts her short.

With one last glance my way, Jenna takes off in the opposite direction, leaving me alone with my thoughts.

The locker room door flies open, and my captain stands with my cell in her hand. "Hart, your phone won't stop ringing."

I immediately panic, thinking something happened to Jack at practice. My pulse rate slows when I see *Ollie* across the screen.

"I assume you're calling to congratulate me on my best performance of the season so far." I bang my boots on the mat, trying to get them clean.

"I knew it, I fucking knew you were dating him! Oh, happy birthday, by the way."

"Oliver, language! Happy birthday, darling. Did you get the flowers we sent you?"

I pull the phone away from my ear to see I'm on a three-way call with my brother and parents.

Delightful.

"Flowers?" My brain catches up, and I remember I sent them Jack's address a couple of days ago, not that they knew whose it was at the time. "Oh, no, not yet. Maybe when I get back home."

"Okay. Well, hopefully, you like them." Mom pauses. "But your brother has a point. When exactly were you going to break this to us, or do you plan on us getting all our updates via ESPN from now on?"

"ESPN?" I repeat.

"Uh, duh. You attended NYPAG with not just a pro hockey star, BUT *the* guy who's just been named the NHL's most eligible bachelor. Makes sense if you think about it. What with his last name and everything," Ollie clarifies.

I shake my head in confusion. "Most eligible ... what are you talking about?"

"Ugh," he sighs. "Check the news when you get a second. I *assume* you've been too preoccupied lately."

"Yeah, yeah. All right, Oliver, that's enough of that," Dad interrupts. "But seriously"—his voice rises a couple of octaves—"are you seeing Jon Morgan's son?"

"Stepson," I correct.

"Eh, potato, potahto," Mom responds.

I look down the hallway like I'll see Jenna and she'll come to my rescue. Instead, I find Jack standing at the entrance to the pitch, rain pouring down behind him, his hands in the front pocket of his Blades hoodie.

My heart rate picks up. He didn't say he'd be here.

I wave to him and then turn back to the family conference call. "Yeah," I say, closing my eyes as the word leaves my mouth, "we're dating."

"Ohmygod! Do you love him?!" Mom bursts out.

"For fuck's sa—"

"Oliver!" Dad scolds.

My eyes are still closed when Jack approaches me from behind, kissing the mark on my neck and wrapping his arms around my waist.

Everything inside me melts away, and I have to fight to keep myself focused on the conversation and not totally engulfed by the tingles dancing in my stomach.

"I'm not answering that question, Mom."

"Well, why not? Should I start speaking to an officiant?"

"No."

I snort a laugh and then look over my shoulder, Jack's eyes sparkling back at me. I don't know if he can hear what's being said, but either way, he's probably got a good idea of the madness I was brought up around.

"Okay, I'm going to go now," I say, already pulling the phone away from my ear.

"Bring him home for Thanksgiving!" Mom says.

I quickly shout, "Bye," and disconnect the call.

"Sorry about that." I wince and wave my phone in front of me. "My family is kind of ..."

"Crazy?" he finishes.

I nod and pull my hair out of its ponytail. "Exactly that."

I look around him and see we're all alone in the hallway when Jack pulls his hands from his hoodie and tips my chin up. "You played fucking awesome today."

"You watched?"

His trademark dimple emerges. "I missed the first half because of practice but caught the second. That tackle?" He gives me a chef's kiss.

I blush. "Thanks."

"So, yeah, about family." Jack reaches out and runs his fingers through the ends of my hair. "How do you feel about meeting mine?"

My eyes grow wide as I thumb over my shoulder. "Like, now? Today?"

He smirks and nods once. "Darce flew in for a few days since she's got a study week, and Mum is ... let's just say, she's insisting she meets you after last night's photos."

I stay quiet. *Fuck, meet his family?*

"I can tell them if it's too soon," Jack quickly adds. "Yeah, it's too soon." He pulls out his phone. "To be honest, this wasn't even part of the arrangement. I don't know what I was thinking." He starts typing a message out.

My hand covers his screen. "No, don't. I'd love to meet them. Just give me a few to get changed, okay?"

I'm pushing through the locker room door when my phone buzzes in my hand.

OLLIE

There was no way you were living with him and nothing else. When you meet Jon, I want a full report.

My brother needs to calm the fuck down.

"Kend?"

I turn back to Jack. "Yeah?"

He looks like he wants to say something, but clearly changes his mind. "I've got my truck; I can drive us."

CHAPTER TWENTY-THREE

JACK

The rain thuds against the windscreen of my GMC Sierra as I sit, drumming my fingers on the steering wheel.

She's going to step out of the shower and straight into clothes, and she'll likely fucking freeze when she walks out into this. Even if it is only a couple of hundred yards to my truck, she'll be soaked to the skin.

I swing the door open and pull up my hoodie, heading for the same security guard who gave me access to the tunnel so I could speak to Kendra earlier.

Apparently, he's a Blades fan.

"Yo!" I tap on the glass, and he startles.

He slides his window open, and I point across to the restricted access directly outside the players' exit.

"I know it's only for deliveries, but my girlfriend, Kendra Hart"—*fuck, that feels good*—"is going to get wet through."

The guy looks at me like I'm from another planet. "Yeah, and? She's a soccer player; she's used to the rain."

I step closer to the window. "She just played the game of her life, and I'm about to take her to meet my family for the first time. I want her to feel comfortable, not sitting there cold and wet." I point over at the gate. "So, can you just buzz me through, and I'll be out of your way?"

He pulls on the bill of his Storm cap, considering my request. "All right. But you have five minutes."

I throw him a thumbs-up and jog back to my truck, firing up the engine. The gate rolls open, and I drive right up outside the players' door.

Pulling off my wet hoodie, I set the heated seats on full and pull her gift from the back. Kendra wanted to save opening it until she got back home, but what can I say? I'm an impatient motherfucker.

JON

Your mom wants to know what time you'll be here.

ME

Maybe, like, an hour. Maybe less. I need to give Kendra my gift first, and then we'll head over to your place.

Gift?

Fuck.

Yeah, I didn't need to know that, Jack.

My face is torn between cringe and amusement.

ME

No, not that. Well, maybe that later. Definitely that later. It's her birthday.

Annnnnd I forgot to tell them.

JON

Ahhh. Cool, cool. So, you thought you'd just skip over the part where you tell us she needs a gift. You know, the woman you're dating and we're meeting for the first time.

I begin apologizing, but another text comes through.

MUM

IT'S HER BIRTHDAY?!!

ME

Don't kill me.

Jon has been added to the chat

JON

Angel, I'm at the door, putting my sneakers on right now. You keep the oven on warm for the beef. I'm running to Kings Plaza a couple blocks away.

Jack, I have zero words right now. Other than I'm updating your contact to Knucklehead.

It must be another twenty minutes when Kendra's teammates begin filing out.

JON

What's her favorite color?

ME

She thinks it's blue, but it's actually, like, a sage green. More olive actually. That's what she wears on her nails.

JON

There's nothing olive in this store.

ME

What store are you in?

JON

Macy's.

ME

And there's nothing olivey in there?

JON

No, Jack, there is not.

Wait, I've found something. Thank the Lord.

I look up from my phone just as Kendra pulls open the passenger door and climbs in.

"How did you get a space here?" Her face drops to the gift in my lap.

"Made friends with Ted." I point at the security cabin.

She pulls on her seat belt and clips it in place. "Wait, so you talked Ted into letting you park here?"

I shrug. "Yeah."

"Why?" She blows out a laugh.

I lean across and rest my palm on her cheek. "Because it's wet and cold, and if you were my girlfriend, you wouldn't be walking in it. Not even two hundred yards."

I keep my eyes on hers before I shift into drive and head for the main car park. "Ready for your gift?"

When I finally park again, she's staring out the passenger window.

"Kendra?"

"Yeah?" She turns to face me with a shine in her eyes.

"Hey, what's the matter?" I reach across and run a hand through her long, towel-dried hair.

She rolls her lips together and twists her hands in her lap. "At what point do we stop this, Jack? The arrangement we made." The tinge of sadness in her voice leaves a lump in my throat.

"Come here." I reach across and unbuckle her belt, setting her card and gift down on the floor.

Kendra climbs across the center section and straddles me,

and my hands find her jean-covered ass. Everything we did last night and then this morning races straight to my dick.

"When do you want to stop, Kendra?" I ask her the question since the answer for me is simple.

Never. I never want to stop. There's nothing temporary about forever, and that's as far as I can see with the girl in my lap.

She winds her hands around my neck and presses her forehead to mine. "Not yet."

With my lips resting against hers, I wish I could reach inside her head and figure out all she's thinking. We're alike in so many ways, but I'm slowly realizing that part of my obsession with this girl is the cards she keeps close to her chest. The parts of her she holds back that I'm desperate to discover.

"When this ends is down to you, Kendra. Just give me the word. But until then, I'm here and next to you." My throat thickens with every word as it leaves my mouth.

I always knew what this was. I knew she wanted to have fun after Tyler. But I wasn't prepared for the way I'd fall under her spell.

I'm playing roulette with my feelings, and there's a chance I'll lose. But I was in deep before, and now that she's been in my bed, I'm all the way over and jumping in with two feet.

Sitting up, Kendra reaches down and picks up her gift and card, a cheeky smile on her face. "This looks like two things."

She tears at the wrapping paper, pausing at the latest AirPods and then at the copy of Chelsea Rayne's recent book called: *A Workout and Nutritional Guide*.

Her eyes grow wide as she flicks to the title page. "T-this is ... signed?"

I nod and kiss her neck. "You had her on the TV that time. Figured you like her."

Disbelief paints her features as she flicks through a few more pages. "She's my favorite. So good. And the AirPods? You really didn't have to. These are so expensive."

Her attention falls to the unopened card, and she pulls open the envelope.

"Bahahaha!" Laughter erupts from her as she takes in the bald eagle on the front. "Oh my God!"

Watching her like this—in fits of giggles and so fucking happy—I find myself staring and push my head back into the rest, wanting a better view.

She's still giggling when I pick up the gift and set it on the passenger seat. Next, I take the card from her hand and place it on top.

"I'll assume this is more about being American than it is how you see me." My girl points to the card, her smile as wide as a fucking ocean.

"You want to know how I see you, Kendra?"

Her laughter fades, and her eyes fall to my mouth. "How?"

"Something like this."

I brush my lips over hers, and the first stroke of my tongue leaves her a writhing mess. Her whimpers only drive me further, hardening my cock with every passing second.

There's nothing fake about this kiss, about the beat of my heart as it thumps against my rib cage. And neither can she fake the flush as it creeps down her chest and travels past the neckline of her sweater.

The heat between her legs intensifies, and she breaks away, her lips swollen from the effects of mine. "I'm having a lot of fun, Jack. You make me happy."

Since I'm addicted to her mouth, I kiss her again. "Me too. I'm even starting to like New York."

A chuckle bubbles out of her. "I have a confession."

I quirk a brow. "Oh, yeah?"

Playing with the buttons on my shirt, she undoes the first two and sets a kiss on my chest.

This girl. This fucking girl.

"I like clotted cream."

I know I look smug; I knew she liked it. Everyone fucking likes it.

"Don't worry, Kitten. Your American secret is safe with me."

"*But*"—she holds a finger in the air—"I still play soccer."

"Bloody hell ..." I brush some hair from her face. "And here I was, thinking you'd learned the error in your ways."

She tips my chin and licks into my mouth, fire turning her brown eyes amber. "I'm not making any mistakes, not right now anyway."

We don't say anything for a few beats, although the silence screams to be filled.

"We should get going," I finally say, realizing we've been messing around and making out for way longer than we should have and it's at least a half hour from here to Mum and Jon's.

"Do you think they'll like me?" Kendra asks, still planted firmly in my lap.

"My family?" I ask, shocked at her doubt.

She nods and plays with the hairs at the nape of my neck.

"What makes you think they wouldn't?"

She twists her lips. "I don't think Tyler's parents liked me that much. He's an only child, and I guess they thought their golden boy could do better."

I bite the inside of my cheek, suppressing amusement at how fucking ridiculous the Bennetts clearly are. "You know what I think? People don't like what they're afraid of. You threatened him, Kendra. You were so far out of his fucking league, and he was way out of his depth with you. Powerful women who do awesome things don't belong with guys like Tyler Bennett. *You* don't belong with Tyler Bennett ..."

You belong with me.

I shove down the thought and take a breath.

"And they knew that. My family knows when they have a good thing. And they are going to love you."

CHAPTER TWENTY-FOUR

JACK

The second the elevator pings and the door opens into the apartment, like moths to a flame, Darcy and Mum come crashing toward us.

Scratch that. They completely ignore me and make a beeline for Kendra.

"Oh my God!" Darcy announces as she launches herself at my girl.

"Give her some space, Darce," Mum instructs, momentarily making me think she's got ahold of herself, but then she does the exact same when my sister steps back.

"Happy birthday! Wow ... you smell so good," Mum announces, reaching up to wrap her arms around Kendra's taller frame. "Doesn't she smell good, Jack? And oh-so pretty!" She braces her hands on Kendra's shoulders to get a better look at her.

I swipe a hand across my face and groan. Kendra is the first girl I've ever brought home. Aside from Darcy's boyfriend, Liam, Mum has been starved of in-law potential.

"Hi," Kendra squeaks out, unsurprisingly overwhelmed at the reception.

And to think she was nervous they wouldn't like her.

Bennett pricks.

"Okay, so I'm Darcy, Jack's sister. This is our mum, Felicity." My sister moves around the group like it isn't obvious who we all are, her honey-colored hair swishing and blue eyes dancing with excitement. "Jon!" she shouts. "Get your arse in here. Kendra and Jack have arrived."

"And I'm Jack." I turn to Kendra and point at myself.

Darcy swats me in the chest and proceeds to wrap herself around me, burying her face in my neck. "It's been too damn long," she whispers, only wanting me to hear what she's saying.

It's been almost four months since I last saw my baby sister. Growing up, we fought like regular siblings, but since our family split across the Atlantic, we realized not only how in tune we were, but how we weren't really built to be apart for long periods.

"Missed you, Bug," I reply.

"Jack"—inconspicuously, Darcy tips her head in Kendra's direction—"I'm twenty-two, I thought you dropped the nickname you gave me when we were five and you chased me with earthworms?"

I shrug and glance over at Kendra as she stares back at us, a vacant kind of look on her face.

"Okay, so dinner should be ready in, like, twenty minutes." Mum claps her hands together. "Jon is just prepping the gravy." She then looks at me. "Jack, why don't you show Kendra the place and then get seated at the table?"

"Did you set up the candles?" Darcy looks at Mum.

She slaps a palm to her forehead. "Shhhhhugar. Forgot."

When I reach out and take Kendra's hand in mine, I notice the trace of a smile as it pulls at her lips. Every night since I bought them and I've been home, Kendra has lit the vanilla candles.

"Okay, no bother." Darcy waves and makes for the dining room. "I can sort it out now."

A couple of seconds later, we're alone, and I take Kendra's other hand in mine, turning her to face me. She might be smiling from Darcy's reference to candles, but I can tell something heavy is weighing on her mind.

"All okay?" I ask, a part of me praying she doesn't come out and say this is too much. That meeting my family is a step too far for what we agreed.

"Yeah." She smiles. "Great."

I step toward her, invading her space in all the best ways. "Here's where I call you out on your bullshit, Kitten. Did I go too far?" I whisper with my lips on the shell of her ear.

Her sigh sounds defeated, and my heart hits the marble tiles beneath us.

"I miss my brother, is all. I haven't seen him in forever. We aren't even on the same continent. Seeing you and Darcy reunite reminded me of Ollie, and I hadn't been prepared for the way it would pull at me. You could say I'm closer to him than I am to my parents." She breathes in and looks down at the floor. "If I'd taken the chance in England, then I'd be a two-hour flight from him and not nine."

My heart breaks for her, and I squeeze our hands together. Not seeing Darcy is hard enough for me, so I can't imagine how hard it is for Kendra, having a pro footballer for a brother. His career rarely brings him to the US. The football season in Europe is as intense as the NHL.

"Do you feel lonely?" I ask, my heart squeezing at the thought.

She pinches her plump lips together, and all I want to do is kiss them, kiss all the anxiety she's feeling away.

"At one point, I did. Now I guess I feel more ..." She trails off and looks toward the kitchen, where Mum disappeared a couple of minutes before.

With her chin between my thumb and forefinger, I pull her

attention back to me. I want—no, I need—to know all that's going on in her head. The mysterious part of my girl leaves me a pining mess.

"Feel what?"

Her brown eyes find mine, searching, uncertainty reflected in them. "Like maybe there's always been something missing, something I didn't know I needed."

That's all it takes for my mouth to find hers.

"What is it you want?" I ask between kisses, really not giving a fuck if I don't give her the guided tour of the penthouse apartment.

Her shoulders drop, and I pull her into me. Desperate for her to interpret the way I hold us close as nothing but want, need, and for her to work out that she's everything and more to me.

I'm this fucking close to telling her I want us to be official. That I brought her here tonight as the girl I'm ten out of ten in love with and not as part of some goddamn arrangement we made to keep some fucking prick off her back.

But thanks to that prick, I'm holding back from everything I want to say, scared she'll bolt on me.

"Ope. Sorry, I—ugh. Okay, I'm going to go." Jon enters the hallway and then spins on his heel, making a run for it.

I rest my forehead against Kendra's and squeeze my eyes shut. "He sure has good timing," I whisper to her as she giggles softly against me.

"Your family is waiting."

I nod with my eyes still closed. "Can we put a pin in this and talk tonight?"

"Yes."

Bringing her left hand to my lips, I kiss across her knuckles. "Just one caveat to that." I open my eyes and find hers. "I want you in my bed when we do."

KENDRA

"What did you study at college?" Darcy asks as I take another bite of the best beef Wellington I think I've ever had.

It's been a half hour since I sat down with Jack's family, but all it took was five minutes for my nerves to fade, replaced with laughter.

I only saw Jon Morgan a couple of times when he coached the college team, and he wasn't someone Tyler particularly liked.

I can see why. Jon's actually nice.

I look over at Darcy—aka pure sunshine. She radiates it from head to toe.

"English Lit."

Forcing down a green bean, she reaches across and taps her brother on the arm. "No way! We studied the same thing. Ah, this is an absolute sign, Jack."

"There's a year between you two, right?" I ask.

"Just under. I fell pregnant with Darcy almost immediately after Jack," Felicity answers with a smile. "Although this one here rules the roost—always has." She points to her daughter with her fork.

A proud smile breaks out across Darcy's face as she sits straighter in her chair. "He's lost without me."

Jack scoffs and sets down his knife and fork. "Based on what evidence?"

"Oh, nothing in particular." Picking up her wineglass, Darcy takes a sip and smiles around the rim. Setting her drink down on the table, she bends down to grab something from the floor.

Standing from her chair, she holds a gift bag in one hand as she rounds the table toward me.

"I hope you like it. We didn't find out it was your birthday until, eh ... well, very recently." Jon side-eyes Jack, and I watch as his cheeks flush.

"This is my favorite brand!" Darcy says as she hands me the bag. "If you like it, I say we sack Jack off and move in together.

Happy birthday!" she squeaks and then gathers up the plates and starts taking them through to the kitchen.

"In all seriousness, we won't be offended if it isn't your thing," Jon says, motioning toward the gift in my lap.

"It's from all three of us," Felicity adds as Darcy takes a seat back at the table.

With four pairs of eyes on me, I push back the soft white tissue paper, and my breath hitches in my throat.

Wow.

"This is, um ..." Reaching into the bag, I squeeze the soft leather between my fingers and notice how it matches my nail color—something to do with Jack, I'm sure.

"A Mulberry!" Darcy bursts out.

Don't get me wrong; my parents have money, as does my brother. Serious money. From time to time, they spoil me just like this, but to receive a Mulberry handbag from Jack's family, whom I've only just met, that's a whole new level of generosity.

"Do you like it?" Jon asks, leaning forward and clasping his hands under his chin.

His mannerisms and caring attitude are so much like Jack's. If I didn't know better, I'd be sure he was his biological dad.

"It's absolutely beautiful," I whisper, still taking it in as I pull it out and turn it around in my hands.

The cost of this bag could probably pay for a month's rent, maybe two.

"Here, let me." Felicity takes the tissue paper and gift bag from me.

"Thank you," I say, still in shock as I look around the table, my gaze finally landing on Jack beside me as he reaches across and squeezes my thigh. "I actually don't know what to say."

"You were right, Knucklehead. Olive is definitely Kendra's color."

I feel my cheeks heat as I set the bag down on the table next to me. I don't think I'll ever be able to look at this color and not think of him or the dress he picked out. But especially last night and again this morning.

Feeling some kind of way over the generosity and the memories of yesterday, I push back my chair. "I'm going to head to the bathroom."

Jack's hand trails down my thigh as I stand up.

"First door on the left," he instructs.

Twenty seconds later, I'm standing in front of a Hollywood-style mirror, my postgame and unstyled hair looking as confused as I feel.

What are you doing, Kendra?

A few weeks ago, you ended it with a guy you'd thought you'd spend the rest of your life with, and now you're playing house with his rival's family.

A part of me feels like I shouldn't be here. Like I have no right to accept this incredible gift from these incredible people. All I've done is take since the day I saw Jack in Rise Up. In my determination not to lean on my family for money, I've done exactly that with the Morgans.

And I feel shitty for it.

So, why does this feel like this is the best birthday I've ever had? And why can I only think about the soft duvet on Jack's bed and being back beneath it tonight?

"Kendra?" a small voice calls from the other side of the door.

I reach across and open the door to find Darcy standing on the other side.

At the sight of me, she cocks her head and immediately steps into the room, closing the door behind her.

"I just wanted to check on you."

"I'm good. Just taking a second," I say, summoning my best smile.

She lifts an unsure brow. "Was the gift too much? I know we can all be a bit over the top." She chuckles. "Mum is probably the most chill of us all."

Gathering my hair in my hands, I let it fall down my back. "No, it was beautiful. I'm just ..." My words trail off because what else am I supposed to say? All that I was feeling a second ago? Hard pass.

"Can I say something?" Her usually light demeanor turns more serious as she lifts herself to sit on the countertop. "I mean, I know we've only just met, but I feel like it might be helpful, girl to girl."

I nod my head once and wait for her to continue.

She inspects her bright pink nails before setting her eyes on me. "My brother loves you."

I practically choke on my own breath. "What?" I spurt.

She winces and drops her hand down beside her. "Ugh, I'm always like this. Brain in first, mouth in fifth gear. But there is no subtle way to say it since it's so damn obvious. My big brother is head over heels for you."

"I-I'm not so sure he—"

"He is. I'm sure of it." She pushes herself off the counter and comes to stand in front of me, our height not too different. "Is it freaking you out? He kind of told me on text that you'd not long ago come out of a relationship, so I did some googling, and it didn't take me long to find out you were with Tyler Bennett, his current teammate and college rival. I remember Jack saying he was an asshole back then. Sorry," she tags on.

I laugh a single laugh and drop my eyes down to her fluffy pink socks. "You're really direct, aren't you?"

"Ugh, I know. It gets me into trouble sometimes. My boyfriend kind of hates how outspoken I am," she grumbles.

Something about that statement resonates with me, lighting a fire deep in my gut. I don't like that he does that.

Without a second thought, I take her hand in mine. "You aren't too much, Darcy. I appreciate you coming to check on me. Also that you gave me your honest opinion about Jack. Things are... complicated right now for the both of us. I know that sounds like a cop-out, but we definitely make each other happy."

Grinning, she keeps our hands joined. "I'm going to the game against the Scorpions tomorrow. Are you free to come watch too?"

Jack and I haven't spoken about me coming to watch his games, but something tells me he wouldn't mind if I did. And an even bigger part of me wants to, not just for him, but for the girl standing in front of me, waiting eagerly for my answer.

Darcy was right when she asked me if I was freaking out. I am. When Jack carried me to his bed last night, I felt things I'd never expected to. Emotions I'd never experienced, not even with Tyler. The more I think about the connection between Jack and me, the harder it is to chalk this all up to fun and making each other happy.

Fun doesn't look at me the way Jack did this morning, and fun doesn't send shock waves to my toes every time I set eyes on him.

If Jack Morgan is in love with me already, then there's a fair chance I'm not far behind him.

There isn't anywhere he goes that I don't want to be, and there isn't a single part of his life that I don't love.

Smiling back at Darcy, I nod my head, already thinking about the way Ollie is going to freak out when I tell him about tonight. "Yeah, I'm free. Me and my Mulberry will be there."

CHAPTER TWENTY-FIVE

KENDRA

ME

So, I know it's, like, three a.m. in Madrid, but I thought you should know I met Jon Morgan today and had dinner at his house. Well, met him officially anyway. Never really spoke to him much at college.

OLLIE

No time is ever inappropriate for these kinds of updates. Literally fanboying over here. Is he a nice guy?

Yeah, he's a nice guy, a real family man. Though, you're not concerned about Jack? You know, the guy I'm seeing.

Nah, I've already established he's a good guy. You have no idea how jealous I am right now; you met my hero.

I'm also going to watch the Blades–Scorpions game tomorrow night.

> Damn, living your best life, Kend. Dining with Jon, dating his son. Soccer career on the rise.

I'm distracted from my phone when Jack walks into the kitchen, carrying a dark blue folded top, a classic smile across his face. One that hasn't left since Darcy announced I was going to the game with her.

I set my phone face down on the island since he doesn't need to see my brother's unhinged messages.

"What's this?" My eyes fall to what he's carrying.

His grin is filled with excitement, like a puppy on Christmas morning.

"You know what's mandatory when you attend your boyfriend's game, don't you?" Jack stops a couple of feet away from me.

Since we got back, he's had a shower and changed into sweats and a white Blades T-shirt. His hair is still damp, and he smells just like the sheets on his bed. My mouth waters at the potential of me being back in there tonight. He did say that was where he wanted to talk.

I shake my head in response since all my brain is capable of processing right now are thoughts of being wrapped around him.

Jack tips his head to the side. "My jersey. Well, specifically my name."

Holding it out in front of him, he lets the jersey unravel to reveal *Morgan* and his number, twenty-two—the same number Jon played with before he retired.

I stare at the jersey in his hands. I guess this is something every girlfriend would expect to wear, but somehow, this feels like the furthest we've gone publicly.

"That's going to drown me." I chuckle, a combination of excitement and desire hitting me at once.

He steps a little closer. "Why don't you test that out now?"

My heart thumps as I look up at him. "Right here?"

He nods softly. "Right now."

Our fingers brush when I take it and pull it over my head. Every sense is on high alert when the material skims past my nose, and the intensity of his cologne hits me again.

When I pull my hair from the collar and reset my focus on Jack, he's already twirling his finger around, asking me to do a spin.

I roll my eyes and do as he asks.

Halfway around, he stops me when his hands land on my waist. But he doesn't say anything, just gathers my hair up and rests it over my shoulder, probably so he can take a better look at his name.

The silence between us is tense and I close my eyes, every muscle in my body squeezing in anticipation.

"It's way too big." I sigh and turn back around to face him.

He grasps a handful of the jersey, shaking his head. "I'd say it was meant for you." The second those words leave his mouth, his eyes bug out and flick up to mine. "Y-you know what I mean. Like, I don't think you'll need much practice wearing it. It's a natural look for you," he rambles.

I take a step toward him, my heart beating faster, adrenaline racing through me. "You think it looks perfect on me?"

I watch the way his pulse point races and his breathing picks up. The effect I have on him makes me feel something I never really have with a guy. Powerful, sexy, desired. I want more of it.

I dip my hand under the hem of his shirt and skim the waistband of his sweats with my fingertips. He's not wearing boxers.

A deep rumble echoes in his chest; it isn't loud, but against the backdrop of nothing, I hear it clearly.

"You don't think I need to test out your jersey anymore?" I ask, knowing the only thing I'm testing right now is how long he can go without putting his hands on me. By the look in his eyes, I'd say, not long—maybe thirty seconds. I pulse at the thought.

Jack runs his thumb across the mark on the side of my neck, one I've no idea if his family noticed earlier.

Just like last night, the switch has been flicked, and a

completely different version of him stands in front of me. One I love just as much as his playful side. One I hope that's exclusive to me.

"What do you want from me, Kitten?" Voice gravelly, he closes his eyes, and his tongue smooths across his bottom lip. "Is it just sex?" He opens them again, pinning me in place. "Or something more?"

Our lips are barely touching, the hot fan of his breath sparking every nerve to life.

"Define more," I reply. Knowing exactly what I want to hear from him.

Jack swallows thickly, pausing for a second that feels more like an eternity. "A kind of more where none of what we do is for practice. A kind of more where my name is across your back for real because we both want that and not for the benefit of anyone else." He pulls me into his body, his hard cock pressing into my stomach. "The kind of more where I lay you on my bed and don't think about whether this is for fun any longer. The kind of more where I can admit my feelings for you and not bury them at the back of my throat."

"Tell me what you feel." I'm breathless, knowing the moment he says this out loud, it can never be retracted. It'll be real.

He drops his forehead to mine; I can tell this is taking every shred of courage he has. "I've always cared about you, Kendra. Maybe even when I didn't have any right to. Maybe more than I should've, given that we barely spoke in college. I can't explain it other than to say I cared about what happened to you. I was fucking gutted when I found out you were going to follow him to New York and give up your dream for some piece of shit. But who was I to say anything? I was no one to you."

I open my mouth to argue, but he stops me with a finger to my lips.

"I *was* nothing to you, and that's okay. You thought you were in love, and you were too damn loyal to ever pay attention to other guys. I deliberately kept my distance too."

"Why?"

He smiles and wraps a piece of my hair around his finger, playing with the strands. "Because I didn't trust myself. I knew that if I got close to you, then I'd do something that would make me feel shitty. Something that wasn't me."

"W-what would you have done?"

"I'd have made a move on you. Thrown my hat into the ring and said, *Pick me*. You weren't ready for that though, and I wasn't willing to show you my cards." He pauses and the hand that rests on my hip squeezes tighter. "Until now."

I take a deep breath and blow it out. "I'm ready to hear it now. Tell me." The pulse in my ears makes it hard to hear the sound of my own voice.

"None of this has ever been fake to me, Kendra. I've wanted you for four years, yes. But not just to see how you unravel beneath me. I've wanted you on my arm for real. I've wanted your candles in my apartment for real. I've wanted you to be my girlfriend for fucking real."

A tear falls down my cheek, and Jack drops my hair, swiping it away.

"Why are you crying?"

I press my forehead into his again, desperate to be closer to him. "After Tyler, I was convinced what I needed was fun. The thought of allowing another guy into my life scared the crap out of me. I was expecting to want to run the moment you said what you just did." My fingers dip further under his waistband. "But all I want to do is let you have me in any way you want. Nothing about the thought of being with you scares me. You make me too damn happy for that." I sniffle a laugh. "Even if you think I'm a brat."

"If you're a brat, then I'm a glutton for punishment."

He brings his hand over mine, and we both ease down his sweatpants.

Next, he pulls down my sleep shorts, dancing his fingertips over the front of my lacy thong.

"Can I fuck my girl?"

"Yes," I whimper, desperation laced in my voice.

I'm ready for Jack to carry me to his bedroom again, so when he doesn't and instead lifts me up onto the island, a squeal of shock leaves my throat, followed by a bubble of laughter.

He steps out of his sweats and removes my shorts and thong completely, leaving me in only his jersey. Reaching behind him, he pulls his shirt over his head, revealing the body that makes me want to study it all night with my hands.

He pushes my thighs apart and licks into my mouth, fisting his cock slowly.

"I want to hear you moan when I push myself inside you, Kitten. Then I want to hear the same name that's printed on your back fall from those pretty lips of yours."

Jack wastes no time as I spread myself further and he slowly enters me. I'm wetter than ever, and my head falls to his shoulder as I take him, and he fills me fully. The ache from where he fucked me earlier reminds me of how he'll make me come hard again.

"Does that feel good, Kendra? Do I feel good inside your beautiful pussy?"

"Ohmygod, yes, you do."

A satisfied groan overtakes us both as he disappears inside, and I lift my head up to face him.

"I can't move yet," he says against my lips. "I need you to hold still because you're clamped so tight around my dick that I'm going to blow straight inside you."

"I need you to move," I beg.

He shakes his head but offers me his fingers, and they stroke my clit gently. "This clit is so perfect. The way it grows beneath my touch. The way it feels on my tongue."

"Move, Jack. Fuck me."

All I get is a cocky grin as he remains perfectly still. "Would you let me bind your legs one day? I could have so much fucking fun with Scarlett. I feel like we'd make the dream team."

He rubs me again, and I shudder uncontrollably.

Teasing the mark on my neck, his tongue swipes across it, and I tip my head to the side, granting him full access.

"I could take your ass; Scarlett could take your pussy. You'd be so full, so wet, so fucking pretty and flushed with lust. Just like you are right now."

The shudders turn into full-on shakes when he pinches my clit between his fingers.

"Jack," I moan. "Fuck me, Jack, please."

"Are you going to come, Kitten? Are you going to soak my cock before it's even moved?"

I nod, my face falling into the crook of his neck.

He pulls on my hair, tipping my head back. My neck is fully exposed to him as he runs his tongue along my pulse point.

"Oh fuck!" I cry out.

The bastard chuckles as he still refuses to move. "Come for me, Kendra. I promise I'll fuck you so good when you give me what I want."

He licks that spot on my neck again, and I unravel all over his dick.

"That's it. You're coming so well for me." He drops his gaze to where we're connected, and as I continue to orgasm and shudder, he pulls out slightly. "I can see you coming. It's so beautiful, watching my girl decorate me like this."

Without a doubt, it's the longest and most intense orgasm I've ever had. But *nothing* compared to the feeling that crashes over me when he slams hard inside, pushing me back on the countertop.

Jack's hands fall to my bare ass as he pulls me into him and starts fucking me so damn hard that I'm squealing, unable to control the intense pleasure exploding on repeat.

"Make a mess of me," I plead, throwing my head back for him to bite and suck where he loves. "Leave them everywhere."

Jack's hands move from my ass to my inner thighs, testing

the limits of my flexibility. "Open this pussy up for me to claim, and I'll do the same with your skin."

The sound of my arousal fills the apartment, and I fight to stay quiet, determined to hear everything as he lives out his fantasies with my body. The way we both finally play out what's always been real.

"Where do you want my cum, Kitten?"

I lift up the jersey and expose my lower half. "Everywhere. I want to see it on me."

Two more pumps, and he pulls out, holding his hard-on in his fist and his eyes on mine.

With a slack jaw, he releases his warmth across me, and I rub it into my skin, gathering what's left and pushing it inside my pussy.

"You're a dirty fucking girl—you know that?" he says with awe.

I swipe the last drops from the tip of his still-hard dick, pushing that inside me too. "Correction: I'm *your* dirty fucking girl."

CHAPTER TWENTY-SIX

JACK

Archer added you to a group chat

Archer renamed the group Shit on the Scorpions

My phone buzzes on the nightstand behind me, waking me from a dream involving the girl currently sleeping in my arms.

Rolling onto my back, I somehow manage to reach behind me and unplug it from the charger while keeping the arm under Kendra still, making sure I don't wake her.

"The fuck?" I whisper, squinting at the screen and waiting for my six a.m. vision to focus.

ARCHER

photo of him shirtless, riding a spin bike

Wakey-wakey. Rise and shine. Been up since five and ready for the biggest game of the season so far.

SAWYER

You realize this isn't your OnlyFans page, right?

Next to me, Kendra stirs, and I shift behind her, wrapping my leg over hers and kissing her bare shoulder.

Fuck, I don't think I'll ever get used to this.

Scratch that. What part of me would ever *want* to get used to this?

She's mine, and I'm hers, and right now, I'm living the dream in a city that's rapidly feeling like the home I never expected it to be.

ARCHER

Nah, the shorts are normally off for that.

SAWYER

Please spare us. I'll need my eyes for today's game.

ARCHER

If Jessie Callaghan thinks he's extending his top goal-scoring lead tonight, he can think a-fucking-gain.

Jon's former Seattle teammates, especially Jessie Callaghan, will be well up for handing our coach and team our asses on a silver platter. Today's game is huge, and I need to get up and start preparing, but for the first time in my life, hockey is a distant second to the girl snoring lightly in my bed.

Our bed.

This is where she sleeps from now on.

ME

Callaghan is definitely thinking it. Probably got one eye on a hat trick.

P.S. typing with one hand is difficult.

SAWYER

I'm sorry, what?

Shit. I start typing another message. My one thumb moving at a snail's pace across the keyboard.

ARCHER

Whoa, whoa, whoa. This isn't actually OnlyFans, you know? Put that away.

ME

LOL. No, my other hand is under Kendra.

SAWYER

I'm calling my agent and putting in for a trade. I didn't sign up for this.

ARCHER

Bro, even this is a bit much for me.

ME

NO! I mean, she's literally sleeping on my arm, and I don't want to wake her, so I'm typing with one hand.

ARCHER

Simp.

ME

I fancy myself for a goal or two today.

ARCHER

Sounds like you've already scored.

SAWYER

Give me strength.

Jack, I know I'm the C and should be all words of motivation, but good luck finding a way past Jensen Jones. He's currently trying to beat his own shutout record in his last pro season. Can't see him making an exception for his former captain's son. Knowing him, I bet he'll go harder.

ME

Added motivation tonight. Will have my mum, sister, and Kendra watching from the box.

ARCHER

Sister ...

ME

DON'T EVEN GO THERE.

ARCHER

Damn, I bet it took you even longer to write that in capitals. You must REALLY MEAN IT.

I know he's joking, but I will castrate him if he even looks at her.

ME

DO NOT TOUCH HER.

ARCHER

That's not very feminist of you. Surely, Emily is her own woman, capable of making her own decisions, no?

ME

Who the fuck is Emily?

ARCHER

The only British name I could think of.

SAWYER

I'm going to weigh in here and say Emily is probably off-limits.

ME

That she is. Plus, she has a boyfriend.

And her name is Darcy.

ARCHER

Darcy, Darcy, Darcy. Like it. Very regal.

ME

Can we stop talking about my sister now?

ARCHER

Sure. I'll see her later anyway.

ME

Unbelievable.

I set my phone on the side when Kendra starts to wake properly.

"You even stretch out like a kitten," I tease, burying my face in her hair before she rolls over to face me. "Open those eyes for me, pretty girl."

She scrunches her nose up. "It's my day off, and I have nowhere to be until I meet Darcy before the game. Can't we just stay in bed?"

I pull back as she cracks an eye open. "Where are you going?"

"Out to eat before we head to the arena."

Something warm flushes in my chest. Not just for me, but for the girl I'm falling in love with. I want her to have everything good in my life, and my sister is absolutely a part of that.

"She invited you out, didn't she?"

Her hands find the back of my neck, and Kendra pulls me toward her for a kiss. "Other way around. I messaged her last night, saying I'd show her some sights before she flies home tomorrow. She's really nice. Your entire family is nice."

I bite back the urge to caveat that—my dad. He's the exception to the rule and the good people I've always had around me, many of them she met last night. Though something tells me that my girlfriend will have minimal exposure to that asshole anyway.

Pushing away thoughts of Elliott Thompson, I focus my mind back on the girl lying next to me. With the difficult time Darcy's having in her relationship with Liam, the invite Kendra extended must have meant so much to her, and I feel myself fall for this girl just a little bit more.

"I really wish I didn't have to get up for morning skate. Because I'd be buried inside you in a second."

She giggles and slides down, disappearing under the duvet. "Go! I'll keep your side nice and warm."

I groan and will myself to move unsuccessfully. "What are you going to do with your morning?"

She giggles again. "Stuff."

"Oh, yeah? Like what?" Reaching a hand down, I tickle her ribs. I've no idea if Kendra is ticklish, but if it's another excuse to hear her laugh, then I'm keen to find out.

Bingo.

"Stop, stop, STOP!" she cries out and wriggles down further until she's out of reach.

I'm immediately on my feet, grabbing the corner of the duvet and flipping it off in one motion, exposing her naked body to the morning air.

Stunning.

Her eyes land on my hard dick as she attempts to pull the duvet back around her. "It's freezing, and I was all cozy and warm!"

Instantly, I'm back on the bed, crowding her with my six-four frame. My dick is lined up with her entrance, and it would take one tip of my hips to be back where I love.

Her fits of laughter stop when she looks down between us and registers the same. "You have to get to morning skate, remember?"

It fucking kills me that I can't take her right now. At a push, there might be time to "fuck her and flee," in Archer's words, but that's not what I want with her. I don't think there'll ever be a time where I'm not desperate to make her come until she's physically incapable of giving me more.

"Meet you after the game?" I say with a kiss. "I don't have any press responsibilities tonight."

"In the parking lot?"

I pull back. "The fucking *what*?"

She rolls her eyes and attempts a British accent. "The car park."

I run a thumb across her cheek, realizing her innocent question just exposed her ex further. "Kendra, why would I meet you in the freezing cold? You meet me in the players' lounge after the game. Then we head out together."

I can sense the realization the moment it slams into her, and my heart breaks at the way she tries to hide her embarrassment. I don't know what Tyler was thinking, but he clearly wasn't interested in his girl being the first person he saw after games.

"You meet me after the game, dressed in my jersey and ready for me to take you out and spoil the shit out of you. That's how it works every time you can make one of my games, Kendra. That's what happens for my girl."

"I DON'T THINK I need to remind you all of how pivotal this game is. A win tonight means we go above the Scorpions on points. I also don't need to remind you of how much we've achieved in the few weeks since the season started. And even more has changed since preseason."

I can't help but cast a glance at Tyler as he sits forward, elbows resting on his knees as Jon delivers his final pep talk before we hit the ice.

He holds eye contact with me, chewing on the corner of his mouthguard. Since the GM didn't put him on the trade list, he's largely kept out of my and Kendra's way and been more professional in games. Although the animosity between us has never been greater.

"You're finally playing like a goddamn team," Jon continues. "But let me tell you this. It's something I've not said in briefings and prep this week, but I think the warning needs to be out there for the rookies." He thumbs over his shoulder, motioning to the rink. "The Scorpions are more like a family. The kind of ride-or-die team that can be three to zero down in the third, and it's not over."

Jon looks directly at me and then Tyler and Matt. "Give Zach Evans half a chance to board you, and he will. His entire game is built on intimidation and strength, but don't be fooled by his distribution capabilities, as I showed you in game footage."

He then looks at Archer. "And I know I've said this fifty thousand times, Moore, but somehow, Callaghan has gotten even better than he was last season. Despite recently becoming a dad, he's faster and stronger, and God only knows he's after some of my own records."

There are a few chuckles from around the room, including one from Archer.

Jon smiles and tucks his iPad under his arm. "But you know what they don't have experience with?"

The room stays silent as we wait for Coach to speak again.

"Most of them can't remember what it's like to struggle. To have fans leave the rink cussing them because their team is going through an overhaul and trying to find its feet again. Most of them have forgotten what it's like to truly fight. So, let's fucking show them!"

Jon leaves the locker room to cheers from freshly motivated players.

I nod my head over at Sawyer, who's doing a last-minute check on his skates. "Ready?"

He nods back, and we both head for the ice, the rest of the team following behind our captain.

I'm nervous every night, but tonight, I made the second line, and I know Kendra will be up there, watching me. I also know how much this game means to Jon personally. Last season, the Blades got wrecked by the Scorpions, and I know he's anxious about it happening again.

"Something on your mind?" Tyler comes to stand next to me.

I shrug and listen to the team announcements. "Nope. Just pumped for the game, is all."

"Not seen her at the arena yet. Kinda weird, don't you think?"

"Kinda weird that you still give a fuck," I reply.

Jesus, I hate this guy and how he still affects Kendra as she learns of all the ways he fucked her over.

With his hands braced on the end of his stick, he leans across to me, still chewing on the corner of his mouthguard, wearing the kind of cocky grin I'd like to remove with a single punch.

One fucking day.

"They say rebounds last around a month, sometimes as long as a year. You're doing well. But I'll be waiting."

One swipe, and I could knock him clean out. I fight with every shred of willpower to keep my hands on my stick. "Yeah, went pretty fucking well last night when she wore my jersey too." We begin walking out, and I throw him a smirk of my own. "If you look up and to the left, you might even catch a glimpse of her in it tonight."

CHAPTER TWENTY-SEVEN

JACK

Jensen Jones is a machine.

Not one damn goal past him, as opposed to the three netted by Callaghan.

Ready for the line switch, I stand and wait for Matt to leave the ice before I'm skating over to position, ready to support Tyler in the slot. This is the most ice time I've had so far this season, and with ten minutes left in the third, the fatigue is really setting in.

When Tyler emerges with the puck, I see Zach Evans make a beeline, ready to board him and spill it for a turnover.

"I'm open!" I shout, banging my stick on the ice.

At first, I think he's too preoccupied with finding a route to the goal to register my position, but then he lifts his head in my direction and makes full eye contact with me.

I crash my stick on the ice and head toward him, making the potential pass even more straightforward.

But he refuses to acknowledge my support, let alone make use of it.

His split-second defiance is met with an Evans-style Kronwall, and Tyler crashes into the side and hits the ice hard.

Fuck.

The turnover is on, and Callaghan must be thinking it's his lucky day as he nets in the top right with a deke and wrist shot as near perfect as mine a couple of weeks back.

I know Jon said we can fight, but my aching legs feel even heavier as we make our way back to center ice.

"Nice assist." I can't help my sarcasm as Tyler skates past without a word.

Seeing red, he spins around and heads straight for me.

Sawyer joins shortly afterward. "All right, guys, let's cool it," he says, trying to calm the building tension.

"Punch me," I goad, all professionalism right out the window as the final threads of my composure snap. "Punch me and get yourself traded. No one fucking likes you."

My eyes flick over Tyler's shoulder and up high into the arena, where the family boxes are located. I know this is being beamed on the Jumbotron, and I know Kendra will have eyes on us. That's the only thing holding me back from going further.

Tyler knocks his helmet against mine, our eyes locked on each other. "You think you're so damn clever, don't you? This is all about getting one up on me, isn't it?"

The ref makes his way over right as Zach Evans arrives, an unusual move for an opposing player, let alone their captain. Major penalties are normally power-play gifts.

"You touch him, and I'll make sure my next hit breaks bones." Zach focuses his attention solely on Tyler as he says it. "I have zero boundaries when it comes to touching the opposition, and when that player is Morgan, I will bury you. No one messes with family."

"Yeah, and you'll have a problem with me too." Jessie Callaghan joins his captain, eyes boring into Tyler. "I'm not ordinarily a guy to Kronwall someone, but for you, Bennett, I can make an exception."

I look between Zach and Jessie. I've spent a lot of time with these guys, especially before Jon retired. Part of me wants to say thanks, but I know they're not doing it solely for my benefit. Jon is a best friend to them both, and there are some relationships that rivalries will never outrank.

When Tyler slides back just in time for the ref to join us, Zach and Jessie spin around, heading back toward their team.

"Have we got a problem?" the ref asks, looking between us all.

"Just a little tactical talk," Sawyer responds.

Checking his watch, he thumbs toward center ice. "Talking's over. Time to play."

When the game restarts and the clock ticks down, the Scorpions fans, who have traveled to New York, drown out the home crowd. And as I switch out for the final time and take a seat on the bench, I notice as Jon visibly deflates.

Zero to four is not what he was hoping for. None of us were.

Emmett Richards, a defenseman, drops his head and whispers under his breath, "Bennett's in the can if he keeps this up."

I haven't spoken to him as much as some of the other guys, but I know Sawyer trusts him. They've played together for multiple seasons.

"He needs to clean up his act," I reply, adding nothing more.

When my eyes travel back to Jon, I follow his line of vision to where it's fixed on the other side of the rink.

The fuck?

Sitting in an ice-level suite generally reserved for VIPs, my dad accepts another drink from the server as he leans across and talks with a dark-haired guy I don't recognize.

All fucking time stands still as I watch on and ignore the game in front of me, the final few seconds playing out.

Dad sits back in his seat, laughing as he runs a casual hand through his dark hair.

Is he even here for me? For the Blades? Because if he is, this is a fucking funny way of showing it.

The buzzer barely registers with me, and Richards knocks my shoulder. "Wake up, Morgan."

I step back onto the ice, shaking a few hands.

Jensen heads over to me, removing his helmet as he approaches. "You played well out there, Jack." He juts his chin down the tunnel toward Tyler, but my focus is on Dad as he walks through a side door. "What's Bennett's problem with you?" Jensen pulls my attention back to him. He clearly witnessed tension on the ice and just like his captain, he regards the Morgans as family.

"Long story," I puff out and then look up to see the family boxes are all empty.

He snarls in the direction Tyler disappeared. "Just watch your back out there, Jack. And if things get too heated and depressing in this rancid place, I'm sure the Scorpions would be only too happy to take you on. You're as good as Jon always said you'd be."

I offer him a smile just before he skates toward the tunnel and knocks fists with Jon, who's already on his way toward me.

"Did you see him?" I ask.

His jaw tics as he focuses on Dad's empty seat. I know he's pissed at the result of the game, but there's one person who fires him up in this way.

"He's here for you," he bites out.

I turn to look at him. "What do you mean?"

He shakes his head and then drops it between his shoulders, a knowing smile on his face. "Your mom and I always saw this coming." He looks at me again, deadly serious. "The second you started to make waves in the NHL and draw in the big paychecks, we always knew Elliott would resurface. It was only a matter of time. Felicity tells me he's here for the week, visiting with his new girlfriend."

I never did reply to his birthday text, and since I pay fuck all attention to the finance empire he runs, I guess I wouldn't know about his unfortunate new woman.

Jon steps toward me. "We're not about to stop you from

seeing him, buddy. We're your family and will be here for you no matter what call you make over Elliott. But if you want my advice, be really fucking careful with what you tell him."

My gaze roams around the empty arena. "I already have my family."

KENDRA

"Okay, so we might've lost, but I will say that was the best hockey game I've watched all season."

"Darcy, it's the *only* game you've watched all season." Felicity winks at us as she gathers some cocktails at the players' bar and walks them across to a few of her friends sitting around a booth.

I recognize them as the wives of Zach Evans, Jensen Jones, and Jessie Callaghan, but there isn't a chance of me heading over there to say hi. Half of them are lawyers, and the other half are just as scary.

"I heard she ties Jensen up with chains and whips him." Jenna tips her head at sophisticated blonde as she giggles with Felicity.

"His wife?!" I whisper-shout.

Darcy rolls her eyes at Jenna, breaking into a smirk. "Yeah, knowing Kate, that's probably accurate."

I say nothing as I take a seat at the bar and cross my legs over.

If only they knew what Jack likes.

When Darcy turns to the bartender to order another drink, Jenna turns to me. "So, are you going to concede now or later?"

I narrow my eyes at her. "Concede what?"

Her hand reaches behind my back and plucks at the jersey. "You can't tell me this is fake too."

"Shhh!" I scold, and she folds her arms over her chest,

tapping her foot as she waits for me to answer. "We kind of admitted we wanted to see where things go officially."

Her eyes light up, genuine elation on her face. "For real?!"

I break into a giddy smile. "For real. We couldn't stop sleeping together. Like, every time we were alone, we were all over each other. Plus ..." I trail off and look down at my boots. "He makes me really happy. I get that feeling, you know? The butterfly one. He told me he's harbored a crush since college, and I ... I really like him, Jenna. I can't deny it, and I'm kind of tired of doing that as well."

Jenna's eyes soften as she takes the stool next to me. "I can see that you do."

"Yep!"

We both look at Darcy as she spins around with two cocktails, one in each hand.

She takes a sip from the French martini and screws up her nose, then moves across to the cosmo. "Much better." She beams.

"What was the 'yep' for?" I ask, loving this girl, along with her happy-go-lucky attitude.

She takes another sip of the cosmo and raises the glass in front of her. "Yep. My brother is head over heels in love, and I'm already picking out my outfit for your wedding."

Butterflies dance in my stomach. I haven't set eyes on him yet, but I know he's close.

"Hey, Kitten."

My chair spins to face the room as a familiar hand wraps around the nape of my neck. Jack steps between my legs and leans down, brushing his lips across my mouth and peeking his tongue out to caress mine.

I'm all smiles and teenage flutters. "I'm sorry about the score."

"Eeeek!" Jenna squeals at the sight of us, slapping her thigh in celebration. "You two are so damn cute together!"

Darcy sets her glass back on the bar and pins her brother

with a glare. "And I've gone off my cosmo. Seeing my brother make out is gross."

He doesn't look at either of them though as he rubs his callous thumb behind my ear, wanting all my attention.

"I'm obsessed with you," he whispers into my mouth. "Is that okay?"

I drag my bottom lip between my teeth, fighting back a jaw-aching smile. "I don't have a problem with it."

He kisses me again, and I hear Jenna sigh from beside me.

"Okay, that's good news because I don't think it's optional for me."

How in the hell did I not see this boy before?

With another kiss, Jack pulls back, and I stiffen when Tyler comes to stand on the other side of Darcy.

I don't know if Jack has seen him or can just sense his presence, but as always, Jack's attention never wavers from me.

"Ignore him. He doesn't exist."

I palm Jack's toned ass and pull him closer, not caring if we're giving others something to watch. "I know. I just wish it were you and me and no complications."

His fingertips trace over my thighs. His touch makes me want to haul him out of this bar and say to hell with socializing.

"He can say, do, and think whatever he wants, Kitten. All that really matters is what we know."

A throat clears from behind us as I drop my hand, and Jack moves to the side.

"You coming to Lloyd's? I know we lost, but figured the team could use a few laughs. Drinks are on me." Sawyer looks between us all.

"Did someone say ..." Rubbing his hands together, Archer bounces up to us, not looking like a goalie who just let four goals past him.

Although from what I know of this guy, he doesn't let anything bother him.

Apart from the honey-haired bombshell—otherwise known as Jack's sister.

It's clear Darcy hasn't noticed a thing or the way Archer didn't finish his last sentence as she raises a finger in the air. "Count me in."

I look back at Archer as Jack continues talking with Sawyer about the game.

He's just staring, ogling her, right next to her brother.

Finally, Darcy's attention snags on Archer, who immediately shoves his hands into his pockets and whistles, gazing around the bar.

Smooth.

On another sigh, Jenna pockets her phone. "So, are we heading out or what?"

CHAPTER TWENTY-EIGHT

KENDRA

Holding my hand, Jack leads me out into the players' parking lot and unlocks his truck, opening the passenger door.

I go to climb in, but at the final second, he spins me around, pressing me into the cold metal. His warm breath heats my cheeks, shooting tingles down my spine.

"Do you think anyone can see us?" He speaks into the dark, a mischievous glint in his eyes.

"Why?"

He drops his bag beside him. Then he opens the back door, lifting me onto the seat so I'm facing him, and his hands rest on my thighs. There's barely anyone around when he checks over his shoulder and his fingers find the top button of my jeans.

"I don't think I can wait until later; I need a little fix of you now."

"W-what do you want to do?"

I watch with intrigue as he picks up his training bag and sets it on top of my thighs, undoing the zip and reaching inside.

"Oh my God! You brought Scarlett to the game with you?" I squeak out, my eyes fixated on the red toy in his hand. "Did anyone see you with her?"

He shakes his head and lifts the bag from my lap with his spare hand, swinging it onto the front seat and shutting the passenger door. Setting Scarlett on the seat, he climbs into the back as I shift until I'm all the way over on the other side, pressed against the opposite window.

"I thought maybe Sawyer caught a glimpse in the locker room after the game, but I buried her good."

I roll my lips together and smirk.

Crawling toward me, he pulls off his tie and undoes the top two buttons on his white dress shirt. "I was only saying I hid Scarlett well. You have a filthy mind—you know that?"

He starts to unzip my pants, and I pulse with anticipation. "Says the boy who's about to make me come with my vibrator on the back seat of his truck."

Removing my boots, he works on my jeans next, peeling them down my legs and pulling me toward him until my back is flat on the seat. He kneels between my thighs, and I watch the way his eyes travel my partially naked body. Only my tiny thong and his jersey cover what I'm desperate for him to touch.

He undoes his dress pants, pushing them and his boxers down until his cock flies free. "Who said anything about only Scarlett making you come?"

My mouth waters at the thought.

"There are so many ways I plan to make you come, Kendra." He hooks my legs around his waist and pushes my thong to one side, teasing me with his hand.

I close my eyes and feel myself growing wetter with each pass of his fingers.

"How long do you think we have until they notice we got delayed?" He's still on his knees between my thighs as his thumb finds my clit and a finger enters me slowly.

"Not long." I groan from the way it feels.

I've never had so much sex in my life, and the delicious ache when he strokes my front wall only fuels my desperation for more.

Since his head barely clears the roof, he reaches over me and braces his palm against the window behind my head, hovering over my body. When his tongue finds mine, he works my mouth and pussy together, and I drop my legs open for him. All I can hear are the needy kisses we share and the sound of how ready I am for him to fuck me.

He smiles and adds a second and then, quickly, a third finger. "Are you desperate for me, Kendra?"

Over his shoulder, I notice the steam building up on the window. God, this is so fucking dirty. "Yes. I want you now."

"Good."

His hand withdraws as fast as his cock slams into me, and I throw another palm over my mouth, positive anyone left in this parking lot can hear me scream.

With his dress shirt partially undone and his pants pushed down over his firm ass, he looks like a dream. His hair falls over his darkened eyes that fix me in place while his hips piston into me.

"That's it, Kitten. Get nice and wet for me. Let me stretch this tight pussy out with my cock."

He thrusts into me again, and we both breathe a pleasure-filled whimper into each other's mouths.

"Come inside me, please," I beg.

I'm so needy, ready to feel the warm sensation as his cum spills into my pussy.

"Not yet." He winks and picks up Scarlett from beside us, a mischievous expression back on his face. "I'm not nearly done with you."

My eyes drop to the silicone wand I've only ever used on myself.

Jack thrusts into me again, and I release all over his cock.

"Good girl. That's what we need."

He holds Scarlett out in front of me. "Spit on her."

My eyes grow wide. "W-what?"

His voice is low, almost a growl. "Do you trust me?"

I nod once. "Yes."

"Then spit on her. Get her nice and wet for us."

Rising up onto my elbows, I do as he commanded.

"Fuck *me*," Jack groans.

He takes my mouth, sweeping his tongue across my bottom lip. He pulls back and spits on the vibrator too, and my pussy tightens as he does it.

He's so fucking filthy.

"Relax for me, Kitten. I need you to be ready for us."

When he guides Scarlett between my legs, I instantly close my thighs around him. "W-what are you doing?"

Jack's eyes soften as he looks at me. "You trust me, right?"

"Yes," I repeat.

His spare hand pushes on the inside of my knee. "Then lie back and let me do all the work. I want to show you how toys are better when your man knows how to use them."

Still inside me, he pulls out just slightly and notches the wand at my entrance. "So goddamn wet. So perfect and ready."

The first centimeter stretches me so fully that I'm sure I'll never take it. "I can't. There's no way."

"Breathe for me, Kendra."

I trust him and open my legs as wide as they'll go.

"Wow. You are so beautiful like this." Jack pushes the vibrator further inside and squeezes his eyes shut, moaning into the silence surrounding us.

"Is that good, baby?" I ask.

He bites on his bottom lip as he looks directly into my eyes. "So fucking good. Do you feel full?"

Another inch, and the sting is replaced with only pleasure. "I feel so dirty right now."

He watches on. "That's because you are. You're my little slut.

On my back seat with your thong pushed to the side, taking me and Scarlett in this perfect, pretty cunt."

He switches the vibrator to its first setting, and we both moan deeply.

"Jesus fucking Christ, I'm going to blow before I start fucking you properly."

"Do it," I bite out.

Jack pushes the vibe in further, and both his cock and the toy bottom out inside me.

"So fucking full."

"So fucking greedy," he rasps.

When he finally starts moving and switches the vibrator up again, I watch as his slick hair sticks to his forehead, partially covering his eyes.

"Kiss me," I plead, overwhelmed with an emotion that scares the shit out of me. "Kiss me."

Balanced on his forearm, he smooths his tongue over mine.

"You've got a strong core to be pulling this off in here," I say with a lust-filled giggle.

He smiles against my mouth and pulls up, bringing his palm back to the steam-covered window above my head. "Baby, I'd do any kind of workout if it meant I could fuck you like this."

And that's it. That's the moment where I lose my mind and come so hard that my vision turns black.

"Mess up my seats, Kendra." Jack flicks the vibrator to its highest setting and fucks me through my orgasm. One that lasts so long that I think it's never going to end.

I never want it to end.

Morphing from smooth to erratic, his thrusts begin to slow, but he never takes his eyes off mine. "I'm filling you so good right now. Can you feel that, Kendra?"

I wrap my legs around his ass as he pulls out the vibrator and tosses it onto the floor.

"Are you still coming?" I ask as his body continues to shake and shudder.

"Yes." Jack's moan is deep as his spare hand grips the edge of his leather seat.

He's lost all control of his senses, and I fucking love the way that makes me feel.

I reach up and push some hair back from his forehead. "That's it, baby. Give me everything you have."

CHAPTER TWENTY-NINE

KENDRA

There are multiple raised brows as we approach our reserved booth in Lloyd's Bar.

"Nice of you to join us." Jenna smirks from opposite us as we take a seat, and she checks her imaginary watch.

"Traffic can be a bitch," Jack drawls, raising his hand to order a drink, and then he stiffens beside me.

I follow his line of vision and land on Archer. He's standing next to Darcy as she sits at the bar. The Blades goalie is exactly like Jack was with me, the night I saw him again for the first time in a year. With his elbow resting on the top of the bar, Archer's body is turned toward Darcy, studying her intently.

You'd have to be living under a rock not to know his reputation. If she has a pulse and is willing, he'll likely leave with her—he's that much of a fuckboy. I guess some could argue that's exactly what he's doing right now—making his move. But something tells me this is different. His eyes don't lie.

"Leave them be," I say, leaning down and kissing Jack's shoulder.

Jack begins ordering from a server, requesting a soda for me.

Jenna taps her finger on the table, attracting my attention. *He drove her here.*

I'm no expert at lipreading, but I'm fairly sure that's what she mouthed at me.

She has a boyfriend, I mouth back.

Jenna shrugs a casual shoulder in response.

From a stool at the end of the booth, Sawyer stares down into his half-full beer.

"Is he okay?" I ask.

Leaning back in the booth, Jack wraps his arm around my waist, tucking me into his side. "We got beaten down pretty good tonight. It affects us all differently."

I don't say anything since I'm not convinced that's the truth. A captain is normally the person to lift their team after a bad performance and the first to celebrate a win. From what I've seen, he's exactly the kind of leader who would do that. But the weight I see resting on his shoulders tonight feels way more than just the result of a game.

A cackle rings from the bar area, and I look up to see Darcy's head thrown back in laughter, but no one responds, only a subtle smirk from Jenna.

A couple seconds pass between us all before Jenna breaks the short silence.

"I guess you got the email," she asks, twisting her drink around on the table in front of her.

I take a sip of my soda. "What email?"

Her eyes flare wide. "Like, an hour ago. From head of team selection." She reaches into her purse and fetches out her phone, tapping the screen a couple of times before clearing her throat.

"*Dear Jenna, as you are aware, we are currently observing as many games as possible in preparation for our preliminary squad selection. This team will also play in a round of friendly matches, which will take place during the international break this February.*"

Her eyes flick up to mine. "*It is our intention to name a squad of twenty-six players in two weeks, and you and your club will be notified if you have been successful.. Please be advised that while the fixtures this winter are strictly friendlies, we anticipate the squad chosen to be similar for the World Cup this summer. Team cohesion and dynamics are a priority, and we want to ensure the selected players are given as much time together as possible. This is, of course, subject to unforeseen events. Kind regards,* blah, blah, blah."

She locks the screen on her phone, and I feel Jack's hand squeeze my shoulder.

"Did you get the email, Kitten?"

"I haven't checked my phone in several hours," I reply, knowing I've been too distracted with hot sex in the back seat of his truck to think about anything else.

Reaching into my coat pocket, I quickly navigate to my emails and immediately land on the one Jenna just read aloud. My heart races in my chest as I check it over for any differences and breathe a sigh of relief when it's the exact same.

"If I'm getting the same email as my established international teammate, that must be a good thing, right?" I tip my head up and look at Jack, then across at my friend.

"You were a shoo-in already." He kisses the bridge of my nose.

"You think so?" I look at Jenna, excitement raising my voice to a squeak.

Grinning, she leans toward me on her forearms. "I know so." She points at my phone as I tuck it back in my jacket. "They're making it out like this is a new process or something, but I texted Hollie right after I got it. You were *delayed* ..." She pauses, and I flush at the memories of a half hour ago. "She said they did this the last time. The players they wanted were pretty much notified in the same way. It all tracks."

"Oh my God." Tears prick in the corners of my eyes as I let it sink in that perhaps my season is turning around. That maybe all the late-night training sessions and Chelsea Rayne Pilates are paying off.

"So fucking proud of you, Kitten." Jack leans down and kisses the side of my head. "If we don't make the playoffs, then I'll come with you to the World Cup in Brazil."

My breath catches in my throat, and I look at him. "That's in, like, seven months."

His eyes search mine, a touch of uncertainty behind them. "Would you not want me there?"

I look down at the bubbles as they pop in my soda. So much of what I've been doing has been about living in the moment. So much of my life has changed dramatically in the past couple of months, to the point where I don't really recognize it anymore.

But none of it feels wrong. There are no red flags when it comes to this boy, and I have to trust that he won't screw me over like my ex did. I flick my eyes to his sister as she continues to laugh and joke around at the bar. I barely know his family, but already, I trust them. I trust her judgment of her brother.

But mostly, I trust my own.

Turning back to Jack, I hold his handsome face in my palms and pull his mouth down to mine. "I want you there."

ME

I think I might be heading to the World Cup in June. Nothing is confirmed yet, but I'm being told it's as good as done!

OLLIE

You act like you're surprised.

I am! There are so many strong options for center back. I thought I'd be last on the list.

You're that good. Which is also unsurprising since you're my sister and all.

Careful. You might trip over your ego.

It's not the size of my ego that's the problem.

Gross.

How's my favorite hockey player?

Jack's good. Jon is also fine. Other than the beating they took tonight.

THE BATTERY SYMBOL on the top right of my screen flashes with a warning.

I gotta go. Are you still flying home for Christmas?

Yep. One of the benefits of playing in La Liga: they actually give you a rest instead of playing you into the ground like the Premier League.

Catch you later, superstar.

"Argh! Fucking bars, fucking phones."

I hear boots cross the restroom as I lean against the side of the stall, and the hand dryer fires up.

"But most of all, fucking *men*!"

I don't make a sound as the girl continues to ramble to herself in a mock voice.

"*All I'm asking for is one drink, babe. I'm not like the other men who messed you around.*" The hand dryer cuts out before immediately starting up again. "And fucking useless dryers!"

Kind of intimidated by what I might find on the other side of the door, I slide the lock open and peer around the corner.

Wavy light-pink hair is the first thing I see, followed by all black. Like, every item of clothing she's wearing is black—from her boots to the skintight black dress that rides high on her thigh. Even her shoulder bag is black.

When the dryer cuts for a second time, she must hear me as

I approach, and she spins around to face me, her striking black eyeliner skillfully applied.

"Oh, sorry!" Her cheeks pinken to match her hair. "Didn't realize I had company."

I smile down at the phone in her hand as she waves it under the dryer again. "What happened?"

The girl I'd pin as a couple of years older than me attempts to pull the back off her phone case—without any luck.

Dropping her shoulders, she frowns down at it and shouts back over the whirring noise, "How long you got?"

I dry my hands with a paper towel and throw it into the trash can beside me. Next, I pull out a tube of hand cream, and finally, the room falls silent. There's something about a bar restroom that always brings girls together. Like, in a place filled with mostly lecherous guys trying to grind against you every thirty seconds, the four familiar walls and mirrors provide a sanctuary to talk shit and sometimes bitch.

"Hit me," I reply, handing her the cream like she's an old friend.

She sets her cell on the countertop, pops the lid on the cream, and squeezes a small amount into her hand. "The usual—boy asks girl out, promising he isn't like all the other douchebags and that he'll definitely meet her right after the Blades game." She hands me back the tube and quirks a brow. "I should have known better than to believe him when he said he wasn't married."

I audibly gasp. "What?!"

She nods. "Yep. Met him at the bike shop, where I've picked up some shifts. He asked me out, and I asked him about the tan line on his ring finger. He said he'd recently separated and was looking for some fun. I turned him down for, like, three weeks solid, but he kept coming back to order parts that I knew he didn't need for the bike he owned. So, eventually, I caved. He was cute, and it had been a while, if you catch my meaning."

The girl rolls her eyes. "Next thing I know, I'm sitting in this bar, waiting around for le douche, when a text from his wife lands in my message requests, saying she's leaving him and I'm not the only woman he's been lying to."

"Fuck."

She lifts her petite frame up onto the counter. "That's all you've got?"

"That's all I can think to say. Other than dickhead."

She smiles, one that reaches her big brown eyes. She's seriously pretty. "Yep, well, that's it for me. I'm twenty-five, and I'll never look at another man again. Or reply to any messages they might send." She picks up her phone and shoves it in her bag. "Not that I have a working one to do that anyway. Or call myself a taxi home."

"Here, you can borrow mine." I pull out my cell to find a black screen. "Fuck."

"Spill a drink on yours too ..." She trails off, clearly realizing she doesn't know my name.

"Kendra," I answer.

She jumps down off the counter and straightens out the collar of her leather jacket, offering out her hand. "Collins. Nice to meet you, Kendra."

I take it and thumb over my shoulder. "I'm here with a group of friends. I'm sure one of them can lend you a phone. You might be waiting a while to use the bar's."

I check myself and remember the people I'm here with are largely famous, including my boyfriend. "Are you into hockey?"

She blows out a single harsh laugh. "Fucking joking, aren't you? Sports are not in my wheelhouse. Bikes? Yes. Sports? Hard pass."

We're out the door, and I'm halfway to the booths when Collins taps me on the shoulder and I spin back around.

"Thank you for this, for helping a girl out. This city can be kind of lonely, and I don't know if I'll see you again after tonight, so, yeah, thank you."

I cock my head to the side. "I know that feeling all too well, babe." Reaching into my bag, I pause when I remember my phone is toast. "Hang on. I should have a pen and paper in here somewhere."

When I find a fine marker, I hold it in one hand and then search for a random receipt I can scrawl over.

"Just write it on here." Collins holds out her palm to me.

"What, like back in high school?" I laugh.

She presses her lips together. "How old are you? People haven't done this since the '90s."

"I wasn't alive in the '90s." I chuckle, quickly writing my number across her palm. "There, just don't wash your hands, or you'll lose me forever."

I expect Collins to laugh, but she doesn't. Instead, she drops her eyes to the floor and mumbles something inaudible against the beat of the music.

Not wanting to push anything, I lead us toward the group. "Can anyone lend Collins their phone? She needs to call for a ride home."

"Sure thing." Jack reaches over with his.

I take it from him and hand it to Collins.

"Thanks so much. I'll only be a second," she replies and starts typing in a number she clearly has memorized.

"Wait. I can give you a ride home if you need one."

Collins looks up and straight at Sawyer. "To my place?"

He scratches the back of his neck and smiles kind of awkwardly. "Yeah, that's where you want to go, right?"

She side-eyes me, clearly unsure.

"He's my boyfriend's captain. You can trust him."

"My face is also pretty well known in town," Sawyer adds.

Punching in the last number on Jack's phone, Collins narrows her eyes suspiciously. "Famous or not, I don't accept rides from strangers. Thanks, though."

She puts the phone to her ear and begins speaking, tuning out the rest of the bar as she turns away.

"Sheesh, bro. Burn, baby, burn!" Archer leans back in the

booth, crossing his arms over his chest, as Darcy giggles beside him. At some point, they must have rejoined the group.

Sawyer leans forward and plants a firm hand on his goalie's shoulder, lowering his voice. "At least I'm not dancing with death tonight." He raises a brow at Darcy, who's busy talking to Jack about her flight home.

Archer shrugs and takes a pull on his drink. "She's got a boyfriend."

"Okay, the taxi will be outside in a second. Thanks so much!" Collins hands Jack his phone and focuses on me. "Thanks again. You never know, if I'm feeling like a random coffee sometime, I might hit you up."

She takes me by surprise as she leans in and sets a kiss against my cheek, shooting one last glance at Sawyer.

"See ya."

CHAPTER THIRTY

JACK

A bottle of Kendra's perfume sits on the side of my bathroom counter. She's only been away for twenty-four hours, but I'm already pining like a puppy when their owner turns their back for a few seconds.

Grabbing my deodorant from next to her Angel perfume, I realize this will be our life on a regular basis—Kendra away with her team and me with mine. It's possible we could find ourselves apart for weeks, especially when our schedules don't align. The only positive? At least the summers will be free. And when she has international tournaments like the World Cup, I'll travel with her.

When it comes to Kendra, everything I see is long-term. There isn't a shred of doubt in my mind when it comes to this girl. I just hope she feels the same way. Last week in Lloyd's, when I said I'd follow her to Brazil this summer, I sensed her hesitancy, the moment when she processed how far away the tournament was. I never want her to doubt my commitment to us—hell, I've been into her since before I was legal to drink.

Nothing about us is temporary, and nothing about what we have lives in Tyler's shadow.

Don't let him get in your head, Jack.

I shake away thoughts of that asshole, finish up packing my bag, and shoot my girl a text.

ME

Do you know how weird it was, sleeping in my bed alone last night?

KENDRA

I woke up this morning to Jenna's snoring. At first, I thought it was you, and I got excited, only to realize I was still in Florida.

I don't snore.

I have recordings that prove otherwise.

Wait, do you actually?

Recording attached.

I hit play on the ten-second video as I walk through the living area and grab my jacket, ready to head to the airport for a three-night series in Chicago.

The tape finishes up, and I frown.

No way. Not buying it. Also, never have I ever complained about the noises you make.

I'm noisy?

I burst out laughing and grab my keys from the console table.

Oh, Kitten, the possible responses I could give to this.

Never mind that. Do I snore?

No.

I do, don't I?

It's cute.

I die.

Recording attached.

YOU DIDN'T!

On a belly laugh, I twist the handle on my front door and grab my suitcase, still smiling down at my phone like a lovesick fool.

"Son. Thought I'd catch you before you head to the airport."

I'm partway to the elevator when the voice wipes away my smile, an awkward feeling settling over me.

"That a girl?" He nods his head at the phone in my hand, and I quickly pocket it.

"What are you doing here?" My voice is ice-cold.

I can't say I harbor hate toward my dad, but I'm definitely not his biggest fan. There isn't much in life we see eye to eye on, resulting in an impasse between us. Which is why I'm surprised to see him here, acting like he actually gives a shit.

"You didn't answer my question," he responds, brushing a few flakes of snow from the collar of his long black coat.

I dangle my truck keys beside me, hoping he'll take the hint that I need to get going. "And you didn't answer mine. I have, like, thirty minutes to get to the terminal."

He smiles and shakes his head in the patronizing way he does.

Dad has always thought a lot of himself. He'd walk into a room and expect all conversation to stop around him. Everything revolved around his agenda, and if yours happened to be full, then you'd better make accommodations.

"Haven't got five minutes for your old man? I came all this

way to see you. Thought it was my only option since you refuse to answer my texts."

I ignore the gibe, along with his passive-aggressive comment. "Not here on work then?"

He runs a self-assured hand through his hair. I wish I could extract his DNA from my genetic makeup and replace it with Jon's, life would be much simpler that way.

He takes a step toward me. "I'm here to check up on the progress of our US hedge fund, but that's not the main reason for visiting New York. I wanted to see you, Jack."

His voice feels sincere enough, but Jon's warning rings true. I can't trust him. There's always something more to his actions. My phone buzzes in my pocket for the second time, reminding me of Kendra's unanswered text.

"I fly back in a few days, and I was hoping to see you before I left. Thought maybe we could grab a bite to eat. You get back early from Chicago on Saturday, don't you?"

I lift my wrist and check my watch. Shit. I wasn't lying when I said I had thirty minutes.

"Debbie, my girlfriend, is here with me. Maybe you could bring yours too?" he continues.

At this point, I'm not really processing his words. "Sure," I say, desperate to get to my truck and avoid the reaming-out Jon is going to give me for delaying the flight.

His eyes light up, like he wasn't expecting me to agree. "Great." He shoves his hands into his coat pockets. "I'll make a reservation for four."

" 'Kay." Grabbing the handle on my suitcase, I stride past him and hit the button on the elevator.

"Jack."

I spin around just as the doors open. "Yeah?"

"You'll remember to bring your girl, won't you? I want to be a part of your life."

His voice sounds borderline defeated, and I fight back the

urge to feel for this guy. Like I said before, I'm at an impasse with him, and that's the best place to be.

The last thing I want is to drag Kendra into my daddy issues, but I also know she won't do anything she isn't comfortable with.

I step into the elevator and hit the button for the lobby. "I'll ask her."

"THAT'S IT, Kitten. You right there?"

"So close."

With my phone propped up on the comforter in front of me, I lean back on the headboard and palm my dick, dragging my hand up from the base in a motion that makes my balls tighten. "Fuck, you look so pretty like this."

She's on her knees for me, her phone lying flat on the bed as she hovers over it, granting me a perfect view of her wet pussy.

Kendra throws her head back and moans, pushing Scarlett further inside her. "I wish you were inside me too."

My dick grows harder. "You liked that, didn't you?"

"So much. I want you here, Jack."

"I know. Me too. Just two more nights, and I'll be back with you, my cock stuffed in your pussy."

On another thrust of her vibe, she moans. Even via video call and in the faint light of my bedroom, I see the way her skin pebbles, the rush of blood to her cheeks as she drops her head forward and comes on parted lips. Lips I'd love to be sucking on my cock right about now.

I'm mesmerized by the beauty sprawled out across my bed, but my hand stills on my cock when I hear Sawyer's key card slide into the hotel door.

"Fuck, fuck, fuck." I pull the duvet up over my waist and grab my phone. "Cover yourself, Kendra. He's back."

Like a fully trained ninja, she dives off the bed and out of sight, and I suppress my laughter when I hear her cussing out my captain. We weren't nearly done with phone sex, and he's back way earlier than he said.

On an arched brow, he steps into the room and closes the door behind him. "Should I ... come back later?"

I drop my shoulders and double-check that I'm not tenting the duvet. "I'd say the moment's passed."

He kicks off his sneakers and moves across to the bathroom. "It's cold as fuck out there. I'm gonna order room service."

He disappears inside the bathroom, and I pick my phone back up.

"Kendra!" I whisper-shout.

When she comes into view, she's dressed in one of my training tops, her cheeks flushed.

"Not helping." I point to her top and then my inflating dick.

She shrugs a shoulder and climbs onto the bed, throwing her hair up in an effortless bun. "First thing I could find to throw on."

Goddamn away series.

"I miss you so much," I say.

She smiles sweetly, tucking a piece of hair behind her ear. "When you get back, we can snuggle all night on the couch."

It sounds like the best idea in history, if only there wasn't one snag. "Actually, I needed to talk to you about that."

She sits up straighter, the collar of my shirt falling over one of her shoulders. "What's up?"

With my dick now fully deflated, I reach over and grab some shorts, pulling them on under the duvet. "I ran into Dad on my way to the airport. He wants to meet up for dinner before he heads back to the UK. He invited you to join us with his new girlfriend, Debbie."

"How does he know about me?"

It's a fair question, but nothing he couldn't work out from the media. "I think there's a fair share of pictures online."

She nods. "True. Do you want to go?"

I scratch at the back of my neck. "Not especially, but in my haste to make the plane, I kind of agreed to it."

She shimmies down under the covers, and, fuck, there goes my dick again, right as Sawyer steps back into the bedroom.

"I mean, I'm okay with it if you are. If his girlfriend is going, it might not be so awkward. I guess I should get to know all of your family."

Every time, even when the conversation is about my dad, somehow, this girl manages to make me fall just a little bit harder.

I open my mouth, the words right there on my tongue.

"Baby, someone's calling me. Can I call you back?" she says.

I clamp my mouth shut; it wasn't the right time anyway. "Yeah, sure."

She blows me a kiss and disappears, leaving me staring at the call summary and running over ways I can tell her that I want the bed she's sleeping in tonight to be permanent.

"Did, err ... did that chick ever contact Kendra?"

I turn my head toward Sawyer as he scans the room service menu from his king-size bed. "Which chick?"

He crosses his feet over at his ankles and flicks the page. "She had pink hair."

I rack my memory for what the hell he's talking about.

Bingo.

The slightest tug of my top lip has him side-eyeing me with a warning.

"She seemed kind of stressed out, was all."

"You're talking about the girl who turned down your offer of a lift home, right?"

He closes the menu and throws it at me. "Don't recall that part."

I immediately select what I want and pick up the receiver to place an order. "Aside from the rock-chick girl with pink hair, what do you want?"

He narrows his eyes at me. "The sirloin."

"Rare or well done?"

He drops his shoulders and tips his head toward the ceiling. "Rare."

I snicker right as a pillow hits the side of my face.

"Order the damn food, rook."

"Want me to ask Kendra if she's heard from her?"

He throws his head back into the soft headboard and exhales slowly. "No, it sounds fucking weird."

The call connects and immediately puts me in a queue, and Sawyer reaches across for the book on his nightstand.

He might think asking after a girl he met for all of thirty seconds sounds weird, but I know he wouldn't have said anything in the first place if she hadn't made some kind of impression on him. Something tells me it took a lot for Sawyer to even ask what he did.

With that knowledge, I decide to do him the favor he didn't ask for.

ME

Did you ever hear from the girl in Lloyd's that night?

KENDRA

Collins?

Yeah.

My eyes flick up to Sawyer as he pulls on his glasses and focuses on his latest crime novel.

Okay, so this isn't weird at all. That was her calling me a second ago. I'm meeting her for the random coffee we talked about.

I look over at Sawyer again. "She's fine. Kendra just confirmed it."

"You asked?" He pulls off his glasses and looks at me, though he doesn't seem annoyed I went ahead when he said no.

"I'm a bundle of love these days."

Fuck, am I turning into Jon?

He got with Mum and instantly went from playboy to matchmaker extraordinaire when it came to his teammates.

He shakes his head at me. "I'm not interested in her, Jack."

I close out the message thread with Kendra. "Why are you so bothered then?"

He continues shaking his head right as the call connects to the restaurant downstairs. "Just leave it."

CHAPTER THIRTY-ONE

JACK

As I pull up outside the restaurant Dad booked for us, Kendra swivels toward me in the passenger seat, her jaw hanging open. "You realize this place doesn't sell anything under two hundred dollars, right? Even the breadsticks require a remortgage."

I shift into park and glance over her shoulder as I watch my dad and his brunette girlfriend walk through the entrance, thankfully not noticing us sitting in my truck. I guess he wouldn't know what I drive.

"You're telling me your dad and brother aren't into fancy places like this?"

She shakes her head instantly and then twists her lips. "Hmm ... Dad? Definitely no. We live on a farm in Ohio, and he keeps bees. Looking at our place and lifestyle, you wouldn't know he earned millions during his career." She chuckles. "But you're right about Ollie. He's a flashy bastard."

I snort a laugh and lean across to run my fingers through her soft hair. "Are you wearing this down for me tonight?"

She lifts a brow. "If I say yeah, will you buy my dinner so I don't spend all that I've saved in rent on an entrée?"

I run my tongue across her bottom lip, and she gasps in surprise.

"You're cute when you're feisty. But for the sake of my inflating dick, can you be a good girl tonight and not give me backchat?"

She's wearing the black dress she wore that first night in Lloyd's, and that, combined with the knee-high leather boots and badass attitude she's giving me, I'm about ready to blow in my pants. Judging by the way her skin pebbles over her bare arms, I conclude we're both feeling similar.

On a wink, I release my hand from her hair and throw open my driver's door, the cold December air hitting me straight in the face, bringing me down to reality as I round my truck and swing her door open.

"Are you nervous?" Kendra asks, clearly sensing my shift.

When she steps onto the sidewalk, I take her jacket from over her arm and wrap it around her shoulders, pulling the collar —and consequently her—toward me. I'm not nervous about seeing my dad, but I am over my girlfriend meeting him.

The wind swirls around us, whipping her hair around my face, her classic scent pulling me deeper under her spell.

"I don't want you to go into tonight thinking he's anything like Mum, Darcy, or Jon. Elliott Thompson is the kind of person you'll hate. The only part of me that's anxious about tonight is making sure you know I'm not the same person he is."

She frowns, and I reach up and smooth my thumb over the crease forming between her brows.

Fuck, I hope she's as crazy about me as I am her.

"And to answer your earlier question"—I interlace our fingers and walk toward the entrance as the doorman pushes it inward and we step into the warmth—"your dinner's already covered. I only need one thing from you tonight."

"What's that?" She shrugs off her jacket as the host makes their way over to us.

I lean down to whisper into the shell of her ear. "Those cute little gasps you make when you unravel for me later."

"SO, tell me, Kendra, do you see yourself playing across the pond one day?" Dad leans forward and refills our water glasses, and I watch as my girlfriend visibly stiffens from beside me.

We've only been in his company for fifteen minutes, but in that time, he's managed to patronize his girlfriend, Debbie, on at least three separate occasions. The second she saw me, she flushed, and it was at that exact moment the pieces fell into place—she was his secretary back when he and Mum were still married. I remember her face from the days when he hauled me down to the office, trying to convince me that my future was in finance.

So far, all she's done is take sips of her wine and smile sweetly at my dad while he focuses his attention on us.

"Maybe. I had an opportunity a year ago, but I didn't take it at the time." Kendra reaches into the middle of the table and plucks a breadstick from the shared pot.

"Not interested in following in your brother's footsteps then, no?"

What the fuck is this? Quiz Kendra night?

I clear my throat and decide to bring Debbie into the conversation, given my dad has fuck all intention.

"How do you like New York, Debbie?"

From the corner of my vision, I watch as Kendra relaxes, the focus away from her and finally elsewhere.

Like a deer being hunted, Debbie startles and looks across at Dad.

Please tell me you aren't seeking permission to speak.

She clears her throat and fidgets with the knife and fork in front of her, never meeting my eyes. "Well, we haven't had much time for sightseeing. Your dad has been busy with work. But, yes, it's really nice. Definitely a lot of people here." She giggles nervously. "It really is the city that never sleeps—"

Like she never existed, Dad cuts across her. "I have to say, I'm surprised you haven't made more changes, given the success you've been enjoying, Jack."

I wouldn't describe Debbie as petite, but she loses several inches as I watch her shrink back into her seat.

Fucking prick.

"Jack," he repeats as I offer Kendra an apologetic smile.

I should've never brought her to meet him.

"What do you mean?" I finally answer as our first course is brought to the table.

Dad picks up his napkin and sets it across his knees. "That agent of yours—I'm not convinced he's got your best intentions at heart."

I bristle. My agent is the same guy who represented Jon throughout his career. He knows the NHL better than the layout of his house, but more than that, he cares about the fate of his clients.

Bracing my elbows on the table, I clasp my hands together and shake my head down at the untouched plate of food in front of me. This was never about seeing me or meeting my girl. I can't say I ever thought it was, to be honest.

"He's a good guy. Not everything centers around money."

I swear Debbie gets smaller as she squirms at my dad's brash approach. If his behavior surprises her, then she can't know him all that well.

"So, passing up hundreds of thousands of dollars isn't a problem for you?"

"What are you talking about?"

Dad shrugs and takes a bite of his food. "I'm just wondering if there's a cut in there somewhere for ex-client referrals."

If it were just Dad and me tonight, this would signal the point where I get up and walk off. But for the sake of my girl and the woman my dad is supposed to care about, I fight with my rage.

"What do you do for a living, Debbie?" Kendra sits up straighter in her chair, dismissing my dad, giving him a taste of his own medicine.

Dad's face twists with annoyance but mainly confusion.

Yeah, it's official. I'm in love with her.

Despite the discomfort she's clearly in, Debbie forces an appreciative smile. "I work for Elliott and his team. Mostly, I work in admin, but I'm training as a stockbroker. I know I said I've not had much chance to sightsee and all, but actually, we're here on business."

Kendra takes a sip of water and nods. "I've heard there's a lot involved in that kind of work. My cousin is a financial adviser back in Ohio. I remember him saying he spent longer training to be qualified than he did at college."

Although my focus is solely on Kendra, I'm distracted when my dad shifts uncomfortably.

"Are you close with your cousin?" he asks.

Kendra nods innocently. She has no idea where this is going, but I've seen enough of it over the years to know exactly what his game is.

What this entire meal was geared around.

"Yeah, he's family, but he works with Dad and my brother. Manages their finances and everything."

A smirk traces his lips. It's not smug or humored. It's disappointed. And with that smirk goes my last shred of patience.

"That's why we're here, isn't it?"

Dad lifts a casual shoulder, his voice completely even. "We're here for a meal as family."

I shake my head, fire burning through my veins. "That's why you came to New York, isn't it?" I tip my head toward my girlfriend. "You'd found out I was dating Kendra Hart, daughter of an ex–pro footballer and sister of one of the biggest La Liga names." I lean back in my chair and look up at the ceiling, throwing my napkin on the table in front of me. "You wanted me to switch agents, no doubt to someone who would sweeten the deal for you personally, and then move in on my girlfriend's family."

I lean forward and rest my elbows on the table as Dad's face burns redder. He can't look at me as his eyes dart around the restaurant.

"Trouble is, Kendra's cousin beat you to it. You and I both know the hardest client conquest is when the current adviser is family."

When I turn to Kendra, my heart hits the floor. All the blood has drained from her face.

"I'd say Jon has twisted your mind up something good, Jack," he replies, his tone still as unaffected.

"Is that true?" Debbie looks at my dad, realization all over her face.

Clearing his throat, he raises a hand to attract a server. "I think we're ready for our mains now."

When Kendra pushes her seat back and stands, I'm not ashamed to admit that despite everything going on right now, I'm hard as fuck at the sight in front of me.

Kendra snatches up her bag and jacket and pins my dad with a glare. "And I think we're ready to leave. Jack was absolutely right when he said I wouldn't like you. I wouldn't want you to do my family's grocery shopping, let alone look after their finances. The only thing I want from you is to stay the hell away from me and my boyfriend."

She turns on her heel and then back around to Debbie, not giving Dad a second glance. "It was nice to meet you, Debbie." Kendra smiles sweetly at her. "I'm not sure we'll ever meet again, so let me say this while I've still got the chance: know your worth because you can do so much better."

As she marches toward the exit, I stand and consider heading straight after my girl, but instead, I pull out the keys to my truck and unlock it through the window.

"Quite the firecracker you have there, son."

"Fucking amazing, isn't she?" I repocket my key and down the remaining water in my glass, setting it back on the pristine white tablecloth.

I know this is likely the last I'll see or speak to him in a very long time, but that thought alone still isn't enough to make me want to look at him.

"I'm sure, at some point, you met my mum." I focus my attention directly on Debbie. "Though I'm not sure if you were seeing my dad while he was still married."

My dad motions to speak, but I hold up a hand, silencing him.

"To be honest, that doesn't really matter, and I don't particularly care. But my girl is right. Get out. Out of my dad's firm and his grasp. Do your qualifications somewhere else and don't look back. Take it from the son who's spent years watching him manipulate everyone around him."

I was convinced I wouldn't, but I do. I look at him. I want him to see how serious these next few words are. "Tonight, you crossed a line I hadn't known existed. No one messes with my girl or the people she loves. I never want to see you again. I'm ashamed to call you my dad."

He scoffs in the condescending way he's honed to perfection over the years. "You talk like things are serious between you both. I always thought you didn't do serious."

I smirk at his pathetic attempt to get a rise out of me. "You're right. I'm not just serious about Kendra; I'm way past that, and I'll crush anyone who tries to hurt her. Shit excuse for a father included."

CHAPTER THIRTY-TWO

KENDRA

When I get really angry, I go quiet.

I don't know why I do, but tonight, I've never been more thankful for that part of my personality. Or that Jack is clearly the same.

Honestly? Nothing good or helpful can come from what I have to say about the guy I just met.

Swinging his truck into the reserved space in the underground parking lot, Jack continues to grip his steering wheel with white knuckles long after he puts the truck in park.

When he spoke about his dad being an asshole, I naively thought he was a prick who thought a lot of himself. No, Elliott Thompson is way more than that, and my heart breaks for not just my boyfriend and Darcy, but for his mom, Felicity. Christ, what must it have been like to live with him daily? I could barely stand him for a half hour.

"I shouldn't have agreed to meet with him." Jack's voice breaks me from my thoughts. "I swear I knew nothing about his intentions with your family."

Slowly, I peel his hand away from the steering wheel and

entwine our fingers. I haven't said anything since I stormed out of the restaurant, and even now, I'm struggling to find the right words. So, I squeeze his hand tighter, hoping he'll find some comfort in my actions.

After a few more beats, I pull open my passenger door and climb down from the truck as Jack does the same, and I hold out my hand for him to retake as we head for the elevators to his apartment.

Up until this point, so much of our relationship has centered around Jack looking out for me. For what I want and need.

Yet tonight feels different. Tonight, I feel like he needs me.

When the elevator ascends past the first floor, I reach over and hit the Emergency Stop button.

"Kendra. What are you do—"

I silence my boyfriend with a kiss as my hands drop to the zipper on his pants.

In my boots, I'm still way smaller than his tall frame, but he doesn't tower over me like he usually does, and that drives my dominance forward.

"Sit on the railing."

As he lifts himself to balance on the brass rail behind him, I cast a glance around us. No cameras.

I know this dress turns him on. I think I've known since the day he saw me wear it in Lloyd's. Even if I was determined to ignore Jenna as she tried to convince me there was something between us.

"This is all for you," I tell him as I pull the straps over my shoulders and lower the dress to reveal my bare breasts, showing him I wasn't wearing a bra tonight.

"Oh fuck, Kitten," he croons. "You're fucking spectacular."

I waste no time as I reach inside his pants and take out his dick. I don't know how long we have before someone works out the elevator has stopped and tries to set it running again.

The first swipe of my flat tongue across his head has him drawing in a sharp breath.

"Grip the railing," I tell him before I swallow his cock.

His fingers plow into my hair while my mouth and hand work in perfect synchronization. I've never blown Jack before, but by the way he moans and tugs at the roots, I know I'm giving him exactly what he needs.

I cup his balls with my other hand and gently massage them. They grow tighter, and he flexes his hips, driving further down my throat.

"I've fantasized about you sucking my dick for so long. Swallowing me down as I make you gag."

I pop off and stare up at him. "Choke me with it."

Jack's jaw hangs open as a trail of spit connects my lips with the swollen head of his dick.

When I take him back into my mouth, he thrusts up into me, harder than before. I gag, just like he wants, and double down, pushing him even further.

"Motherfucker," he gasps. His hand falls to one of my nipples, playing with it between his fingers.

I want to hear him roar when he comes and releases not just himself, but all the pent-up tension he's felt tonight down my throat.

"Gonna blow." Jack puffs the words out breathlessly.

Right before he fires off, I feel his dick harden and his balls contract to the point of no return. He hangs his head, his face full of awe and his body completely at my mercy.

I pull off briefly. "Good boy, baby."

The first shot to the back of my throat is fucking delicious. I can't lie. He tastes as good as I thought he would, and my body pulsates with raw need.

When I've swallowed him twice and he's still coming, I bring his cock out of my mouth and continue to pump, spilling his hot release all over my tits.

"You called me a good boy," he whimpers.

"I did," I reply, his cum still squirting onto me. "Do you like it when I praise this pretty cock?"

"Yes, Kendra."

His face is flushed, his eyes are wide, and his jaw is slackened with desire as I rub him into my skin. His relaxed body is everything I hoped for when I stopped the elevator, and when I stand up straight and hover over him, his cock still hard in my palm, I swipe my tongue across his bottom lip and let him taste himself.

"Actions speak louder than words, and tonight, I couldn't find the right thing to say about your dad. Other than he's an asshole."

Dropping off the railing, he cups the sides of my face in his hands, his forehead resting against mine.

He reaches across and pushes the Emergency Stop button to set us going again and then pulls my straps back over my shoulders. "No part of this was fake to me, Kendra. Not when I asked you to the gala and not now that I have you as my real girlfriend. I always knew you were incredible, but somehow, you've taken that word and leveled it up to the point where I'm on my fucking knees for you." His lips tremble as they find mine. "I know so much of what we share is fun and exciting, and that's absolutely the truth. It's just that, now, I'm falling in love with you too."

THE BAROMETER for a good blow job has to be your mascara and how smeared it is afterward.

Well, mine is fucking streaming.

While Jack lies passed out on his bed, needing to "take a minute to recover from that masterpiece"—his words, not mine—I take the opportunity to cleanse my face and soak in my smug feeling.

Mission accomplished. And fuck you, Elliott Thompson.

I'm finishing up on my eye cream when my phone lights up

from an unknown caller, and my heart falters when I recognize the international dialing code.

"Hello?"

"Hi. Is this Kendra Hart?" A British female voice, not all that different from Darcy's and Felicity's accent, immediately speaks.

"Yes, it is." I spin around and face the en suite door, waiting with bated breath for her to reveal who she is and where she's calling from.

"Oh, great. I deliberately called at this hour since I wasn't sure what time was best to catch you. My name is Sarah Watkins, and I'm the head coach for London Villa."

Oh fuck, I know who she is. Only one of the best coaches in the world, now heading up arguably the best team in Europe right now.

"How can I help you?" I ask, trying to steady my phone in my shaking hand.

"I hope you don't mind me calling you directly. Your agent gave me his permission. I felt this would work better, coming straight from me since I've had you on my radar for a long time."

"You have?" I turn back around and face the mirror.

She chuckles lightly. "Oh, yes, absolutely. But due to financial rulings, we couldn't make an offer to the Storm until now. Well, actually not officially until January, when the winter transfer window opens here in the UK. The point behind my call is to let you know of our intentions. Come the new year, we plan to trigger the release clause in your contract and invite you to join us." She pauses. "If that's something you want."

My mouth runs dry, and I struggle to formulate a response. Instead, I stare at my reflection, motionless.

"I understand this is a little out of the blue," Sarah continues. "We are just concerned that this is a big move for you, and we understand it might take some time to think it over, so we wanted to give y—"

"I don't need any time to think about it," I interject, finally finding my voice.

"You don't?" Her voice is excited.

I shake my head and stare down at Jack's toiletries lining the counter. Swallowing thickly, I pray that my decision is the right one. I can't make the same mistake again. But my gut has never been stronger on anything, and I can't ignore that either.

"I can't accept whatever offer you make."

She exhales slowly. I can sense her disappointment through the phone. I close my eyes and pray to anyone listening that I didn't just set my career up in flames.

"Can I ask the reasoning behind your decision?"

"It's nothing to do with your club, the team, or you as a coach. The setup you have over there is phenomenal." I swallow past the lump in my throat. "My decision is a personal one. I ..." I drop my eyes to the tiled floor, and Jack's smile is right there in my mind. "I recently entered into a relationship with someone and have found a lot of happiness that I didn't have for a long time. This isn't a situation where he can move across the Atlantic with me, and neither is it one where I'd ask him to."

She hums in understanding. "Jack Morgan?"

"Yes," I answer, realizing my boyfriend isn't exactly a secret.

"So, your intention is to stay and play out your career in the US?"

I open my eyes and think over the gravity in her question. We're both the same age, and the NHL doesn't exist outside of North America, whereas soccer does. Part of me wants to decline answering her question, but I know why she's asking—she wants to know if there's a possibility of me transferring to Europe anytime soon or if I see my long-term being stateside.

Thoughts of my brother twist my stomach. Moving to England would mean I'd be much closer to him. I'd also get to see him on the regular since he'd play in the UK far more than he does the US. Memories of my dad racing backward and forward to Mom also play out in my mind. They made it work, but is that what I want for me and Jack? Between our away series, we already spend way less time together than we want.

I know there are no guarantees for us working out, and I can never tell Jack about this call. I have zero doubt he'd tell me to follow my dreams, but what he doesn't realize is, he's rapidly become a part of them.

I don't realize I'm crying until the first tear hits my cheek, and I swipe it away quickly. "Yes," I say with way more certainty in my voice than I expected. "Things are really serious between us, and I have no plans to leave the US anytime soon."

CHAPTER THIRTY-THREE

JACK

"Looks like we're paired up again." Archer throws his towel on the weight bench beside the one I'm using.

"Do you believe in clothes?" I ask him. "Or maybe just a shirt."

He lifts up his cap and replaces it backward. "Does it make you feel inadequate?" He drops his gaze to his pecs and tenses each one in turn, making them dance.

"Does that impress the ladies or something?" I say, sitting up to straddle the bench and swiping my water from the floor.

His grin is cheeky. "Speaking of, how's your sister?"

I shake my head on a gulp. "Those kinds of questions are ill-advised when her brother is about to spot you. All it would take is a slip or loss of concentration, and fuck knows where that Olympic bar could end up."

A snicker from neither Archer nor me joins the conversation.

"Quit bothering my winger, will you?" A shirtless Sawyer rests his arm against the bench press machine. "Besides, aren't you seeing Chelsea?"

I pop the cap on my bottle and lie down, ready for my next rep. "Who's Chelsea?"

Archer shakes his head at our captain, and for the first time, I see an emotion other than playful. "Where did you hear that? I haven't seen her in months."

Sawyer shrugs and thumbs over his shoulder. "Couple of the guys said they thought they'd seen you leave with her that night in Lloyd's."

I've lifted the bar around an inch when I set it back down and sit up again. "The same night you were flirting with Darcy?"

Archer twists his lips, a doubtful expression on his face. "I wouldn't say I was flirting with her. Just trying to make her feel welcome."

"Uh-huh," Sawyer adds.

Archer throws his hands out to the sides. "What? I wasn't." He pauses and rubs the back of his neck with a towel. "She did tell me all about Liam though."

"Seriously?" I side-eye him, not believing a word, convinced he's trying to goad me. Although how else would he know her boyfriend's name? "Why would she tell you about him?"

Archer nods once. "We got talking and she opened up to me. Seriously, he's kind of a prick."

Sawyer bursts out a laugh. "Of course you'd think that. He was the only reason you didn't get what you wanted that n ..." He trails off and looks at me.

I glance between them both and pinch the bridge of my nose, closing my eyes slowly to will away the thoughts. "Archer, do you want to fuck my sister?"

Silence. He should be denying it straightaway.

I open my eyes and pin our goalie with a glare. "I'm not kidding around. Do you want to fuck my sister?"

He holds his face still before he doubles over in laughter. "Oh my God! I had you. You were ready to lay me out, weren't you?"

I'm not laughing. Not one fucking chuckle leaves my mouth. Eventually, Sawyer joins in.

My head darts to my captain. "Anyway, you can talk." I clear my throat and go for my best Southern American accent, pulling it off to perfection. *"Jack, is she okay? Maybe she didn't get home all right. Can you check on her? No, actually, don't check on her. That would be weird. Instead, I'll sit here and be all broody and shit and pine over the pink-haired girl and pretend I can't recall her name or the fact that she blew me off when I offered her a lift."*

"My name is well known around here," Archer adds on a wheeze, holding up his hand like he needs a minute. "Jesus, when you said that to her and she said she didn't accept lifts from strangers, I nearly collapsed with secondhand embarrassment."

Sawyer crosses his arms over his chest and raises a single brow. His face is stoic as he continues to watch on as we laugh like a pair of hyenas.

"Jesus, if only you trained your bodies like you do your mouths, we'd be buying an extra trophy cabinet." Jon comes to stand in front of us.

He looks as unimpressed as Sawyer, and gradually, our laughter trails off.

Jon tips his chin at me. "How many reps have you done, Morgan?"

Leaning down, Sawyer wraps his hand around my upper arm. "Not enough. It's kind of skinny."

Archer starts up laughing again, and Jon swivels his head to him.

"At the risk of overstepping my coaching boundaries, you do know she's not just your winger's sister, but technically, she's my stepdaughter too. Jokes aside, that's pretty fucked up. Even for you."

Archer blushes—full-on fucking blushes—as he tries to pass it off as nothing. "Ah, I'm just messing around with the rookie."

"You know how it is, Coach," Sawyer adds.

Jon looks doubtful as he clicks his tongue and pulls his iPad from under his arm. "At some point, do you plan on heading for the massage you booked in with the trainer?" He raises his other arm and looks at his watch. "Fifteen minutes ago."

"Shit!" Archer announces, grabbing his towel and hightailing it toward the exit.

Jon shakes his head and takes a sideways glance at me as he makes his way around the gym, continuing his observations.

I lean back on the bench. "Since I lost my spotting partner, fancy teaming up?"

"Sure." Sawyer rounds the rack and comes to stand behind me. "How are things going with Kendra?"

He passes me the bar, and I pump out a few reps before he takes it back and gives me a breather.

I can't lie; she's been a little different over the past couple of days. Initially, I chalked it up to her being nervous since she has a wait until the team USA squad is announced in the next couple of days, but when she told me she was feeling okay about that, my mind started to wander. When she gave me the insane blow job in the elevator, she told me she hadn't had the words to describe what an asshole my dad was, but she did make it clear that she could see I was nothing like him. Maybe she isn't so sure now.

I push away any doubt.

"We're good," I answer, taking the bar back and moving through my set before Sawyer increases the weight.

"I'm thinking about asking her to move in," I add.

Sawyer pauses with a weight, and I swivel around to face him.

"But you already live together?"

"Is it Groundhog Day or something?"

I close my eyes at the sound of Tyler's voice. *Not again.*

"What do you want, Tyler?" I ask, turning to look at him as he stands at the end of the bench, hands propped on his hips.

He bites on the inside of his cheek. "Why don't you have the balls to tell me stuff to my face? Everything I've found out is because I overhear you."

I shrug and rub my hands together, wiping some of the chalk from my palms. "I don't tell you because it has nothing to do with you."

"So, you're living together?"

I nod. "Since her apartment was condemned and she needed a place to stay."

He steps forward until his shins press against the end of the bench. "Wait, so you're telling me you invited her to live with you before you started dating?"

I nod again, not giving a fuck at this point. I'm in love with his ex-girlfriend, and I'm ninety-nine percent sure she feels the same. There's fuck all he can do about it.

"Yeah, right after you split."

His face twists with the usual anger I hope Kendra's never seen. "It all makes sense—all of it." He leans forward, pure hatred flowing off him. "You're nothing but a predator. You waited until she was at her most vulnerable and then decided to strike."

Yeah, I mind that.

I leap from the bench and head straight for him. "Say that again, asshole!" I spit as Sawyer grabs my arms from behind.

I look to my left and see that Jon has left the room—thank fuck.

"Predator," he repeats calmly, a smug smile on his lips.

My anger boils, and I know if my hands weren't pinned behind my back, they'd be in his face right now.

"You don't know the first thing about me and definitely not the girl you lost. You can't stand the fact that she's moved on and upgraded to a man who doesn't just make her happy, but who she's also falling for. That's right, Tyler; she loves me. She can't get enough of us and the way I make her smile."

I know he wants to hit me, but he can't. Not if he values his career.

"And guess what, Einstein." I smile brightly, my dimple

popping good and well. "I'm so far gone for her that I'm going to ask her to turn my apartment into our home. Then I plan to fuck her on every surface we own together." I blow out a relaxed breath, mocking him and his dead-ass depressing situation just a little more. "Then, when the time is right and she can't even remember your name, I plan on giving her mine."

CHAPTER THIRTY-FOUR

KENDRA

Rise Up—better known as Kendra's meeting room.

The place is way quieter than I've seen it before though, and it doesn't take me a second to spot all black with a mass of pink hair sitting on a stool in the window.

"All right, Kendra?" Ed—the café owner who Jack has introduced me to a few times when we've snuck in here for a post-sex treat—waves his hand at me.

"Hi," I reply and make my way to him as he motions for me to approach.

I prop my hands on my hips when a scone comes into view. "Let me guess who put you up to this."

Ed chuckles and hands me the plate. "He said you'd be here this afternoon and asked me to have your favorite ready. Cream on top, right?"

"Yes. Yes, that's right," I say on a defeated breath, pretending I'm not fucking swooning the entire time.

"Oh, and tea for one." He sets a tray with a ceramic pot, cup, and saucer down in front of me.

I frown. "Wait, you don't even sell this kind." I pick up the tea bag and look at the paper tag hanging from the string. "Yorkshire? I've never had this brand."

Ed shrugs and smiles. "Jack asked me to get it in especially, so I did. Selling like crazy, to be honest."

Yeah, I'm in love with him.

Flutters shimmer throughout my body as the memory of him telling me how he feels comes racing back. *He's falling for me too.* The guy who said he didn't do serious when it came to girls is falling for me.

I set the scone on the tray and take the whole thing from Ed. "How much do I owe you?"

He drops his shoulders, and he knits his brows, giving me a look that needs no further interpretation.

"Was he in here this morning?" I ask.

He nods and takes a sip of his own Yorkshire tea, and I fight back a laugh.

Jack Morgan—slowly turning New York British.

"Stopped by when we opened. Said he needed to stock up for his week away series."

My heart sinks as I remember him leaving me in bed this morning. One whole week. Seven long days. He spent the entire time inside me last night, determined to make up for how much he'd miss me. Still wasn't enough. It's not like I can distract myself with soccer since we have four rest days after a stacked playing schedule and ahead of a crazy run of matches before the holidays.

It looks like I'll be busying myself with TV repeats and waiting on an email confirming what I'm praying for—a place in the national squad this February.

"Question."

I look up at Ed as he sets his cup down and smiles.

"When you two tie the knot, you'll be coming to me for the cake, right?"

I stare back at him, not speaking since I'm unsure how to

answer that question. I'm only just getting my head around how fast I'm falling.

"Are you coming over or what?"

I spin around to find Collins drumming her fingers on the bar in front of her.

She smiles as I make my way over and set the tray down in front of me. "What is this? Alice's tea party?"

I snort and pick up my scone, taking a bite and humming with appreciation. "Want to try it?" I offer her the other half.

She scrunches up her nose and picks at her brownie. "I'm good, thanks."

"Did you ever hear from Mr. I'm Not Married?" I ask, getting straight into it since I get the impression Collins doesn't stand on ceremony. She's the kind of girl who doesn't do small talk either.

She shakes her head. "No. I did send him an invoice for the parts he kept coming back for though."

"Obviously," I say, bringing the cup to my lips and hating the fact that this is the best tea I've ever tried.

Damn him.

Collins winces. "Didn't go over too well with the boss though."

"Why? You did nothing wrong."

She winces harder. "I added Asshole Tax."

I choke on my tea, a few splashes hitting the window in front of us, and I quickly wipe it away with a napkin.

"And, yeah, that was the end of that job."

"Wait, so you're unemployed?"

She shrugs like it's no big deal. Maybe it isn't. I know very little about her.

"Are you some kind of millionairess and jobs are just for fun?"

She stirs a spoon of sugar into her coffee and laughs. "No. Not all of us are pro soccer players."

When we spoke over the phone, Collins told me she assumed I was a hockey player and that's how I'd met Jack. I quickly corrected her with soccer, still, it's obvious she thinks I'm rolling in cash.

Dream on, Kendra.

"Yeah, the big bucks are reserved for the men," I reply.

"Ah, yes, it's a man's world. I forgot that part. Silly me."

I love her.

Still stirring her coffee, she sits back in her stool and brushes some brownie crumbs from her jet-black jeans. "I live my life how I want. I don't spend much time in one particular area, and therefore, I don't place any particular importance on a job. It's a means to an end."

As much as I respect her and kind of envy her attitude, I can't help my heart from sinking a little. "So, you won't be staying in New York?"

She shrugs and then laughs. "Depends if I can find a new job."

I laugh along with her. "But seriously, I've spent half of this year worrying about money. What will you do?"

Her brown eyes find my own. Her carefree expression is kind of refreshing. "I don't know how much of my life you're interested in knowing."

I'm taken aback by that. Why would she think I wouldn't want to know more about her? Sure, I haven't known her for long, but I can't deny the instant connection between us. Some people you speak to like you've known them for years, and Collins definitely falls into that category.

"I'm all ears," I reassure her.

She rests her elbow on the table, supporting her cheek in her palm as she looks at me from the side. "I guess I have been fortunate in some ways and not in others. Life's been a bit of a mixing pot."

I take another sip of tea and let her speak, already relating to that statement on a visceral level.

"I won't bore you with too many details, but my grandparents effectively raised me in Ohio."

I set my cup down quickly. "No kidding. I'm from Ohio! Where are you from?"

Her eyes light up at that. "Just outside of Cleveland. You?"

"Cincinnati," I reply.

"So, we didn't attend the same kindergarten and then forget about each other's existence?"

I snort. "No. Anyway, you were saying about your grandparents."

"Yeah, so they raised me and then died."

I look around as she falls silent. "Is that ... is that the end of the story?"

She lifts a shoulder. "Pretty much. Died when I was eighteen and left me a stack of cash. I was an only child, so I didn't need to share it. Since then, I've used it to travel. Both around the US and to countries a lot of people haven't visited. Didn't bother with college since it's a load of bullshit. Then got into bikes. Bought my first one after my grandparents died and nearly killed myself on the freeway one night. Finally put some of their money to good use and qualified as a mechanic. Rest is history." She takes another sip of coffee. "But, yeah, the money's running out now, so jobs are becoming more necessary."

My mind whirls at the influx of information. I don't want to ask what happened to her parents since that feels a bit invasive.

"So, yeah," she continues, "I guess I see myself as a bit of a free agent. I don't have any family, and people generally let you down, so I keep to myself. Seems like the easiest way to go."

Arguably, there's a lot of sadness packed into what she just said. But I don't really see it reflected in her demeanor. I think Collins is the type of person who has genuinely found peace with who she is and the life she leads.

A bit like Jack in that way.

Reaching across, she picks up the half scone she previously refused and takes a bite.

"What do you think?" I ask.

She moves her head from side to side. "*Comme ci, comme ça*. It's alright, I guess."

"Well, whatever you do, tell my boyfriend they're the best thing you've ever tasted, okay?"

"Here's the first confession in our friendship." She sets the scone back down and wipes her hands together. "Remember how I told you I have zero interest in sports?"

I nod once.

"Well ... that's not strictly true, not in the appreciative sense anyway." She winks at me. "Pro athletes do have fine butts."

"Yep, I can definitely confirm they do."

She frowns at a thought she's having. "I couldn't enter into a relationship with one though. I think I'd be happy just to palm it every now and then."

I burst out laughing. "Like a firm-butt-with-benefits kind of arrangement?"

"Yeah." She smiles and then throws her head back. "Ugh, it's been way too long."

"You kind of only have yourself to blame for that, you know?"

Her head whips to me. "What do you mean?"

"You remember turning down a ride offer from the Blades captain. Let's just say, I've kind of known the guy for a while, and I'm not sure he's ever made an invitation like that."

Collins fluffs out her hair. "Oh, no, I remember the offer and interpreted it as a potential booty call. That's why I turned it down."

"But you just said it's been a while?" I counter.

"He's not my type," she immediately responds. "He must be ten years older than me, and—I dunno—he sealed the deal when he reminded me of how famous he was. Like I wasn't already aware. Hockey fan or not, Sawyer Bryce is known."

"You called him a stranger?"

"Did I?" She smiles, clearly remembering that she did. "Did it dent his ego?"

I roll my lips together to prevent the evil giggle I want to release. "I'm not sure what it did to his ego, but I do know he's been asking about you. Wanted to make sure you got home all right."

She downs the last of her coffee. "I go for younger guys. Generally, there's less baggage. *Generally*."

I rest my chin in my palm and study her. "So, what's your plan? Find another job and stick around so we can meet for more random coffees and bitch like two old women? Or will you be loving and leaving me?"

She picks up her phone from beside her and checks the screen. "Can I answer that question in a couple of hours? I have an interview at another bike shop. If I don't fuck it up and they aren't bothered with previous employer references, then my tiny apartment and I should be golden for another few months."

She slides off the stool and grabs her leather jacket. "I like you, Kendra. I think you're in danger of becoming the first friend I've made in a while."

I tip my head to the side and smile. "Better make sure you're offered the position then, right?"

She gives me a little salute. "Doing it for you and me and our blooming love story. See ya!"

When she pushes out of the café and passes by the window in front of me, she blows a kiss before disappearing out of sight.

I sit there in a daze for a few seconds. She's like a whirlwind but in the best way. The kind of person you meet and then wonder if that actually happened.

I'm still staring out the window when my phone buzzes on the bar, and I swipe it up, knowing all too well it's too soon for a Collins-related job update.

JACK

So, our flight got delayed. It's going to be tight between landing and the game tonight. I'll call you when I can, Kitten.

P.S. Away series suck.

P.P.S. You looked beautiful this morning.

ME

picture of teapot

When are you taking me to the UK so we can stock up on Yorkshire tea bags?

I thought you'd never ask.

I'm typing out a response when the text chat disappears, and my happy mood instantly shifts to kind of pissed.

"Aren't you boarding a plane soon?" I answer, not bothering to say hello.

"Don't hang up on me," Tyler says quickly. His surroundings sound quiet, and he's whispering.

Feeling uncomfortable, I push off my stool and grab my bag, waving to Ed on my way out. "Well, that depends on why you're calling. If it's to ask if we can be friends, then no, we can't. You set any chances of that alight when you acted like a prick the other day. Jack told me what you said to him in the gym. No one is preying on anyone."

There's a short pause as I step out onto the busy sidewalk and head back to Jack's apartment.

"Believe it or not, Kendra, and despite the fact that you hate my guts, I still care about you."

I blow out a disbelieving breath. "Word of advice: I'd up your caring game for the next girl you meet."

He doesn't say anything as I reach a quieter part of town and root around in my pocket for my key.

"Is that all you called to say?"

"I need you to see something. I get that it's coming from me, and you don't exactly see me as a credible source, but like I said, I care about you, and I can't let you make a mistake without letting you see it. I don't think I could live with myself." Tyler sounds kind of pained as he delivers a sentence that makes my stomach roll with nausea.

"Tyler, what are you talking about?" I'm agitated—a product of how vague he's being and how anxious it's making me feel.

"Look, I might be a lot of things, and I genuinely accept there's no way back for us." He exhales deeply when my phone buzzes in my hand, and a message with an attachment comes through from him. "But I've known about this for a long time. An old college buddy of mine showed it to me back then because he thought I should see it. I did nothing about it, but kept it close to me since ..." He trails off. "Since I always knew there was something I didn't trust about him. The last thing I want to do is hurt you, Kendra. But whether you think of me as a friend or not, I do you. And friends wouldn't let you make a fool of yourself like this."

I bristle at the last sentence. "I'm not making a fool of myself. I'm happy."

"Just ... look at what I sent you and then ask yourself again if you really believe this whole thing is real to him. I was always about you, Kendra. Not sure if he can say the same thing."

Dread crawls through my bones as I stand motionless and a few hundred yards from Jack's apartment.

"Open the message, Kendra. I gotta go."

When the line goes dead, I keep the phone to my ear.

I don't trust a word that left his mouth, but that isn't going to stop me from reading whatever he sent. I know it isn't.

In slow motion, I open the thread with him and then click on a compressed file of messages.

The first thing I notice is the date stamp from over three years ago. We were just finishing up on our second year of college.

The next thing I see is Jack's name, along with a couple of other guys from his former team. I knew he hung out with them at the time, and one of them was also friendly with Tyler.

My heart beats wildly in my chest as I scroll through the first few. There's nothing here but typical nineteen-year-old boy banter about girls.

Until there isn't, and my back thuds against the wall behind me as I slide down and sit on the cold, damp ground, drawing my knees up in front of me.

I've read this all wrong. There's no way it says that.

I look up and blow out a calming breath, trying to steady my shaking hand before I center myself and read it again.

BEN

So, to be clear, you want to fuck Kendra Hart?

KURT

Don't deny it. It's obvious.

JACK

Yeah, I do.

BEN

Called it!

KURT

She's with Tyler.

JACK

So? It would be as easy as taking candy from a baby. Flash her my smile, promise her a good time, and she'd be in my bed in seconds.

KURT

Wait. You're serious?

JACK

Deadly. I get to fuck the hottest girl on campus and then see his face the next morning. With any luck, might make her scream loud enough so he can hear it too.

CHAPTER THIRTY-FIVE

KENDRA

The soles of my feet burn as I enter Jack's apartment, having walked the streets of Brooklyn for hours, trying to clear my head and calm down.

Not bothering to switch on any lights, I welcome the stillness as I make my way to the couch and sit down absentmindedly, pulling the blankets across my lap.

This is the exact spot we've shared multiple times. The couch where I straddled his lap, wrapped in the same blankets as we made out properly for the first time. The first time he kissed me for real. It was the start of everything between us.

Wasn't it?

I know he was nineteen when he sent those messages, and I know we'd barely spoken, but that shit really hurts.

"Was I always just a pawn?" I whisper into the darkness, unlocking my phone and rereading the messages Tyler sent me.

These can't be from Jack.

JENNA

Have you gotten the email?!

With my heart in my mouth, my adrenaline is already at an all-time high as my attention snags on a message that drops down from Jenna.

I immediately open my emails, pulling down on my inbox several times, trying to refresh it.

ME

No. There's nothing here.

JENNA

Maybe it's taking a minute for yours to come through.

I get up from the couch and start pacing the length of the living area. I can't take this. I'm spinning out with thoughts of messages I never expected to receive and an email I'm desperate to see, but won't come through.

When my phone buzzes in my hand, I almost drop it in my haste to open my inbox.

From: *Team USA Selection*

To: *Kendra Hart*

Subject: *Squad Announcement*

Dear Kendra,

Following our recent communication, we write, as promised, to advise you of our decision.

You should know that all positions were highly contested, which showcases the vast array of talent we have and the progression our sport has made over the past twelve months.

The position of center back was one of our most difficult decisions, and we know you're aware we can only take a limited number.

Unfortunately, we do not feel you are quite ready for international selection. Our scouts have been incredibly impressed with your work ethic and skill set, but we do harbor some concerns about your physical condition. The soccer season is long and stressful, and when we consulted with your physical trainers, they have advised that you are undergoing a strengthening program to help with instability to your ACL. We do not believe it would be fair or ethical to place added stress on your existing injury. Additionally, from a squad point of view, the risk of selecting a player with a potentially serious injury could have major repercussions, especially if Team USA goes deep into the tournament—which is, of course, our aim.

We understand this is disappointing, and by no means are we saying future selection is out of the question. Our main priority is your physical condition and securing the longevity of what we know will be a very successful career.

Your club has been notified, but please do not hesitate to contact us if you have any questions.

We wish you all the best for the rest of the season.

Team USA

LESS THAN A DAY.

That's all it took for the blissful walls to come tumbling down and my life to go from tea and a scone with a new friend to a devastating realization.

I pull at the neck of my sweater. I feel hot and claustrophobic, and I need to get the fuck out of this apartment. Stay in a hotel. Stay anywhere but here.

Heading to the bedroom I haven't slept in since the night of the gala, I pull out my suitcase from under the bed, open it up, and make for the dresser.

Jenna: So ... did you get the email? Brazil, baby!

Through blurry eyes, I read the message from my teammate. The one I longed to get. I feel crushed, depleted. I've got nothing left to give to anyone or anything.

ME

I didn't make it. They said my knee wasn't worth the risk.

JENNA

Okay, stop joking around.

ME

I wish I were.

I drop my phone on the duvet and swipe a handful of clothes from the top drawer of the dresser before throwing them into my suitcase. When I spin around to grab a couple of things from the nightstand, that's when I see them. Two candles half burned and staring straight at me. The code to his apartment is next to them, scrawled in his handwriting with a smiley face below it.

There's no way he sent those messages.

"Fuck it."

I snatch up my phone again and scroll for Jack's number. I just need him to tell me the messages were fabricated and that it's all going to be okay. That I'm not a complete failure for not being selected. That I made the right decision when I turned down another shot in the UK.

That my gut was right to dive into something so soon with him.

That everything I felt between us was real and not a game.

Sitting on the bed beside my suitcase, I wait as his cell continues to ring until it connects to voice mail. I consider hanging up but change my mind at the final second.

"Jack, hi. It's me. Um ..." I bite down on my bottom lip and steady myself. "I need to talk to you about something that happened earlier today, and I really need you to call me back, okay?" My voice breaks, and I try to fight the sob as it spills free. "Yeah, I just need you to tell me it's all bullshit."

I hit End Call and wipe furiously at my eyes. Two more messages light up my screen.

JENNA

I'm throwing hands. No, actually, I'm refusing to play. You are the only center back I want. This is insane.

COLLINS

Got the job! Piece of cake.

"Jack?!" I answer the phone on the first ring.

"Hey, hey. I just stepped off the ice. The game just ended. We won, and I scored two!"

There's so much background noise and shouting that I can barely hear him. But it's obvious he hasn't listened to my voicemail.

"Great," I force out. "Did you get my message?" I ask anyway, my stomach turning in on itself.

"No, I didn't." He sounds way less animated as he picks up on my flat tone. I hear a door close behind him, and the previous noise disappears. "What's the matter, Kitten?"

I swallow hard, bile rising, making it difficult to push down the nausea.

"I need to ask you something, and I need you to be completely honest with me."

"Kendra, what's this about?"

I pull my phone away from my ear, bringing up the file Tyler sent me. Attaching it to a message, I forward it to Jack.

A ping rings down the line.

"I need you to tell me you didn't write these messages."

Silence passes between us as I wait for him to read them.

"Jack," I whisper, unable to stand the tension any longer, "I know things were different back then. I know we didn't know each other that well, but did you really say that you could fuck me easily?" I fight back the tears and dig my nails into my palm so hard that I know they'll leave crescent-shaped marks. "Did you tell Kurt and Ben that fucking me would be the best way to get at Tyler?"

More silence.

"Kendra ..." His voice is soft, just like it was that day in this very room. The day he asked me to go to the gala with him as his fake girlfriend.

I thought it was because he cared.

"Kendra, I—"

"Did you send them, Jack?" I ask again, my voice harsher this time. "Or is Tyler the bullshitter I hope he is?"

"Kendra, I don't know what to say ..."

"It's easy. Yes or no?"

"Yes, I sent them."

My phone drops to my lap as I cover my eyes with my palms. All the while, I can hear Jack's voice repeating my name.

On a deep breath, I pick it back up.

"I was nineteen and a fucking idiot for what I said. I was pissed at the way he was treating you. I don't have the evidence because it was from years ago, and to be honest, I forgot all about the messages, but what he sent you wasn't the whole conversation."

I angry sob. "Oh, yeah? What else did you say?"

"I don't remember the exact words. I just know he clipped that to make me look bad ..." He trails off. "And I know it looks bad, Kitten. But I promise you that's not what this is about. Those messages aren't how I feel about you."

"You know what I feel? Humiliated," I whisper-hiss. "Like I'm being taken for a fool."

"I promise you aren't. I feel so much for you."

I shake my head, not knowing what to believe anymore. "How much of this was about your issue with Tyler, and how much of it was about me?"

"It's *all* about you, Kendra. All of it. Every single fucking piece," he grits out.

I want to believe him. I want to hear him out. But honestly, at this point, I don't know how to. I don't know what to trust or judge anymore. My career's imploding and the very arms I'd seek for comfort are breaking my heart.

"I turned down a contract with London Villa for us."

"W-what? When?"

My head involuntarily drops between my shoulders. "A few weeks ago. The head coach called me and said they wanted to trigger my release clause in January. But I told them no. I said I had a new life here. I said I didn't want to put us at risk." More tears hit my cheeks. "I didn't hesitate when I made my decision. I didn't tell you because I thought you'd try to convince me to go after my dreams. Was I wrong, Jack?"

"I—I don't know what to say, Kendra. I wish you'd told me."

"I didn't make it onto Team USA either. Got an email earlier to say they couldn't select me due to my ACL injury. I was too much of a risk."

"Kendra, I'm so fucking sorry. It's their loss. They're the ones missing out."

I pick my head back up. Anger swelling in my gut. "Is that what you think, Jack? That I'm worth taking a chance on?"

He goes to speak, but I cut him off.

"Because right now, it feels like I'm not worth much to you."

"Kendra, there's so much that I want to say to you. But I can't do it properly over the phone. I need to come to you."

"Was it real? Were we real? Maybe everything was too soon.

This whole thing has gone from zero to a hundred, and I've barely had time to catch my breath."

"We're real, Kendra. I promise you we're real."

I shake my head despite him not being able to see it. "I don't know what to think. I'm lost."

"I know it's been fast, but that's because it's right. All of this—you, me—it's all right."

"I—I just don't know what's happening anymore."

The tears emerge again, and I suck in a big breath, blowing it out slowly.

"I think I need time." The second the words leave my mouth, my heart protests. Though I know it's what my head needs. "I need space."

"W-what are you saying to me, Kendra?"

I never thought someone could sound nauseous, but Jack proves me wrong.

Pinching my lips together, I squeeze my eyes shut. "I don't know. That's the point. I don't know anything other than I need space. From everything. I'm going to Ohio."

CHAPTER THIRTY-SIX

JACK

Yeah, violence would feel good right about now.

It takes me two strides to make it to the treatment room door and rip it from its hinges.

Another three strides before I'm parallel with the benches and I can throw my phone into my training bag.

And on the seventh stride? My fist connects with Tyler's face.

He stumbles backward, blood pouring from his nose.

I hit him again, this time aiming for his jaw. The unmistakable crack of two teeth is the only noise in the deadly silent locker room.

I take one final stride, but Archer makes it to me first with Sawyer hot on his heels from the shower.

"You—you broke my fucking nose!" Tyler screams.

No regrets. Not fucking one.

"WHAT THE FUCK DID YOU SAY TO HER?!" I've never felt this kind of rage—I'm uncontrollable, seething.

Archer's grip around my waist tightens. "Breathe, Jack. For fuck's sake, breathe."

I genuinely think if anyone else had said it, I wouldn't have listened. My anger would still be rising as the voice of reason washes over me.

But this is Archer—the guy who's usually all jokes and playtime—now asking me to cool it.

I pause on trying to hit him again when Tyler spits blood in my face.

I smirk, raising the hem of my jersey and wiping at my cheek. "Like I said before, sloppy seconds never felt so good."

He growls like some kind of fucking Doberman. "She read the messages then," he says, blood streaming down his face and over his jersey.

"Fuck, Tyler. What have you done?" Sawyer comes to stand beside me.

"What I should've done months—no, years ago." This time, he steps toward me, and Sawyer gets between us both. "You really think I didn't know your game back then? How desperate you were to get under my skin? I told you this has never been about Kendra. It's always been about me."

None of that is true, but it shakes me to my core regardless. I couldn't give a fuck what Tyler thinks. Except he's poisoned an already-vulnerable and heartbroken Kendra against me.

She needs me now more than ever, and there's nowhere else I want to be.

Panic overtakes me as I hold Tyler hostage with my glare. We've always had a rivalry, never been able to stand the sight of each other. Though this time, he knows he went too far. As I said to my dad, I'd burn anyone who hurt the girl I loved.

And I'm in love with her. It didn't take the thought of losing her to conclude that. But it did take this moment right here to realize I can't live without her.

I refuse to let my idiotic teenage behavior be twisted and used against me.

My molars are practically dust as I fight against Archer's grip, ready to hit Tyler again. "You and I both know that text thread was clipped to make it look even worse. You know what my next message said—that she deserved better. She deserved to have a guy who'd show her what it was like to be worshipped. Even at nineteen, I could see that, and you knew I could make her happy. The truth in my words threatened you. Why didn't you send the full thread, Tyler? Not man enough?"

"Fuck off!" he spits.

I've seen and heard enough.

When I turn away, Archer releases me, and I rip off my jersey and pads, throwing them down on the bench.

"Where are you going?" Sawyer asks, one brow raised with worry. "You can't go after her. We're in the middle of a series."

I snatch up my bag. "I'd say, the second I hit him, I landed myself in hot water with the GM. Nothing—and I mean, *nothing* —is going to stop me from going to her. She didn't make the national squad, her career is imploding, and now I've just broken her heart."

He claps a hand on my shoulder and squeezes—his way of asking me to take a second. "My Papa always told me to fight battles I know I'll win, and I can see my chances aren't good with this one."

My jaw tics, Sawyer's absolutely right, he can't stop me. "She's going home to Ohio and that's where I'll be in a matter of hours," I reply.

He reaches into my bag, fetching out my phone and handing it to me. "Send me Kendra's number."

I take it from him. "Why?"

"Just send me her number."

Hitting forward on her contact, I tip my head over my shoulder and watch as Tyler attempts to stem the bleeding from his nose. "Where's Jon?"

Sawyer runs a hand across his jawline. "Prepping a debrief a few rooms down."

I nod and make for the door.

"Jack?"

I turn toward Archer as he sidles up next to my captain. "Yeah?"

"Darcy knows Kendra's home address in Ohio. When we were hanging out in Lloyd's that night, I was there when she asked her for it. She wanted to send a Christmas card to her family. So, all I'm saying is, if you need to know where her parents live, then your sister can help you out."

I don't know where her family home is, though I'd have knocked on every door in the state until I found her. Despite the fucking turmoil I'm in, I manage an appreciative smile before I'm out the door and heading for Jon.

The empty player hallway only serves to feed my panic as I check each room and come up empty.

I'm going to lose her. I am losing her.

When I finally find Jon sitting at a long boardroom-style table, I take a breath and watch him through the door window, observing different clips of game footage.

He spins around as I push into the room, the smile on his face from rolling over Nashville completely gone, along with his coach persona.

He drops his pen to the table when he sees the pain in my eyes. "Jack, what the fuck has happened?"

My bag hits the floor with a thud as I collapse against the wall beside me. "It's all fucked. Everything."

He rounds the table in less than a second, his hands on my upper arms as his eyes search me from beneath the bill of his cap. "Talk to me. Does this have to do with Kendra? Because you just played the game of your life out there. The media wants to speak with you." He tries to lift my spirits. "They're calling you the next Jon Morgan."

I remember the first time Jon showed up at a college practice session. I was in my freshman year and one bad drill away from calling it quits. My game wasn't where it needed to be. I was miles behind. All I could do was skate fast and excel in agility tests.

It got to the point where most of the guys avoided talking to me since not only did I not fit in on the ice, but Tyler made sure I was as foreign as my nationality off it too.

Mum has said to me on multiple occasions that Jon changed her life, and I know he feels the exact same way about her. They were strangers to each other when they met but were instantly magnetized.

That's how I feel about Kendra. How I've always felt about her. And that's how I feel about the guy standing in front of me. He changed my life that day. All my teammates wanted pictures and autographs, and when he finished up being the true professional he'd always been, he quietly went about giving me the coaching he knew I needed.

He didn't give up on me, and he taught me not to do the same when it came to my dreams. He showed me that I could be whoever I wanted, and he guided me both on and off the ice.

When my mum bought those season tickets for my eighteenth birthday, she thought that would be the best present I'd ever receive, and it was damn close to it. What she didn't anticipate was the man she met as a result would eventually become the father figure I craved.

There was never any other name I'd play under, and there's no other girl I want to pass it onto.

She's endgame for me.

"I need to go to Kendra."

His eyes drop to my red knuckles, and I brace for him to ream me out.

It doesn't come, and I look him directly in the eyes.

"I fucked up in college, and Tyler has twisted it against me."

Jon exhales slowly, not saying a word.

"I know. I know this is the NHL and I have responsibilities. But she just got bad news about the national squad, and now she thinks I've been using her as part of this fucking stupid rivalry with Bennett." I push my hand harshly through my hair. "I need to go to her in Ohio."

I've been waiting for him to hit coach mode since I walked through the door.

He surprises me again when his face turns softer. "Is she the one, Jack?"

I don't hesitate. If she weren't, I wouldn't feel like my organs were being doused in acid.

"Yeah. I need to show her that she can trust me and she's my girl, and I can only do that face-to-face."

He presses his lips together. "Say no more."

"I hit Tyler," I tell him. "Twice."

His eyes drop to my knuckles again. "Off the record, I don't fucking blame you. If anyone messed with Felicity, I would ..." He trails off and regains his professional exterior. "Well, you know I hit Elliott. When you told me what he did the other night, I was all for going there again. Your mom thankfully distracted me away from that idea."

Despite the shit show I find myself in right now, I roll my eyes. "Yeah, not helping with the nausea."

He tips his chin over my shoulder. "Go. You've got two days before we play again. I'll clean up this mess and smooth it over with the GM." He drops his voice, a deadly expression on his face. "This goes no further."

I nod once as he releases me, and I waste no time in grabbing my bag and getting ready to chase after Kendra.

"Bennett's last chance was tonight. He's been on a warning for a while. His training and game aren't up to par, and his attitude fucking stinks. We're shipping him to the farm team in Connecticut."

I don't say anything. Internally, I'm fucking buzzing. He deserves to be dropped.

"Who's going to replace him?"

Jon pulls his cap off his head and leans toward me, placing it on mine. "You've got incredible playmaker abilities, and you're one hundred percent future captain material. When you aren't punching your teammates, that is. The day you signed with the team, you were being doubted left, right, and center. Now every single guy, bar one, can see the value you bring to each game and practice. Including the GM. If I can convince him you won't make a habit of getting into it with your teammates, then I have no doubt you'd be his first choice."

My jaw pops open, and he points to the door behind him, picking up his pen and preparing to push on with work.

"Now go. Get your girl and tell her about the apartment."

CHAPTER THIRTY-SEVEN

KENDRA

ME

I'm coming home.

OLLIE

Like, right now?

Yes. When will you be at Mom and Dad's?

In around twenty-four hours.

I'm at the airport now, waiting for my flight. Shit has hit the fan, Ol.

Talk to me.

I don't know what to say.

Tell me whatever it is upsetting you.

That's the thing. I don't know where it all went wrong. About six hours ago, I found out I didn't make the squad because of my knee. Then I told Jack I needed space after I read some pretty fucked-up messages he'd sent about me. Oh, and I turned down another shot in the UK because I didn't want to fuck up the relationship that feels fucked anyway.

I have strong thoughts on the squad decision, and all of them are that they're fools for not choosing you. But right now, what can I do to make this better?

Sitting in the empty departure lounge, I watch as a couple hands over their boarding passes to the attendant. Wrapping his arm around her shoulders, the guy pulls his girlfriend into him, setting a kiss in her hair.

Thoughts of Brazil and traveling to the UK to stock up on tea settle in my eyes, turning them glassy.

I reach up and wipe the wetness away with my sleeve. It's been hours since I told him I needed space. And the truth is, I do. But that still doesn't stop me from missing him. Up until Jack, I felt confused and at sea with my life. He and his smile brought some clarity, and I stopped questioning everything. I just went with it.

I had fun, and it was showing in every part of my life. My soccer especially.

I just don't understand how I arrived back here—lost and confused and fucking alone in a city that once again feels as cold as the frost lining its sidewalks.

ME

I think I need my brother.

OLLIE

That I can help with. I just moved my flight up. I'll be there in twelve hours.

I know I give you shit, but you're kind of okay.

Screenshot taken.

Want to talk about Jack?

I told him I need space because I literally don't know what to say to him. I'm pissed, I'm hurt, I'm humiliated, I'm sad, and I'm just so fucking confused, Ollie.

I don't know exactly what happened, but I'm not sure I really need to. You're in love with him. When you fought with Tyler, you were so unbothered that you forgot to tell me. When it comes to Jack, you're flying to Ohio, and I'm moving my flight up.

I read his message three times over, every word making complete sense, even in the midst of my meltdown. I know I'm in love with Jack.

OLLIE

The question is, are you running from Jack or the fear of getting hurt again?

I'm still wrapping my head around his last question when another comes through.

OLLIE

Give it some thought. I'm going to pack and catch my flight. We can talk more when I see you.

"KENDRA? What can I get you to eat, honey?"

My stomach growls, but I couldn't feel less hungry. "I'm

good, thanks," I shout back at Mom as I look around my childhood bedroom.

Pink walls, pictures of family, and one massive print of my favorite soccer player decorate the space around me. I haven't been home in a while, and my parents haven't changed a thing in my room since I moved out before college.

Mom pushes on my door, her face full of concern. "You didn't eat when you got here last night, and you're refusing again this morning. You need to keep up your strength."

I sigh and flop backward onto my bed, and she comes to sit next to me.

"You've always been fiercely independent. From the age of three, you were determined to do things most five- and six-year-olds were still struggling with."

"I don't like being a burden on anyone," I say. I place a palm over my eyes as a headache builds behind them.

"What made you come back home this time?"

I peer up at her from behind my hand.

"Would the strong and independent woman lying in front of me like a bit of advice from her older mom?" she asks, picking up a framed picture of us at a local water park one summer.

I nod and reach down to take her hand. She's absolutely correct in her assessment of my stubborn independence. Though, sometimes, I still need my mother's words.

She strokes her thumb across the back of my hand. "I never told you this. Maybe because I've been wrapped up in your dad for thirty years and I'd all but forgotten him. He didn't seem relevant anymore, but maybe my hindsight could benefit you right now."

She sets the frame down carefully. "I once dated a guy similar to Tyler Bennett. His name was Jason Matthews, and he was the hottest boy in high school. Honestly, I was with him for four years, and at one point, we were pretty serious for saying we were still so young. He was from a well-thought-of family with the classic white picket fence and parents who painted the perfect, serene picture. He was the complete opposite of your dad and his upbringing. As you know, your grandfather wasn't a kind man."

I sit up on my elbows but remain silent.

"I was too young to work out why Jason cheated on me that day. I caught him making out with someone else in the back seat of his car. It was right outside his house, and I'd shown up to surprise him after his baseball game. For years, I projected inwardly, thinking I wasn't good enough for him. But then I got older and wiser, and then I met your dad. It still took me a while, but you know what I figured out in the end?"

I shake my head, my brain locked in and focused for the first time since Tyler's text landed in my inbox.

"I don't think Jason appreciated what he had. I don't think he ever took a step back and thought about how sacred and precious those who loved and cared for us were. I don't think he'd ever been shown or experienced what it was like to want for something like the security of trustworthy, loving arms."

She falls quiet and meets me with her eyes. "Tyler Bennett gave me Jason Matthews vibes. So many times, I wanted to tell you to tread carefully, and sometimes, I felt like I'd overstepped your independent boundaries when I did hint at it. Tyler never made you happy or injected pure sunshine into your voice. Not like I heard that time on the joint call with your brother. You sounded light and full of life. It radiated from you. Even from thousands of miles away, I could tell."

My senses sting with not just emotion, but realization. "And you think Jack makes me happy?"

She lifts one shoulder slowly. "I'm just saying that you're right to be angry at Jack. You were right to be hurt, and your feelings are absolutely valid about that. What I also think is that you don't need space at all. That's not what you're searching for. I think you want him to *show you* that he's worth the fact that you turned down the UK and put your relationship ahead of a shot in the Super League. And for what it's worth, I personally think that he is. Call it mother's intuition."

She releases my hand and rises from the bed, turning around to look at me.

Like finding the missing piece to a puzzle, something clicks into place.

Elliott.

Jack has watched his mother and family be manipulated by a man who I couldn't stand the sight of, not for even thirty seconds. Maybe because of his asshole father, he's grown to appreciate the important things in life.

Maybe I don't need to worry about him hurting me at all.

Mom smiles as she watches me think everything over. "I hope there's something helpful in what I said."

Her eyes flick back to my nightstand, and she hands me my phone. "Someone named Darcy is calling."

With my thoughts still whirling, I sit up and take it, and she makes a quick exit, allowing me some privacy.

"Hello?"

"Kendra? It's Darcy."

The sound of her soft British accent forces me to bite down on the inside of my cheek, emotions overwhelming me as I hear the natural kindness in her voice.

"So!" she says excitedly. "Guess who's heading back to New York after Christmas? Long story short, I have another reading week, and I thought, *What the hell? I'll come back and see my favorite person. Along with Jack.*" She giggles. "He has another game, and I figured we could go together again. Last time was kinda fun, and being honest, I haven't seen him play enough."

I swallow thickly. She doesn't know. I guess she wouldn't. Not even Jenna knows what's happened. Only my brother and parents.

Working hard to hide my emotional crisis, I clear my throat. "That sounds great! I have a really stacked schedule around Christmas, but if I can make it, then I—"

"What's the matter?" she cuts me off dead in my tracks. "You sound upset."

I shift my phone from one ear to the next, trying to figure out what to say. "I-I ..."

"He didn't break it off with you, did he?" Her voice is incredulous.

I shake my head. "No, no. We're still together—well, sort of together. I've just had the worst twenty-four hours in history, and we kind of had a fight, and I came back home."

"Wait ... you're at your mum and dad's. Right now?"

I look around at my pink bedroom.

"I came home to think everything through," I say on a broken sob that I can't help. "It's been a shitty twenty-four hours."

She sighs softly into the phone. "Oh, babe. Jack called me earlier, asking for your exact home address. I figured he was going to send your parents something for Christmas. But now I'm thinking something else."

"Kendra?" My door creaks open, and Mom reappears, standing in my doorway. Her face is flushed a little pink, and she wears an unmistakable smile. "Are you expecting visitors?"

She steps to one side, and a white sneaker appears, followed by the bill of a Blades cap.

"Hey, Kitten," he says softly. His eyes are red, and his jawline is scruffier than I've ever seen it.

"He just got here," I say to Darcy, not taking my eyes from him as he walks into my room and sets down a bag of something by his feet.

"I'll be right back with drinks and food." Mom's still smiling as she closes my door behind her.

"Does he look apologetic for whatever he did?" Darcy's deadpan tone pulls my lips upward.

Clearly hearing her, Jack rolls his eyes and shoves his hands into his jean pockets.

I chuckle and feel the butterflies as they react to seeing him for the first time in days.

"Okay. I'm going to go and let you talk out whatever it is you need to. But let me finish with this: There's no way I'm letting go of you now—you got that? Even if my brother's a big enough asshole to lose you, then I sure as shit am not. Understood?"

I smile at her positivity. Just like her brother, she's infectious. "Loud and clear," I reply.

I look up at Jack as he takes a single step toward me, his eyes burning into mine.

"Okay, cool. Make him grovel, babe. Lots of love. Bye!"

When the call disconnects, Jack reaches down and takes the phone from my hand, setting it on the nightstand. He takes a seat on the bed next to me, the mattress dipping with his weight as he rests his elbows on his knees.

"You're on an away series."

He pulls off his cap and runs a hand through his hair. "Technically, yes. I have forty-eight hours before I need to be back. Well, more like thirty-six now."

The energy between us feels awkward, though not in the way I can't stand. More like there's so much to be said, and he's nervous to approach it. The conversation I just shared with Mom has brought me some clarity, but I need to hear his uninterrupted thoughts. I need him to show me what I'm praying is true.

Drawing in a deep breath, he looks around at my room. His trademark smile is evident, though it's clearly buried beneath a weight of worry. "I had to come to you. I know you said you needed space, but I wanted you to hear everything I have to say before you decide what to do, what it is you want."

He runs a palm up the side of his face, stress flowing from him. "Seeing you hurting is the worst kind of torture. And knowing I made you feel this way is fucking unbearable. It makes me want to crawl out of my skin."

He drops his head between his shoulders and turns to look at me, his blue eyes not as bright. "There's a chance I'll say this, and it won't change anything. Still, I don't think telling you will ever be in vain. You need to hear the words, and I need to walk out of this door, knowing I left it all in these walls. I can't control the past, but I can control the present."

I hold my breath, unable to inflate my lungs as I wait for him to continue.

"I'm not just falling anymore, Kendra. I'm fully in love with you. With every part of you. From your incredible talent on the pitch to the way you mess with your hair, not knowing whether to wear it up or down. Truth is, you could wear it any way possible, and you'd still be just as beautiful."

He reaches his hand out to my upper thigh and then quickly retracts, not sure how far to go.

"When I saw the messages Tyler sent you, I felt sick. Sick because I knew how badly they would hurt you. Manipulated and cherry-picked for his benefit or not, I should never have said what I did. I don't have any excuses, and I'm not about to make any either. You are in your rights to be pissed at me, and I have to wear that."

He sits up and edges slightly closer until I can feel his warm breath as it tickles my lips.

"You can be angry with me for as long as you want. You can have as much space as you need. There isn't anything I won't do for you. Even if it means I have to disappear for a while, I will. But I won't be gone. I refuse to walk away from the undeniable pull between us. I'm not even sure it's possible, to be honest."

"I felt like a pawn in a game," I breathe out, my heart hammering in my chest.

Unable to stop himself, he softly traces the back of his hand across my cheek. "It's impossible to play games over something so serious. Without even trying, you knocked me right on my ass; you made it hard to think straight when I was in your proximity." He huffs a soft laugh. "All without even looking my way. That's the hold you've always had on me, Kitten."

Flutters shimmer through me, all the way to my toes.

"The past three months, you've looked at me how I always fantasized you would. You've given me the chance I wanted so badly, one I had to watch some prick waste away for four years. You haven't made any mistakes, Kendra. Not one. You lit up my goddamn world when you said you chose us and New York because I chose us too. Every single *real* second of us. It's never been about Tyler or the rivalry. Just you. All I've ever wanted or cared about is you."

CHAPTER THIRTY-EIGHT

JACK

Yeah, I'm verging on a heart attack.

I've got the girl of my dreams sitting next to me on her teenage bed, her palms over her face and her head full of every thought possible.

I'm tempted to repeat the words I've never said to anyone before. I always thought they would be hard to say out loud, and when I finally uttered them, some kind of fireworks display would go off around us.

Instead, it was as easy as ordering a scone from Ed. It rolled from my tongue like it was the most natural thing in the world.

Loving Kendra Hart is as easy as breathing.

"Penny for your thoughts?" I ask on a whisper as her mum knocks on the door and steps back in with two sandwiches and bottles of water.

She sets them down, and I offer her a smile.

"Do you want me to put this in the fridge?" She points to the bag on the floor.

Kendra pulls her hands away from her face, and my heart bleeds out when I see the pain in her eyes. She's been through so much this past twenty-four hours, and some of that is on me. Though I'd take it all on and away from her in a second.

"What's in the bag?" Kendra asks.

I reach over and pull it toward me so she can see inside too.

"Wait." Her hand dips into the bag and pulls out potatoes, carrots, onions, and ground lamb. Her eyes flick up to mine. "You brought the ingredients for shepherd's pie?"

I know my dimple is popping when I pull out three more ingredients for a trifle. "I did promise you." I look between Kendra and her mum. "I have enough to make it for everyone." I put my focus on the girl beside me. "If you want me to stay, that is."

Kendra passes the items to her mum, and she puts them back in the bag, clearly sensing it's her time to leave when she picks it up and makes a sharp exit.

A few beats of silence stretch between us, but I'm determined for her to be the next one to speak.

Her mobile buzzes on her nightstand, making us both jump, and she tentatively reaches for it.

I can't see the screen, but I'm not looking at it anyway. Only the way her lips roll together and the tear as it hits her cheek.

I want to reach out and swipe it away.

"Oh my God," she finally breathes. Another tear falls from her eye as she looks at me. "How did he get my number?"

My brows draw together in confusion, and Kendra passes me her phone.

UNKNOWN

Kendra, I know we haven't spoken all that much in the past year, although I'm not sure that really matters. I wanted you to see something too. Something that counters the bullshit Tyler sent.

I once told your boy that I don't much believe in love. I don't, and I have my reasons. But I do believe in friendship and good people, and my boy Jack is both of those things to me.

You might be making out right now, and if so, discard and go ahead. But if seeing a copy of this thread, which I know Jack won't mind me forwarding to you, helps, then I'll gladly do what I can. I'm a good judge of character, and let me tell you, Morgan is golden.

Attachment from Unknown

ME

Kendra and me—well, we're fake dating. I offered to take her to the gala to help keep Tyler off her back and so she wouldn't feel so uncomfortable if he turned up with a random date. That kiss you saw earlier—it wasn't exactly real.

It's real. Trust me when I say, you can't fake that. I don't care if you've won a hundred Golden Globes and Oscars line your trophy cabinets. That shit was real.

JACK

I won't deny that it was for me. I felt everything between us. I'm in deep with her. But how can you tell with Kendra?

Because that's the way my wife used to look at me.

Slowly, she takes her phone from my hand and sets it on the duvet beside her. Then she reaches up and pulls at her topknot, letting her hair cascade around her shoulders.

"Kiss me."

Two words are a wave of relief as I bring her face closer to mine, her chin gently gripped between my thumb and finger.

"Do you want my tongue, Kendra Hart?"

She wets her bottom lip, and at the same time, her pupils dilate. "I want whatever will last the longest."

"I've missed you, Kitten." My voice is raspy as I feel her lips for the first time in what feels like forever.

I kiss her again, sweeping my tongue inside her mouth. "You taste like mine. Are you mine?"

She whimpers as her body practically collapses beneath my touch, and I bring a steadying hand to her waist, pulling her body into me.

"Because if not, I might start up a relationship with my captain."

The smile she releases against my lips makes me want to lay her down right here and demonstrate in multiple ways how much I love her.

She pulls at the hem of her sweater. "Take this off. Take me."

I shake my head, pissed at myself for doing it. "I'm not going to fuck you while your brother and parents are downstairs."

My jeans are tented, and her eyes drop to the obvious bulge.

"Your dick says otherwise."

"Yeah, well," I whisper against her swollen lips, "I'm a respectable English boy."

I watch the way she melts.

"You have no idea how hot that is."

My face is all cocky smirk. "Why do you think I said it?"

I run the back of my knuckles across her jean-covered pussy. "You're soaking through your pants, Kitten."

She whimpers with more need.

"But I want you to eat something while I ask you a question."

Her hooded eyes grow a little wider as I hand her a sandwich and then wider again when she sees the olive-colored key in my other palm.

"What's this?"

"What do you think it is?"

"Well, it looks like a key to your apartment," she says, taking her first bite.

I shake my head. "Technically incorrect. It's a key to *our* place. If you want it."

She swallows her mouthful and stares right at me. "Are you …"

I nod. "I don't want you to save up for another apartment because I want you with me. In our place, watching reruns of your favorite programs and arguing over football."

She narrows her eyes, and I kiss her before she can say it.

"*Football*," I drawl.

I kiss her again because what the hell? I missed the shit out of her.

"Move in with me and sign the deed that is currently sitting on the kitchen island at home. I bought the place from Jon, and I want it to be ours. Just you, me, and our castle."

"Like royalty?"

Her eyes sparkle with the answer she hasn't yet said, but I don't need to hear it. I can feel it already.

I push her hair behind her left ear. "Yes, Kitten. Because you're my queen."

KENDRA

"You know you need to close your mouth to chew, right?" I say to Ollie as he sits, slack-jawed, shepherd's pie piled high on his plate.

"All this just feels like a dream. Like Christmas came early or something." He points at Jack with his fork. "What was it like when you met him for the first time and *then* found out your mom was marrying him?"

I look across at my boyfriend as all five of us sit around the dinner table.

I can tell what he's thinking—*Why in the hell is this guy, one of the biggest names in soccer, fanboying over my stepdad?*

I mean, I get it—Jon is a big name. But my brother is arguably bigger worldwide. That's Ollie though. While he might be flashy with his cars, you'll never find a humbler person.

I take another bite of Jack's dinner. Damn, this is good.

"How are you feeling, honey?" Mom asks me as she leans across and refills my water glass.

My brother pauses on his swoon session and immediately shakes his head. He's been pissed off with the national squad decision since I told him.

I shrug, feeling anything but relaxed over missing out. "It's just another four years to wait."

I swear I see Mom grow heart eyes when Jack rises from his seat and rounds the table.

When he reaches me, he leans down and presses a kiss to my cheek. "I promise I'll make this summer unforgettable for you ..." He pauses and brings his lips closer to my ear. "Fuck Brazil. We'll have an amazing time together, whatever we do."

"Do you think the Blades will make the playoffs?" Dad asks Jack.

He remains standing behind me, massaging my shoulders as he answers, "I think we have a shot, yeah. It's going to be a close call though."

"I think you'll do it. Jon has worked wonders with that team." Ollie nods his head at Jack. He never interacted with Tyler like this about hockey. The difference is night and day. "Although you've proven all the doubters wrong."

I feel Jack's weight shift from behind me as he leans down and wraps his arms around my shoulders, his chin on top of my head.

Fuck, I love this boy.

"Can you all keep a secret? I'd say my balls depend on it."

Mom giggles, and Dad fights back a smile.

"Ooh, insider knowledge." Ollie rubs his hands together with glee.

"What is it?" I ask, sensing Jack's excitement.

"Jon told me I'm getting my shot on the first line as center. They want to see how I go."

"No freakin' way!" I audibly squeal, and my dad's hands fly up to cover his ears.

I leap from my seat and wrap myself around my six-foot-four boyfriend.

"Wait." I pause and pull back. "That's Tyler's position, right?" I'm so not sorry when a grin spreads across my face.

And judging by his current expression, neither is Jack. "Again, top secret, but he's being shipped to the AHL. It's been a long time coming."

"Fucking shit anyway."

"Oliver Hart!" Mom announces as she stands from the table with her empty plate. "Congratulations, Jack. You have such a bright future ahead of you—I know it." She glances down at our joined hands and smiles. "You both do."

CHAPTER THIRTY-NINE

JACK

"It was at this point right here when I concluded that Jon is a better coach than he was a player." Ollie pauses the footage and jumps up from his chair. He points at me, Tyler, and Matt Rice on-screen. "Nashville was not expecting this overload, and you fucking nailed that slap shot!"

He crouches down in front of the TV, and I sit on the sofa, my eyes feeling heavy. It's almost midnight, and we're the only ones still up. If it had been an option to head to bed with Kendra, that's exactly where I'd be. Despite liking her brother immensely.

I lean forward, resting my elbows on my knees. "Are you sure you picked the right sport?"

He stands from his crouch, shoving his hands into his pockets. "Can't skate for shit. Plus, when Dad was home from England, he had me on a pitch before I was even talking."

He walks back over and sits down, hitting play on the footage. "While I have the chance and Kendra isn't here, I just want to say thanks for what you did. For helping her out. She's too stubborn to come to me or Mom and Dad, so, yeah, thanks."

He keeps his eyes focused on the screen as he runs a palm down his sweatpants, clearly deep in deliberation over his next sentence. "Tyler broke her heart. Maybe not at the point of their breakup, but definitely when she realized what a ball sack he was."

I know what he's saying. I'd be saying the same thing when it came to Darcy, and I'm positive she would, too, if the shoe were on the other foot.

"I won't hurt her," I say, giving him the answer he needs. "The only time I'll leave her life is if she asks me to."

He visibly relaxes into the cushion behind him. "She'd hate me if she knew I was being the protective big brother. It's only because I care." He flicks his eyes to me, and I see the sincerity. "I like you, Jack. I get the feeling I'll see a whole lot more of you over the years, and I can't say I'm mad about it."

I nod once. "There isn't anything I wouldn't do for her. I told her I was addicted, and I'm not ashamed to admit the same thing to you."

Can men swoon? Clearly, they can, judging by the way Ollie is looking at me.

On a stifled yawn, I reach across and grab my mobile from the end of the sofa. "I won't see you for Christmas since the NHL isn't the La Liga and we have to work for our wages."

He rolls his eyes, and I smile at the video message that just came through.

"So, consider this my gift to you."

Walking the few paces, I pass Ollie my phone and hit play.

"Noooooo!" he exhales when he registers what I did earlier.

"Hey, Ollie. Jon Morgan here. Jack tells me you're a huge fan, and since he's head over heels with your sister, I figure we'll essentially be family at some point. Anyway, consider it my future father-in-law duty to send you a couple of items, including a signed puck from when I made a hat trick against the Blades a few seasons back." Jon grins at the camera. "Have a great Christmas and go kill the Champions League this season. I have a hundred dollars on you making top goal scorer."

The video ends, and Ollie remains transfixed on the dark screen. "That was undoubtedly the coolest thing I've ever seen."

I take my phone back from him and pocket it. "All in the name of big-brother brownie points."

He stands from his chair and offers his hand out to me, pointing toward the door I'm about to head through for bed. "Jack, I will carry you up there myself if it means you'll propose."

I snort a laugh and shake his hand. "Don't fucking tempt me."

I KNOW I previously said having Kendra sleep in the room next to mine was torture. But having to walk past her room, knowing she's likely half naked and all mine?

Yeah, I'm not hard at all.

In around twelve hours, I need to board a flight back to Nashville, and I'm painfully aware of it as I stand, fixated on the spare bedroom door.

Respectful English boy. That's what you are, Jack. You can't fuck her in her childhood bed. You've gotten off to a great start with her family. Don't blow it now.

And don't think about blowing.

Undressed and now in bed, I flip onto my back and stare up at the white ceiling.

"Fucking idiot," I whisper to my nineteen-year-old self. "The fuck were you thinking?"

"You know they say that's the first sign of madness, right?"

Kendra stands in the doorway, dressed in an old New York Storm jersey which falls to just below her pussy.

Fuck ... is she wearing underwear?

I go to ask her what she's doing when she presses a finger to her lips, strutting into the room and closing the door behind her. "Shhh.'"

Her hands fall to the hem of her top, and I reach out and stop her, squeezing my eyes shut and thinking about all the dirty things I'm desperate to do.

Screw the respectable-boy image. I'm fucking her.

When I set my eyes back on my girlfriend, I see the same fire burning in hers.

"Leave it on. You might be made to wear my name, but I have a competence kink, and the sight of you in this"—I pluck at the material—"has me harder than ever."

Her grin seals my fate as she climbs under the covers and straddles me. "I'm not wearing any panties."

The heat radiating through my athletic shorts told me she wasn't. "Come here, Kitten."

She braces a palm on the pillow next to my head as her hair falls around us.

"Can you be really quiet for me?" I ask after several swipes of my tongue into her mouth.

She whimpers when I pull her bottom lip between my teeth and bite down gently. "I wouldn't be here if I didn't think I could. My brother's next door, and these walls are thin."

I lift my hips into her. "Do you think he'd still like me if he knew what I planned to do with his baby sister while he slept a few feet away?"

My girlfriend's on her back in seconds as I hover over her body.

"Though, just to be clear"—I swipe my hand through her pussy and let her taste first—"I might fuck you like it's the last time I'll feel you underneath me, but I'll always love you like it's forever." I steal a taste from my fingers as her eyes shine in awe. "Because it is forever, Kendra. I'm done, finished, on my knees for you."

She swallows thickly as I push down my shorts and thrust

into her. She gasps at the shock, and I throw my palm over her mouth, muffling the sound.

"Take this cock like the silent slut I know you can be."

I drive into her again and grab the top of the wooden headboard, preventing it from banging against the wall.

"How's that, Kitten?"

She stays perfectly silent as I roll my hips again.

"If I remove my hand, can I trust you to come all over my dick in secret?"

Kendra blinks once, and I interpret that as confirmation, pulling my hand away before bringing it down between us.

"Even if I do this?" Using the release dripping from her pussy, I tentatively circle her ass.

Her eyes grow wide. "That's my ..." She trails off, overcome with pleasure when I slowly and carefully insert one finger.

Frantically, she pushes the duvet back and exposes us, and then—like a good girl—she lifts both legs in the air and spreads them as wide as they'll go. "I'm going to come, Jack."

My name tumbles from her lips as she arches into me, taking my dick and fingers so perfectly.

"Is this what you wanted when you snuck in here? To have your ass and pussy come like this? Because they are, Kitten. I can feel you all over me."

My own filthy mouth is my undoing, and I drop my face into the pillow beside her, groaning and moaning through the best orgasm I've ever had.

"Thank you," I breathe out quietly. "Thank you for giving me the chance to prove I'm not the jackass he made me out to be. I'm not, Kendra. All I am is in love with you."

She runs a hand through the hair at the back of my head, and I lift up to look at her. "Do I have to wait a little longer before I win your heart over?" I place my palm over her chest as it rises and falls rapidly.

She cups each side of my face in her hands, stroking my cheeks with her thumbs. "You have it, in its entirety. Truthfully, I think you always have, even if I just didn't know it. Even if it never felt like it. I always knew you were around; I could always feel your presence from across the room at parties." She kisses my forehead, and my heart detonates. "I love you, Jack. Forever."

My knuckles tighten around the headboard as I roll into her again. Despite the fact that I just came, I'm still hard, and she's soaking from us both.

"I reckon we have a few more hours before everyone wakes up. Let me show you what it's like to be the center of someone's world."

CHAPTER FORTY

KENDRA

"You know, I've always thought I could never move away from England." Darcy looks around the arena and then back at us all sitting in the family box. "But I see the appeal of New York. It kind of feels like anything can happen when you're here. Sort of like you have the world at your fingertips."

Collins snorts a laugh as the Dallas goalie stretches out on the ice. "Oh, there are some benefits all right. You can invite me along to as *many* hockey games as you like. Speaking of eye candy ..." She pulls a packet of jelly beans from her coat pocket and pours a ton out on the table next to her, sorting all of the red ones into a neat pile.

I quirk a brow as Darcy and Jenna watch on from beside her.

"What are you doing?" Darcy asks.

She slides the rest into the packet, leaving only the red ones to eat. "This color tastes way better."

"Or you could just buy the red ones?" Jenna suggests, looking out onto the ice.

Collins shrugs a shoulder and pops a few more into her

mouth. "Where would the fun in that be? I think there's something to be said for working for it."

"Speaking of which, how's the new job?"

She waggles her brows at me. "Well, the head mechanic offers a great servicing package."

Jenna throws a hand over her mouth as Felicity returns with a tray of drinks for us all.

"You are not getting into it with your boss?" Jenna gasps. "That's never a good move. I remember back in high school, the principal started dating the head of science, and let's just say, it didn't end well. She had to leave and—"

"He's not my boss," Collins clarifies. "We're just messing around, and like I've been telling Kendra, it's been way too long. I needed the light relief."

"Yeah, I get that," Jenna says, taking a sip of her soda and practically serenading it. Sugary drinks are a rarity for her, especially now that she's stepping up her conditioning for international duty.

My heart drops a little. It's been three weeks since I received the email from Team USA, and it still feels just as raw.

"You and Lee are constantly at it," I gibe. "When I was living at your place, that's all I heard. Literally."

Darcy waves a dismissive hand in front of her. "Let me tell you, that all dies down after a while. Give it a few more months, and you'll be waking him up for snoring rather than round two."

I open my mouth to argue since I can never see a time when Jack isn't laying me on a random surface and "stealing some sexy time," as he calls it, but Felicity gets there first.

"Jon and I go at it most nights."

Darcy holds up a hand, feigning to puke, when her attention snags on the Jumbotron. The players are skating off the ice after warm-up, and the camera pans to Archer as he pulls off his helmet.

Jenna side-eyes me, curiosity written all over her face. I look at Felicity and she wears a similar expression, but none of us says anything.

Silence stretches for a few more beats before Collins breaks it.

"I didn't know Sawyer Bryce had a kid."

We all turn to look at her in unison.

"Told you, Kend. Baggage," Collins adds.

"And you felt it necessary to look into his personal life because ..." I trail off, waiting for an answer.

She lifts one shoulder very gently, pouring more jelly beans onto the table. "He did this interview in a magazine I was randomly reading on the subway the other day. It was about him raising a child as a single dad." She blows out a breath. "Snaps to him. I couldn't do it. I can barely take care of myself, let alone have a kid."

"Liam had that talk with me the other day. He asked me if I wanted a family. I told him maybe when I'm forty," Darcy adds.

"For real?" Exasperated, Felicity throws her head back. "I was banking on you two for my first grandchild."

"Yeah, well, don't look at me either," I reply. "These ovaries are on lockdown for the next five years. Paris is the year I make it to the World Cup—I can feel it."

Jenna leans across to offer me a high five. "Your ACL issues will be but a distant memory."

My mind travels back to last night. Every time Jack joins me for a Pilates workout, it finishes with him ripping off my Lycra shorts and fucking me on the new mats he bought us.

"Sit on my face and fuck it, Kitten."

I squeeze my thighs together as his commands literally come flooding back to me. I've got his mom sitting a couple of chairs down from me, watching as her son takes the ice for his first game as starting center, and I'm tingling from head to toe as I swoon over other talents he possesses.

Collins leans into me and whispers, "You're thinking about fucking him, aren't you?"

I snatch a red jelly bean and bite down. "Yep."

She snorts softly. "Can't say I blame you. I would take that butt to town."

"The nausea is overwhelming tonight." Darcy squeezes her eyes shut. "I'm going to pretend like I didn't just hear what you said."

I narrow my eyes playfully at her and mouth, *Sex god.*

She shudders and dips into her pocket, pulling out her phone. "That's it. I'm canceling our dinner reservation. Appetite has officially left the building."

"I CAN'T BELIEVE you actually canceled dinner." I pick up a fry and dip it in ketchup. "I'm starving and eating everything I shouldn't in this bar."

I grab another fry as Jack slides in the booth beside me.

"I can help you work it off later."

Darcy scrunches up her nose but is soon distracted when Sawyer and Archer join.

Sawyer's eyes find everywhere but Collins as she busies herself with a text conversation, and I'm willing to bet it's of the booty-call variety.

"You, um ... solved your phone situation then." Sawyer clears his throat and takes a seat next to Darcy, earning a look from Archer.

Collins is the kind of girl who exudes confidence. Literally nothing or no one fazes her. So, when she looks up and tucks a lock of pink hair behind her ear, I conclude she might not be telling whole truths when she says the Blades captain isn't exactly her type.

She resets herself in a flash. "Yeah, weeks ago."

The stilted conversation between them reaches around the

table as Archer takes a seat on a stool at the end of the booth and his eyes fix on Jack's sister. "How long are you in town for, Darce?"

Jack hasn't taken his eyes from mine. Up until now.

"*Darce?*" Jack spins from me to his goalie.

The slightest tug of Archer's lips leaves no doubt as to how much he loves winding my boyfriend up. And I'm sure that's what he passes it off as too—banter between teammates over the rookie's hot sister.

Whatever you say, Archer.

Darcy breaks off from her conversation with Jenna and wears her usual bright smile. The kind she would offer me as a friend. There's no reaction to him calling her Darce as she flicks her honey hair over her shoulder. "I need to be back by Thursday since it's Dad's birthday this weekend."

I feel Jack stiffen beside me. I know he didn't tell Darcy what happened that night at the restaurant. Reading between the lines, I can tell Darcy has always been closer to Elliott, and I think it's something Jack wishes he could change, but he doesn't want to be the brother who turns his sister against her dad.

"You okay?" I whisper into Jack's ear.

He runs his hand through my long hair, pushing it away from my face, and I can't help my eyelids from fluttering at the contact.

"I'm good, Kitten. Actually just thinking about the first time we were in this bar together." His eyes drop to his jersey I'm wearing. "Trying to figure out if I prefer the little black dress or what you're wearing now."

I press my forehead into his. "For me, it's neither."

He pulls away just slightly. "Neither?"

"Neither," I repeat on a headshake. "The black dress makes me feel sexy, and I gotta admit, when I saw you here that night, I was happy Jenna had talked me into wearing it."

He plucks at my jersey, the conversation going on around us reducing to a mere murmur. "And what about this?" he kisses my pulse point. "Is it because I fucked you in yours while your family was sleeping?"

I giggle like a teenager. "Oh, don't get me wrong; I enjoy wearing your name."

His eyes flash with heat and possession. "Maybe that's the perfect combination then—my name, your jersey."

"I could see that happening one day," I say, pushing my hand through the short strands of his hair.

"So, tell me, Kitten"—Jack tips my chin to look directly at him—"what's your favorite thing to wear?"

I pause and think about NYPAG, a night I initially planned to survive but turned out to be the start of everything between us. "The dress you bought me."

"The green one?"

I nod slowly. "I'll never forget your face when you saw me in it, and I'll never forget when I spun around to find you standing right in front of me. I think that was the moment I felt it—the pull between us. I think that was when I started to believe that maybe nothing was fake. At least, that's when I hoped it wasn't."

Jack brushes his lips across my mouth, his tongue teasing mine. "If it's okay with you, Miss Kendra Independent Hart, I'd really like to buy you some more."

"With your big starting center salary?" I tease. "I don't know if I can allow that to happen. I might need a little more convincing."

He smiles against me, his dimple popping and blue eyes sparkling with mischief. "When I bought you that dress, I was fantasizing over the way it would look while pooled around your feet. And what I promised back then still stands, Kendra. Now that you're my girl, there will be nothing left to the imagination."

EPILOGUE

July

JACK

"Jack! Can you help me with this zipper?"

I step into the hotel bathroom to find a flustered and red-faced Kendra.

I could pretend and say she's worked up because of the zipper on the stunning black dress I'd talked her into letting me buy a couple of months ago, but that would be a lie. She's been nervous since the organizers asked her to give a speech a few weeks ago. Kendra wanted to come back to Seattle to catch up with her friends since she didn't get a chance to attend the college reunion last year, and I convinced her we should go. Shortly after we booked the tickets, she was contacted and asked to share her career and the journey it's taken so far.

Bringing my hand to the zip, I slowly glide it up her back and then fasten the clasp at the top.

She stands, watching me in the mirror, and when my eyes meet hers in the reflection, she spins around to face me. "Should I have worn my hair down, do you think?"

I shake my head and kiss her neck. "Gives me better access to do this."

Beneath the touch of my lips, I feel her body relax, and she leans into me, looping her arms around my shoulders.

"I've never given a speech before. I'm one hundred percent going to fumble my words."

I rest my hands on her hips, the satin material soft against my fingertips. "You're going to kill it."

Her brown eyes, framed with thick black lashes, soften in response. "I just can't believe Tyler decided to turn up. Seems a little too convenient if you ask me—I'm confirmed as the speaker for this year, and he suddenly announces his attendance."

I set a kiss on her forehead. "I can't say I blame him."

Her eyes grow wide. "What do you mean?"

"Stuck in the farm team over in Connecticut. This is the only chance he'll get to see you. Unlikely he'll be invited to NYPAG this year."

It's even more unlikely he'll be returning to the NHL anytime soon since I've had the greatest season of my life as center. Sure, we didn't lift the Stanley Cup, but we did make the playoffs, and that's insane progress from where we were in September. Right now, the team has no use for him.

She bites down on her bottom lip, and I take her hand in mine, pulling her out of the bathroom and heading for the door.

"Wait." She stops in her tracks as my hand reaches the door handle. "Do you think I should practice again? One final run-through so I can be confident I haven't forgotten everything I want to say?"

I planned on doing this when we got back up to our room later tonight. But from the anxious look on her face and the way she grips my hand, I conclude that maybe it's the distraction she needs.

Releasing the handle, I reach into my pocket and pull out a folded piece of paper. "Sure. Last night, I noted down all the areas you wanted to cover. Women in sports, the rise of *football* in the US."

I hand her the slip, and she narrows her eyes at me.

Eight months together, and she still won't admit I'm right.

"Thank you. That's really thought ..." She trails off and stares down at the paper in her hands. "T-these aren't notes for my speech."

I step toward her and bring my hands back to her waist, dropping my head so I can read the flight confirmation once more. "Is it not? What does it say, Kitten?"

"Two first class tickets to Heathrow. Leaving in two days." Her voice is a mixture of excitement and wonder as she reads the details.

Bingo. Relaxed Kendra is back.

I take the paper from her and throw it on the bed beside us. "It will be a quick turnaround when we get back to New York, but Mum and Jon have lent us their cottage in Oxford for two weeks." I duck my head to meet her shocked gaze. "Just you, me, the English countryside, and as much tea and cakes as we want."

Kendra rolls her lips together and lets out an excited squeak. "I love you so much!" She throws her arms around me and goes in for a kiss. "Ope. Shit, you're wearing my gloss now."

She goes to wipe it away, but I reach up and run my finger across my bottom lip, bringing it to my mouth.

Her eyes hood at the sight. "And now I'm going to be horny when I deliver my speech."

I tip her chin up to meet my eyes. "Let's go downstairs and see our friends. Then I'll bring you back up here, and we can play with Scarlett."

"WOMEN HAVE ALWAYS HAD a place in sports and will continue to thrive not just over here in America, but across the world and in many disciplines. Young girls should be inspired to reach for their dreams of becoming a famous marathon runner, gymnast, tennis player, hockey player."

With my jaw agape, I watch on as my girlfriend knocks her speech out of the park, just like I knew she would.

For a brief second, she flashes me a cheeky grin. "Or *soccer* player. I'm stoked to see more girls with aspirations of turning their incredible talent into careers, and I'm honored to be one of the many athletes helping to push female sporting excellence forward." She pauses and swallows thickly. "Unfortunately, my teammate and good friend, Jenna Miller, couldn't be here tonight since she's traveling back from Brazil with the Golden Glove."

She pauses while a few people in the crowd cheer and applaud Jenna's incredible performance in the World Cup. They narrowly missed out in the final to England.

"But I wanted to take tonight as an opportunity to announce our plans to establish an academy for girls up to the age of sixteen. This will be backed and funded by the New York Storm, but over time, we hope to expand its accessibility across the country."

The crowd morphs from applause to full-on cheers as Kendra steps back from the microphone, and I take a second to look around the room. Her college friends all push back their seats and rise to their feet, clapping and appreciating her incredible delivery. And as I stand along with them, I can't help but notice the only person not offering their congratulations is Tyler.

I don't know what smart-ass sat him there, but when we reached the table and she clocked his place card next to hers, I offered to switch things around, which earned me a firm no.

Like some kind of goddess, she takes the final couple of steps down from the stage, and I'm not ashamed to admit the slither of thigh I catch, coupled with the power speech she just gave, has my dick twitching in my pants.

Not now.

Paying zero attention to Tyler, she sits back down and waves to her friends before focusing her attention on me.

I reach across and pull her chair toward me. Dinner is done, the speech was nailed, and now I want to have some fun.

"Aside from the fucking amazing job you just did up there, do you know what's got me looking like a Cheshire cat?"

She smiles around the rim of her champagne glass. "What's that?"

I lean in a little closer and catch Tyler pull out his phone, trying desperately to ignore us. "The last time we were on this campus, surrounded by all these people, you were only the dream girl I could never touch."

Dipping my hand under the white tablecloth, I'm confident no one will see us since there's only a wall behind us and everyone else is deep in conversation.

"But now, tonight, and for-fucking-ever if I have my way ..."

I trace my fingertips up the outside of her thigh, and she pulls in a sharp breath when I reach the edge of her thong. When I hook my index finger under the slender waistband, she lifts her hips, and I peel the tiny excuse for underwear down her legs. She steps out of them and sets her glass back on the table, wearing a look of pure lust when I pocket her thong and bring my hand to her inner thigh.

I can feel the heat there. Needy, wanting heat.

"Last time I asked you not to scream, you did such a good job and kept so quiet for me." I find her pussy as it immediately drenches my fingers. "Can you do the same for me again?"

She whimpers, and I push a finger inside, turning my body to face her fully. To the onlooker, I'm simply devoting all my attention to the hottest girl in the room. But in my reality? I'm fingering the woman I'll, one day, ask to be my wife.

"I can do that, Jack," she says, hooking her nearest leg over my knee.

Her mouth forms the perfect O as I add another finger and feel her walls tighten around me.

With my spare hand, I pass her glass back, and she takes another sip while I curl my fingers and stroke her perfect cunt.

"I'm going to play with your clit and make you come now, Kitten. Is that okay?"

She nods once, and I pump my fingers slowly, aware I can't make any sudden movements and risk attracting attention.

When she starts to spasm around me, I take the glass as it shakes in her hand and set it carefully on the table.

"That's it. Give me all of what you have." I soothe her slowly as she fights to stay upright, her face flushing a cute crimson.

The music is relatively loud, but the sounds her wet pussy makes as she releases all over my hand is unmistakable, and my balls tighten, pressure builds at the base of my spine, and my self-control unravels.

As Kendra comes, her pussy floods my hand.

"Want to know something?" My voice is breathy and barely a whisper.

"Yes," she gasps.

"I just came in my pants, watching you come apart for me like this."

Her eyes drop to my crotch. She can't see the wet patch since it's hidden beneath the table, but it's there.

"Thank fuck I wore black pants." I chuckle.

She draws her bottom lip between her teeth. I know exactly what she's about to say before she's even opened her mouth.

"I want to go to bed now, Jack."

I pull out my fingers and then her thong from my pocket, wiping her release on it. "Okay, Kitten, I'll take you upstairs right after you put these back on and do one final thing for me."

She does as I asked, and I interlace our fingers. But before I lead her upstairs for a night where I plan to have zero sleep, I take one more look at the girl I never thought I'd get.

"Repeat after me: *football*."

THE END

Sawyer's story is coming in July 2025. Pre-order his book now!

ACKNOWLEDGMENTS

My Husband: Thank you for putting up with me and my incessant talk of Jack Morgan. I know I've been insufferable over him. But mostly, thank you for being you, for holding me on late nights when I'm exhsuated and always believing in me no matter what.

My Dad: You're forever my cheerleader, and I'm forever grateful for every phone call, message and email you send, encouraging me to chase my dreams.

My little boy: To my very own golden retriever—the boy who races along shorelines and smiles even on the hardest of days. This one is for you, LB.

Sariah: Forever my Jon girlie. I'm so happy to bring you a whole new Morgan era with levelled up swoons and heat. P.S. Don't tell him, LOL.

Tina: I'll never forget when you sent me the "no notes" message. I think I fell a little harder for Jack—if that's even possible. Thank you for your love and support, as always.

Nay: I mean, he's even listed in your bio. Thank you for screaming along with me. Forever grateful for our friendship and unhinged messages.

To Autumn and all at Wordsmith Publicity: I'm running out of ways to thank you and superlatives to describe the incredible work you do alongside the amazing support you provide me. I know how excited we've been for this series, and it's finally here!

To the Bookstagram community: JACK MORGAN

HAS ENTERED THE CHAT! I know how excited you've been for him, and I'm so thrilled to share his story—and mouth—with you. This boy has had me in a chokehold for months, enjoy him. Thank you so much for all your love, forever and always.

To all my readers: Most importantly, thank you to all my readers who open my books and immerse yourselves in love for my stories and chracters. I wouldn't be here without you all, and I wouldn't have this wonderful opportunity to share the words I love and escape into worlds where book boyfriends reign supreme.

ABOUT THE AUTHOR

Ruth Stilling is an avid romance reader turned writer. Having spent many years reading about and dreaming of her ideal book boyfriend, she finally decided to create her own and to share them with the rest of the world.

Living in a small town in Derbyshire, England, Ruth is an introvert by nature and spends much of her time talking with her equally book-crazy friends from across the globe.

When she isn't writing your next book boyfriend, Ruth enjoys watching all kinds of sports and is an Aston Villa and Derby County fan. The outdoors is a real favorite, and if the British weather were kinder, she would spend all her time writing outside.

Ruth is a wife to her best friend and number one cheerleader, whom she married in 2015, and a mom to her beautiful son, who has shown her a new perspective on life—enjoy and celebrate who you are as a person and cherish those who are there for you through rain and shine.

Ruth is incredibly excited to share Perfect Deke, the first installment in her second generation series, The Blade Kings!

You can follow Ruth and keep up to date with what's coming next via Instagram and TikTok by searching @authorruthstilling

Printed in Great Britain
by Amazon

58832435R00192